Raising the Dead

by

Lisa Compton

The Olivia Osborne Series, Book Four

The Wild Rose Press, Inc.
PO Box 708
Adams Basin, NY 14410-0708
Visit us at www.thewildrosepress.com

Publishing History
First Edition, 2024
Trade Paperback ISBN 978-1-5092-5443-9
Digital ISBN 978-1-5092-5444-6

The Olivia Osborne Series, Book Four
Published in the United States of America

Dedication

To my kids and cats.

Prologue

Before Olivia Osborne hunted monsters for the FBI, she worked in a place just like this one.

The smell of lemony antiseptic tickled her nose as she stepped inside, a failed attempt to mask the odor of stale urine. Olivia breathed in through her mouth, a throwback from her nursing days. The technique didn't spare her from the layers hanging beneath a patchwork of lives clinging to faded hopes and dreams. Those who lived here lingered in the middle ground, one step away from a hospital room or a grave where death loomed in the wings, ever watchful, biding its time.

Olivia knew the walkabout was an introduction, but she wasn't there for the tour until she was. She felt the room before she got there. It stood out like a beacon. Despite the need for occupants, it was unoccupied but not empty.

"That's just storage," Graham Banks said. He looked like an insurance salesman or a funeral director with thinning gray hair, colorless skin, and a tailored gray suit, much too dressy for a simple tour guide. He introduced himself as a member of the facility's board of directors, making it clear he had the authority to speak for the collective.

"Not just. Open the door," Olivia said. It wasn't a request.

The pasty Mr. Banks wasn't used to taking orders.

Still, he complied by entering numbers on the keypad and stepping aside.

Olivia crossed the threshold and drank in the energy of the room. She could feel the tattered remnants of death. The end had been peaceful, welcome even. But not before.

Olivia weaved her way through the maze of discarded medical equipment standing in the room like silent sentries to reach the other side. She pulled aside the thick folds of fabric blocking the sun. Olivia discovered white crystals standing like small peaks still holding their place against the window. With a tentative finger, she touched the first one and felt a whisper of magic stored within. Remnants of its power wove up her arm like vines spilling words in a language she did not understand. It was an invocation. Some might call it a spell. To her, it was a binding. Old but not evil. Olivia risked dipping her finger in the trail among the crystals. Salt. A pure substance made of the earth and sea. The taste lingered in her mouth, the hint of a familiar stranger. Whatever lurked here before wasn't coming back. It had been banished.

****

In the boardroom, under the cover of a perfectly polished mahogany table, Olivia slipped off her shoes and dug her toes into the carpet. The room looked like it could comfortably house a dozen, but it was just her and Banks. He didn't seem pleased with his duties for the day, and Olivia wondered what he had done to earn them.

Since severing her ties with the FBI, Dr. Olivia Osborne traded killers for patients, but today's client wasn't like the others. While the discovery in the locked room was well within her skillset, it told her this matter was something else entirely. Olivia couldn't help but wonder who knew to request her services. Certainly not Mr. Banks. He lived in a world of numbers, not shadows.

"Father Dominic assured me you were the one to call."

****

Olivia slipped out of bed, careful not to wake Silas. Barefoot, she padded downstairs to her office. 3:00 AM – Dead Time. It was a familiar hour. She slid her hand down to her growing midsection, reveling at the life inside. The gentle stirring brought a smile to her face. She wasn't the only one up. She would need to feed her little night owl before she went back upstairs to join her husband.

Olivia logged onto her computer and began her search. There were still monsters to catch, but she wasn't the only one hunting them.

Chapter One

Her feet were bare. The silk shirt she wore was untucked. Her skirt was held together by a safety pin. Those were the first things Walter Meeks noticed. Sometimes they meant nothing. Sometimes they were everything. He had been attending death long enough to know the difference.

As the Bexar County Chief Medical Examiner, he rarely went to crime scenes anymore, but today's adventure was a special request. By the time he arrived, the parking lot was already overrun with media vans and a throng of onlookers. Additional patrolmen had been called out to separate the looky-loos from the residents. At least the privacy tent was in place by the time he arrived. Now that there was nothing to see, he hoped the pulsating sounds of the helicopter would stop. Meeks could only hope the same was true for the attending lieutenant. Renard hadn't shut up since he arrived.

"I googled this place. They have one unit for sale. Two million is the starting price," Nathan Renard made small talk when he was nervous. He had just been promoted and he was excited and horrified that his first big scene was in such a swanky place.

"You know when they built this place fifty years ago, it was mostly professors who lived here." It was an easy sell with two nearby Catholic universities. "No professor could afford to live here now." It was only after the educators left did the building evolve into a set of luxury condominiums. The high-rise was one of the first places outside of downtown to employ a full-time doorman.

"Rumor has it a cop lives in this building."

Finally, Renard said something interesting. Now Meeks knew why he was called out of a meeting he didn't want to attend. Renard was better at playing politics than he was at lieutenant.

"No cop I know could afford to live here." Renard was fishing now because he knew Meeks had been around a long time. What he didn't know was Meeks had gotten the chief position not because he wanted it, but because he outlasted everyone else. "That's why I asked for someone senior," Renard explained.

If Meeks was working this with his favorite lieutenant, he would clap back, asking if senior was a euphemism for old. Unfortunately for him, Bartholomew didn't catch this one.

"Did anyone move her?" Meeks asked. It was a standard question. It also gave him time to think and maybe signal to Renard he should stop talking and let him do his job.

"No. According to the officers, all they did was pat her down looking for ID," the EMS attendant explained. He'd only stayed behind until someone else could take over and was glad when Meeks relieved him with a nod of his head. He preferred his patients breathing.

Lieutenant Renard watched the EMT go, thankful he hadn't been left alone with the body. "The first officers on scene did a quick perimeter search. They didn't find a purse or shoes."

She was tucked in a fetal position as if she had a last-minute change of heart and was trying to shield herself from the fall. Her arms were tucked under her. Her hands weren't visible. Meeks wondered if there was a wedding band in there somewhere. Was someone looking for her right now? Meeks searched for some kind of identifier. So far, he could only skim the surface.

The bunion on the side of her misdirected foot told him she had been a fan of inappropriate footwear for years. No doubt the heels accentuated her toned calves, but they were murder on the feet. She had traded comfort for fashion. Appearance was important to her. The pinned skirt was out of character. Meeks wondered if the weight gain was unexpected.

Renard shifted from one foot to the other, not liking the quiet. He was relieved to find the scene less gory than he had expected. Fortunately, he couldn't see the dead woman's face. It was obscured by her hair, which was long and black and looked expensive to keep up. She could be mistaken for someone taking a nap. The only thing out of place was the weird angle of one of her feet. The EMS guy described her insides as a slush pile. Luckily, that was Meeks' department.

"How high do you think?" Renard asked.

"How many floors in this building?" Meeks wanted to know.

"Fifteen."

"Anything above six would have done it," Meeks told him. "When flesh and bone meet concrete from that height, there is no coming back."

"So, she was serious." Renard's words were

nothing more than a stream of conscience.

Jumping wasn't like sticking a loaded gun in the mouth. The jumper wasn't taking any chances at not getting the job done. This wasn't a call for help. This was a sign-off. Still, Renard's question tickled the back of Meeks' brain. This one was hiding something until the very end. Why? Or maybe someone else was the deceptive one. Maybe that's why no one had come to claim her. Is that what was bothering him about the shoes?

"We don't know where she came from? No one saw her fall?" Meeks asked.

"She almost hit someone's car on the way down, other than that, we've got nothing. Not the apartment. No ID, nothing. I have officers inside going door to door, but it's going to take time. Middle of the workday, a lot of people aren't home."

Meeks looked up. The ratio between the jump point and point of impact made all the difference in the world. With the damn tarp over his head, Meeks couldn't get a visual.

Renard realized too late it was something he should have done already. "You think someone pushed her?"

"I didn't say that," Meeks said, speaking slowly as if to a newbie. A landing farther from the jumping point suggested a push. It was why he needed measurements.

Meeks squatted down to get a closer look. She was a petite woman. It wouldn't have taken much to push her. He estimated her weight to be no more than one hundred and twenty-five pounds and no more than five feet five. The heels she liked would have given her the height nature didn't. If she jumped, she would have taken her shoes off to climb over the balcony. If an early morning dive wasn't her idea, she would have kicked them off to run. Either scenario explained her bare feet. Meeks needed something more.

****

"I can't believe you know so little about your family."

"That's why I have you," Olivia smiled at her next-door neighbor. She enjoyed their morning visits on her porch. Lily Forester was her buffer, recanting family history she was too afraid to read for herself. The family research project was all part of Lily's effort to repay Olivia for getting rid of whatever was haunting her house. The growing friendship between them was a bonus.

"Gran never liked to call magic what it was." Magic had become a normal part of her and Lily's conversations. Demons were still off the table, even though there had been one in Lily's house. Not that Olivia would ever tell her. It wasn't there for Lily or her husband Ross. It was there for her. Since being banished from the Foresters' house, *Alleracsap* had taken up residence in Olivia's backyard like a sentry.

"At least your gran taught you everyday things," Lily said. "That little window garden you've got in the kitchen is practical. As a nurse, I believe the power of nature is a lost art."

"I got the inspiration from Abitha." She was Olivia's great, great-grandmother. The original owner of Lily's house and a former Apothecary.

"Is that how you knew about the ginger root? It's great for nausea, a dead giveaway you were pregnant, even before you said something."

Olivia remembered the compulsion to buy some

just before she and Silas learned the news. She'd been munching on it before she got out of the produce section. "No one taught me. It was just instinct."

"It was the whisper of an ancestor, I'm sure." Lily smiled. "If Abitha could talk to the dead, then I'm quite sure she could talk to you. It's why her own daughter, Ella refused to learn. She forbade Abitha from teaching her granddaughter, your gran."

Olivia wondered if that was the reason Gran passed on nothing but fear. She acknowledged Olivia's gifts but also avoided them. As she grew older, Olivia stopped sharing them. She had vowed not to take the same path with her own daughters, thus her long overdue family education.

Lily saw the car pull up in front of the house. It might not be marked, but she had lived next to Silas and Olivia long enough to know how to spot an unmarked police car. The new arrival meant their history lesson was over for the day.

"Lieutenant Bartholomew," Lily smiled as she passed him on the walk.

"How are the feet?" Barry asked.

Lily blushed. He was there the night SAPD came to her house because she shot up her bathroom. Not one of her best moments, but at least he remembered her. He was an attractive man. "Good as new," Lily said with a smile a little too bright.

Barry approached Olivia with his hands in his pockets. It kept her from seeing the clench of his fists. His heart beat a little faster at seeing her. She was glowing, looking happy and healthy. Impending motherhood suited her.

"Hope you don't mind if I don't get up," Olivia

greeted him, her bare feet resting comfortably on the footstool in front of her.

"Don't bother on my account." The sexy red on her toes caught his eye. Flashy for her, then again, they were something she normally kept tucked away. Olivia could be very different in private. Despite the growing space between them, that was something he couldn't forget.

"I wasn't expecting you so soon," Olivia told him.

"I was in the neighborhood."

Olivia questioned the validity of his statement but said nothing. She poured him a glass of what she was drinking and slid the plate his way. "Then have some iced tea and a cookie."

The cookie melted in his mouth. Barry couldn't remember the last time he tasted something homemade. Not unless he counted the taco truck outside SAPD headquarters. "That's good," he said, catching the crumbles tumbling out of his mouth. "That's really good."

Olivia pushed the plate closer with a finger. Her nails were clear, not the hypnotic red of her toes, and not nearly as distracting. "Gran's family recipe. Made with real butter."

"She taught you well." Barry's eyes narrowed, chewing slowly, savoring every bite. "Is that cinnamon I taste?"

"Just a hint," Olivia beamed. It was her secret ingredient as a child.

Barry's hand hovered over the plate in front of him.

"Go ahead. I've already had three," Olivia admitted.

"You have an excuse."

"Maybe, but these calories aren't free," she said, showing off her ever-expanding midsection. "Growing humans makes me hungry."

Barry grinned at her. "What's my excuse?"

Olivia opened her mouth but swallowed her words. *You can't resist me.* Their lives were irrevocably intertwined. She had made peace with it. She wondered where Barry was in the process.

"So, a nursing home, that's your new client?"

Her first two had been large medical complexes. The multi-million-dollar county hospital where Jamie Smythe escaped, followed by the local state psychiatric hospital also known for its escapees. With a nursing degree and a background in law enforcement, Olivia could meet all their needs. Neither of her clients had any association with the FBI. Barry wondered if the scaled-down venue of an old folk's home had been Silas' suggestion.

"Technically, it's a skilled nursing facility with a memory care center," Olivia corrected him. "I used to work the Alzheimer's units, back when I was a nurse." Before she chased monsters.

"You can tell me the truth. What really got you curious about the old people? Please don't tell me it involves Smythe." The Good Samaritan Killer had once worked at a facility just blocks away from her new client. The scenario had been on Barry's mind since she asked for his help.

"I hope not. Unless you have something you need to tell me?" Olivia quizzed him. She knew Jamie had been Barry's pet project since he escaped custody, but there hadn't been an official meeting of the task force for months.

"No news," Barry assured her. Trolling the neighborhood where it all went down had become a habit for him. "No sign he's been back to the house." Even though they had no definitive evidence Smythe was the one who was behind the break-in at his abandoned childhood home. In Barry's mind, it had to be Smythe. Who else would have known what was hidden away under the floorboards of the closet? In Barry's mind, it was most likely cash, something a man on the run would need. Especially since Smythe had been flushed out of his hiding place at the state hospital. Smythe may have escaped custody, but he had never left the city. Barry was sure of it. With a million and a half people, San Antonio had a lot of places to hide.

"Is he still...?" Barry paused. They hadn't talked like this in a long time. "You know, possessed?"

The fact the kid wasn't killing again was a good thing, but Barry feared over time, people would forget the monster he was. Barry wished he could forget, but the image of his best friend's murder was seared into his memory. St Bartholomew—the patron saint of tanners had been flayed alive, just like Mark Austin. Only every cut on Mark's body had been meant for Barry. The scene would haunt him to his grave.

"No." The sharp edge to Olivia's tone brought Barry back to the present. "The demon is gone." From Jamie anyway.

Barry looked over at her. Her gaze was trained on the street, but she wasn't there with him. Gone was the glow from before, replaced by the cold resolve of the monster hunter she was.

She bought Jamie's freedom from the demon one

night in a barn in the middle of Atascosa County. The demon only asked for one soul, but she gave him twice that many. One of those had wanted her as an offering of his own. But Olivia had been the strongest of them all. The demon included.

She turned to Barry. "Back to why I called you. If it makes you feel any better, the referral came from Father Dominic."

Barry looked surprised. Dom hadn't mentioned anything to him. Not that the priest had to tell him, but Dom did know his place in her life. Barry was her assigned Watcher. How could he look after her if he didn't know what was going on?

"I took a tour, and I found someone like me."

"I didn't think there was anyone like you," Barry reminded her. If that were true, that would have been an important bit of information to share.

"Not exactly like me, but related," Olivia clarified. "I told you Pittman said there was a collective."

Larry Wayne Pittman. Barry was still getting over the fact the source of her information was a confessed murderer that had somehow gotten inside her head. It was the cop inside of him. It didn't help that he and Father Dominic had just started exploring Pittman's claims when the priest was dispatched to Rome.

"There are others who are gifted. That's what I meant."

Barry didn't need the reminder. He couldn't shake the feeling that she knew more than she was saying. It reminded him of the Archbishop. Mendoza had stepped in to fill the void of Dom's departure. Despite confirming Pittman's story of other gifted ones, the man of the cloth was strangely mum. Just like Olivia was now. With her, Barry knew it was because she knew how he felt about Pittman. The Archbishop, however, was a whole other matter. Barry would feel more comfortable if he had an additional source of information. It also bothered him more than it should that Dom didn't say anything about a referral. Now the priest was a continent away and unavailable for comment.

"There was evil there," Olivia told him.

It was scary the places his mind went these days. "A demon?" Barry asked, shedding the cop persona as quickly as he had applied it to Pittman. If Dom were here, would he tell him to listen to what Pittman had to say?

"Yes, but it had been banished."

She wasn't holding back now. Not when it involved demons.

"The room felt like a void, vacuum sealed against evil. Only magic from someone gifted could have done that. I felt them."

"Did you find this person?"

Olivia reached back to that time and place, letting her senses wander. The energy to return to recent events was strong now, a gift on loan from one of her offspring.

"A staff meeting was ending." She and Banks had to wait for them to pass just as they exited the converted closet. Olivia felt the tingle along the nape of her neck that she knew came from the familiar who lined the windowsill with salt. "Whoever had been in that room was there." With the collective energy of so many, she couldn't pinpoint who.

Barry was at an impasse and in need of direction.

He heard himself asking her what Dom should have told him before he left. "So, is this a police matter or something else?"

Olivia shook her head just as lost as he was. "You did the digging. You tell me."

Chapter Two

Agent Jon Sharpe angled the Bureau suburban alongside the red pickup truck with the Bexar County fire inspector's seal on the door. Sharpe left Silas behind to walk over to talk to Ruben Cruz. Sharpe and Cruz had overseen the cleanup of the original investigation while Silas returned to Virginia in preparation for his move from the BAU to his current position as the local FBI station chief.

Silas took a moment to survey the surroundings. The last time he was here, he had been racing toward a burning building, wondering if he would ever see Livie alive again. Today, all that remained of the barn was a pile of rubble. Silas watched as the backhoe driver pushed the charred remains into a freshly dug pit. There was something satisfying about the finality of it. If ever a case needed burying it was this one.

"So, why are you here?" Sharpe asked, loud enough to draw Silas' attention.

"It's the case that keeps on giving." Cruz had been the unlucky one on loan to the nearby smaller county from the beginning. Starting with Ferdinand Roche. "The owner, Mr. Sampson, kept calling about a fiery glow."

Sharpe turned to catch a glimpse of the backhoe driver. He had climbed down to take a break and uncover his face. That's when Sharpe noticed the mask.

It wasn't a simple one. It looked like something from an apocalyptic movie. "What's really going on?"

Cruz shrugged. "Just a precaution."

Silas stepped up. "Against what?"

"Ramblings of a crazy old man," Cruz spoke his mind.

"You don't sound concerned," Sharpe said.

"Sampson's calls are always late at night, after stumbling in from the bar. Who knows what he's seeing? Could be something, could be nothing at all." It was a well-known fact Abram Sampson liked to drink.

"Atascosa County only has volunteer fire departments. They were dispatched several times but never found or saw a damn thing. Given the sensitive nature of the site, I obtained soil samples before the tear down began and will do so again when that guy over there is done." Cruz sounded like he was quoting from a higher authority.

"Find anything?" Silas wanted to know.

"The dirt showed an unusually high amount of lead," Cruz said.

"Is that a concern?" Sharpe asked.

"Before it was banned in the late seventies, lead was commonly found in paint. Lead paint lasts longer and is moisture resistant, everything you'd want for an outside dwelling such as a barn. My guess is it was the paint used on the barn that accounted for the lead content in the soil. It was a little unusual considering that thing hadn't been painted any time in the last forty years, but nothing to be concerned about."

Silas was the one who looked concerned but said nothing. Sharpe figured it was because, so far, they hadn't found what they came for.

"The house is gone, too," Cruz said.

Silas knew the one. It was down the road and should have been visible. He hadn't noticed until now that it was missing. Maybe because he wanted to forget.

Originally built in the twenties, the house came with a root cellar used to store canned fruits and vegetables. Andre Roche locked Livie in there with plans to sacrifice her in the barn. How she survived any of it was lost in a string of unanswered questions leftover from that night.

"I heard the cellar was overrun by rattlesnakes. Snake wranglers were involved, I shit you not," Cruz said, letting out a low whistle, rousing Silas from the memory. "Glad I wasn't involved in that one."

"Speaking of shit, what about the trailers?" Sharpe asked.

The trailers were included in Abram Sampson's weekend hunting leases, but after Andre Roche came into his life, the space was used as temporary housing for some of the girls Roche collected. The others were kept in the bunker that was attached to the cellar. That's where Livie found Kimberly Burleson and Rose Corey.

By the time Sharpe and company arrived, there were no more girls, just the head of a former Atascosa County deputy stuffed in a freezer. The theory was Andre Roche killed the deputy because he no longer trusted him to keep quiet. Roche's accomplice, Ana Lutz, assured Barry Bartholomew the missing girls were alive, just relocated to someone who knew what to do with them. So as far as Silas knew, none of them had ever been found.

"The trailers are still standing. Luckily, I have nothing to do with them, either," Cruz explained. "They belong to your pal Ranger Gaines." Since the murdered deputy was local law enforcement, the investigation of his death fell under the purview of the Texas Rangers.

"Have you been contacted by an FBI agent named Mason Deveroux?" Silas finally spoke.

"Sure have."

"Did Agent Deveroux say what he wanted to speak with you about?"

"Did he ever. Man, I don't know what else I can tell you people."

Silas guessed *you people* was code for Feds.

"I can't tell you or him what happened in that barn. What I can tell you are the basics. Fire is simple. All you need is oxygen, heat, and fuel. There was a wind raging that night making the inside of that place the setting for a perfect storm. Roche was using lamps fueled by kerosene. Something caused them to break or spill. Mix that with dry hay and a rotting structure and poof." Cruz threw his hands up. "How two people escaped and two didn't is on somebody else. I'm just the fireman."

"Is that what Deveroux wanted to know?" Silas asked.

"Yea. He's like a dog with a bone. He asked me the same damn question about fourteen different ways. I can't tell him or you, what I don't know." The frustration in the fire inspector's voice was palpable.

Silas nodded. Cruz had been pushed far enough. He was also right. He couldn't tell what he didn't know. There were only two people who could.

"So, where is he?" Cruz asked. "Deveroux told me to expect him today or tomorrow. I sent him a text on my way over to let him know it needed to be today because we're done here."

"What did he say?" Silas asked.

"Not a damn thing."

****

"Take me through your morning, Mr. Castell."

Same request. Different cop.

"Everybody calls me Manny."

"Okay, Manny, take me through your shift."

"I got here at six thirty. I grabbed a cup of coffee before the other guy left."

"That would be Mr. Gibson?"

"Yea." Ron was on his way, but he lived across town on the west side."

"Then what happened?"

"Only a few people came through. Things don't get busy around here until afternoon." It was one of the reasons he liked the gig. Anything beat the other place on the Riverwalk with the constant foot traffic. "It was a normal day. Until, you know." Manny's gaze strayed outside. Every time he looked there were more cops.

"Manny, look at me and think," the cop interrupted. Outside, they had called for measurements. Officers were now blocking all the exits. This guy could be their only hope.

"These people you saw. Were they coming or going?"

"Residents don't come through here. They use the parking garage. It has its own set of elevators."

"Who were the people you saw?"

"Two kids from upstairs. They went out the front door."

"I thought you just said residents don't use the front door."

"Kids use the front door. They go to the high school across the street. They don't drive. They walk." The officer looked like he wrote that down or at least pretended to.

"Do you know what unit?"

Manny shook his head. "No, man. This is barely my second week." He didn't know shit. It's not like there was any real training for this job, especially when the other guy quit with no notice.

"So, if you didn't know them, how did you know where they were going?"

"It's a private school. They wear uniforms."

Manny at least had that part right. Maybe this guy knew more than he thought he did. Still, this was taking too much time. The onsite commander wanted another count, in case he needed to call in more reinforcements. The residents weren't going to stay on lockdown all day. "How many units in the building?"

Manny did the math in his head. Fifteen floors, four units per floor, except the top two floors. Those were penthouses. Due to their size, there were only two per floor instead of four. He only remembered the detail because one was for sale. Manny wondered if the dead woman in the parking lot was going to affect the price. "Fifty-six."

The officer relayed the information through his walkie and turned back to Manny. "Then what happened?"

"I had another cup of coffee. There was a delivery." The box was still sitting on the counter. "Then I went to the bathroom. When I came back out all I remember was the lady screaming."

The officer looked interested, for the first time.

"Was the scream inside or outside?"

"Outside." Manny gestured to the corner where the lady had been sitting before the paramedics took her away. "She came running in the door screaming about someone falling from the sky. I thought she was crazy."

"This was the woman who reported the body?"

"Yea, Ms. Montez."

"I thought you said you didn't know anyone. How do you know Ms. Montez?"

"I don't know her, know her," Manny said, starting to feel flustered. It's not like anyone introduced themselves. Not to the hired help who stood behind the desk. Still, Ron said it was a good gig at Christmas. Most residents dropped off goodies or gift cards as if that made up for ignoring them the rest of the year. "Her name's on the list."

"There's a list? What kind of list?" The officer snapped, interested again.

"People who don't live here but are allowed to come and go. The lady, Ms. Montez, is some kind of personal care attendant for one of the residents. A lot of old people live here."

"So, you had seen her before?"

"Yea. Anyway, she looked like she was going to faint." He owed her one. She saved him from seeing the mess outside. "Right after that, one of the lawn guys opened the door and started yelling for me to call 9-1-1, so I did. Then you guys showed up."

"Manny, that's a lot of time unaccounted for." The original call didn't come in until more than three hours after Manny arrived. "You forgot to tell me about the list before. Is there anything else you're forgetting?"

"It's a boring job. It's why I like it." Manny looked

toward the resident entrance. Did someone slip past?

The officer snapped his fingers, rousing him from the memory. "Manny, you still with me?"

"I didn't forget. She did," Manny mumbled.

"What do you mean? She who?"

"I saw her in passing when I was on my way to the bathroom. She held up a set of keys and kept walking like she was in a hurry." But so was he. That second cup of coffee always did the trick.

"Had you seen her before?"

"No."

"You sure about that?" the cop asked.

"Yea. She's the kind you would remember."

"Remember, how?"

Manny felt the heat rise in his cheeks. He was married. He wasn't supposed to be looking. "Come on, man, you know." He really had noticed her hair first, until she walked away.

The cop didn't ask. "Does she live here?"

"I don't know. I told you. Residents don't usually come through here." Manny's gaze wandered back outside. Something was happening. An officer was sprinting toward them. He pushed past the officer asking the questions and shoved a phone in Manny's face.

"Have you seen this woman?"

Manny stared. His mouth went dry, and his tongue felt thick. "Yea. That's her."

The officer's face was intense. "Her who?"

Manny hoped he wasn't going to start with the questions. He didn't seem nearly as patient as the other guy. He started to back up but had nowhere to go. "She's the one."

"What was she was wearing?"

"Navy jacket, short skirt, red heels."

The new guy nodded to the other one. The original officer took the phone. He took a look and shoved it back in Manny's face. He was mad now, too. "Where was she going?"

"I don't know. She had keys like she was supposed to be here." Manny had a sinking feeling he had done something wrong. He wouldn't have forgotten her, but he should have asked.

The cop shoved the phone toward him again. The picture looked like something off of a professional website. The cop's finger covered the name, but not the bio. Doctor.

Shit. She wasn't supposed to be here and now he didn't want to be.

Chapter Three

Barry pulled out a batch of papers he'd stuffed in his shirt pocket. He was afraid of where they would lead because wherever it was, he knew he would follow. "Several months ago, the Jones substation dispatched a patrolman to Oak Hollow Nursing Facility to answer a security alarm for an unauthorized entry. They found nothing suspicious. They were called back two more times. Different patrolmen; same results. No forced entry. No suspicious persons located."

"The facility put in a work order with the alarm company to inspect the doors and change the entry codes, etc. Their findings were also negative. The document was in a file provided by Mr. Banks," Olivia told him.

"So not electrical?" Barry had been around her long enough to learn electrical disturbances could be a sign of paranormal activity. It's what happened at her neighbor's house.

"What Mr. Banks didn't give me was a new contract with a new alarm company and a clear inspection from the local electric company."

"If he didn't give it to you, do I want to know how you got it?" Olivia Osborne had many gifts, but last Barry checked, computer hacking wasn't one of them.

"Kevin Branch found it when he did a cursory review of the facility financials. He has a keen eye and the skills of a detective." Kevin liked to hunt, much like his older brother. The skill was instinctive. Olivia believed everyone inherited something from those who came before them. Some ancestral gifts were more obscure than others and thrived best in the shadows. That's how they survived.

"So, no more calls to the Jones sub-station?" Olivia asked.

"No. Now they call the coroner. Pretty unusual for a home full of seniors if you ask me."

Barry was correct. The coroner only came into play when the death was suspicious or unexpected. Death in a nursing home was part of the circle of life. Part of the intake process involved notification of family upon death, followed by the deceased's physician and then the preselected funeral home.

"I checked with Meeks." Barry trusted the medical examiner to keep the inquiry to himself, especially when he added Olivia's name to the request. The old man had a soft spot for the former FBI consultant.

"What's bothering you?" Olivia could tell something was.

"These had to be experienced nurses familiar with death. Yet they were suspicious enough to call the coroner."

"They might not have been as experienced as you think. There's a severe shortage of nurses," Olivia offered. "You would be surprised how many inexperienced nurses are thrown into situations they never should be in just because they have a license." She had been away from the bedside for more than a decade. Things had only gotten worse since then.

"None of the families elected to do an autopsy, so

those same concerns didn't trickle down to the family."

"By then most families were prepared. Or another nurse could have been equally convincing that one wasn't necessary. For long term patients, some of the nurses become like family," Olivia countered.

"Then you should see this." Barry reached over and took back the papers he had given her. He thumbed through the reports looking for what caught his eye before. "There was one last call for an officer. It came with the last call to the coroner." Barry found what he was looking for and handed the paper back to Olivia.

Their old friend, Officer Brad Harris, filed the report. The signature was legible, as were the neat block letters beneath his name. Acronyms were commonplace in both of her vocations, but Olivia didn't recognize this one.

"JDLR?" she asked.

"Just doesn't look right."

****

San Antonio didn't get many jumpers. The last couple used an overpass, not a pricey place like this one. They were in the middle of a quiet suburban neighborhood where things like this weren't supposed to happen. Jessica Tate had a bad feeling about this. As a reporter, she had honed those skills and felt confident enough to listen to them. Someone was dead, and she was on the brink of a big, messy story.

Jessica studied the building and felt the writing process kick into full swing. Even if the plot was fuzzy, the setting was familiar. She was recently here for dinner. Despite his bachelor's status, he could cook. Jessica imagined he could do a lot of things. He just chose not to. Even before he became one of her favorite people, Jessica knew he was one of the good guys. She had spent enough time around cops to know. He truly cared about people, and he was protective of those close to him. He took Will under his wing and became both a mentor and a friend. Because of his support, Will was off chasing another dream.

If Will was in town, Jessica would have texted him. If he didn't know what was going on, his boss would. She could text him herself, but for all she knew, he was already here. At least, he should be. Her finger hovered over her phone, but she decided against it. Jessica worked hard not to cross lines, even though some of them were blurred in her world. She lived with a cop. Even before that, when her niece Kim was missing, Jessica didn't use her position with the media to gain preferential treatment. Instead, she used her own resources and reached out to a woman she once interviewed. Dr. Osborne ended up saving Kimmy's life.

Her cameraman Reggie nudged Jessica out of the way to make room for the car speeding past. Unlike all the others, this one wasn't patrol. It was command. Jessica wondered what was happening now. Earlier, a cop she didn't know, came out and pushed the crowd further away, making room for more uniforms. According to parking lot gossip, the building was on lockdown. Were the residents complaining, or was it something else?

"At least it's not SWAT," Reggie said. Still, it felt like so much more than a jumper.

Jessica saw movement up ahead. Something was happening. With Reggie leading the way, she secured a spot at the front of the line. She finally caught a break when she found a cop she did know.

Jessica flashed him a smile that used to go further when she was single but still managed to work. "Hey, Mikey, help me out here." It was a subtle way of reminding him he owed her. "Look, I already know someone took a dive. Rumor has it the jumper is female. Confirm or deny."

Mikey looked around to make sure no one was listening. "Confirm." Mikey leaned in close. "I'll do you one better. It will more than square us."

Jessica pulled out a small notebook she carried with her. She made a show of writing down the date and time with his source name. "Go."

"Tell your boy, Will, he needs to find his boss."

"Will's not here. He's at Quantico. Why?"

Mikey sighed. "That's too bad."

****

"He could be a hunter."

This time the tale didn't come from only Pittman. The Archbishop had also mentioned ones he called Hunters. What better to hunt than demons? Still, Barry wasn't ready to commit. His information was incomplete. Vague. Intentional or otherwise. He needed to stay with what he knew. He was back to being a cop.

"I just told you I found a nurse who had the most patients die in the last year and that's all you have to say?" Barry stopped himself and took a breath, tempering his mood. "By your lack of reaction, I'm assuming you already knew." Barry wondered if it was more data mining or something more. Olivia valued her senses. Her unnatural abilities were what complicated her relationship with the FBI.

"I did not. Not exactly." Kevin Branch was still

compiling employee records and cross-referencing them with employees on duty at the time of the staff meeting.

"Profile building is a good place to start." Olivia didn't mind admitting Barry was right. "But again, you have to take into account the location, and the population we're dealing with. Alzheimer's units, skilled facilities. People go there to die."

"Or hunt for victims," Barry stressed. "It wouldn't be the first time."

"No, it would not," Olivia hated to admit it, but nurses made very skillful serial killers. They certainly had the means and a pharmacopeia at their disposal. They also had victims who trusted them.

"Rogan Poe is originally from Louisiana but he hasn't lived anywhere permanently since graduating nursing school fifteen years ago. That's a long time to be on the move. If it wasn't for his work history, this guy would be a ghost. He fits the profile of someone who doesn't want to be found," Barry told her.

"I'm not denying that he checks a lot of boxes, but nurses are in demand. Travel nursing is a lucrative career," Olivia countered.

"Yet this guy owns nothing except a vehicle." Barry was frustrated his warnings were falling on deaf ears.

"Pittman said I would have crossed paths with a hunter during my time as a nurse. I just didn't know it." Alzheimer's disease pulverized the brain leaving the patient a shadow of their former self. Sometimes they were erased altogether, morphing into a stranger even their family didn't know. Mild symptoms masked as confusion. Severe cases led to transcendence into another world, leaving the individual vulnerable, their actions and thoughts no longer their own.

Olivia's experiences as a nurse showed her it wasn't her imagination and that she wasn't crazy. There was light and dark, and their world was trapped in a shade of gray. With scientific validation, combined with her unnatural abilities, Dr. Olivia Osborne blazed a new path in forensic psychology. Still, there were missing pieces for her personally.

"You have to understand. I grew up thinking my gifts were a curse or a debt owed by an ancestor to a demon. Meeting Larry Wayne Pittman changed everything. He lived in a world I was denied." Learning she wasn't alone was an awakening that came when she needed it the most.

Olivia cradled her growing belly. Her daughters had their own gifts, and the babies would be here before she knew it. She had a lot of catching up to do before then. She had turned her back on the FBI to embrace who and what she was so she could guide them. "Oak Hollow is the first client who came to me specifically for my gifts. It's a proving ground."

Or divine intervention. The thought slithered across Barry's mind. For all the moving around, here was the only place this hunter had ever been more than once. The first time was four years ago. Barry wondered what made Rogan Poe come back three years later. He had been here longer than he had been anywhere else. There had to be a reason.

"A broken mind is a playground for demons. Pittman said hunters are there in the end to protect those who can't protect themselves. I have to follow this lead. I've been sleepwalking through my whole life. Now that I'm awake, I can't go back."

Barry remained quiet, unwilling to commit.

His silence wasn't what she wanted. "Say it," Olivia insisted.

"I want you to be careful. I know what you found in that room was significant, but it doesn't mean Rogan Poe is the one who left those things behind." Barry hesitated, not wanting to say what he really felt. "Rogan Poe might not be an angel of mercy."

"Are you saying he's an angel of death instead?"

"If I didn't know what I know now, I would think this Poe guy has all the makings of a killer. He has means and opportunity."

"And motive?" Olivia asked.

"You." The realization hit both of them at the same time. Maybe it was why Father Dominic knew this was a job for her. "What if you're the motive? You attract killers. These kinds of killings, if that's what they are, were sure to catch your attention. And Dominic's." He had worked at the same kinds of places in between being a priest.

"It would be an easy trap to set." Olivia acknowledged.

"Pittman said I'm your Watcher. Like it or not, that means I'm here to protect you. That's what I'm trying to do here. If you believed Pittman," which Barry knew she did. "Then that means you have to trust me."

The buzzing noise saved them.

Barry reached for his phone, checked the screen, and ignored it.

It reminded Olivia of another time. Then it had been Amanda he was avoiding. Who was it this time? "You're not going to get that?"

"It's Zavalla. I technically haven't checked in for the day. He'll call back. Besides, I'm about to shove off." He reached for another cookie.

Barry believed in her but not Pittman. The fact he even brought him up told Olivia he was struggling. She had been living with her gifts her whole life. For Barry, his whole world had changed since meeting her. The last year had been a steep learning curve. Still, Olivia needed them on the same team. She changed the subject to something they could agree on.

"I saw her the other day."

The confession came out of the blue, but Barry knew who, even without a name. Still, it sounded like Olivia was talking about the other woman. Maybe she was. Amanda Greene was the one who shared his bed after he and Olivia were what? Almost lovers.

Dr. Greene was a psychiatrist in a practice that counseled police officers suffering from post-traumatic stress. After finding his friend dead at a crime scene, Barry could have been one of Dr. Green's patients. Instead, she became something else.

Amanda tried without success to be Olivia's friend, but Olivia saw it for what it was. An insecure woman's feeble attempt to learn more about the one who got away. Experiences like that were why Olivia preferred dealing with monsters. They didn't hide their intent. Dr. Amanda Greene was a mirage, full of smoke and mirrors.

"I was at an appointment." Instinctively, Olivia felt Barry shift into full watcher mode. "We go to the same OB practice," Olivia assured him.

"You know it's not mine," he rushed to remind her. It was his secret; the one he chose to share with Olivia instead of the woman in his bed.

"Did you tell Amanda that?"

Not in so many words. "I told her I knew there was someone else," Barry said.

"I'm so sorry."

Barry showed up at her place after hearing a shots-fired call over the radio. The incident happened next door at Lily's, but Barry's visit prompted a conversation he and Olivia needed to have. The unresolved feelings between them were still evolving. One way or another, Barry would always be a part of her life. Her thoughts earned kicks from both babies. They seemed to agree.

Barry stared straight ahead, chewing his cookie. "I'm not sorry. You made me promise to do what I needed to do. If I hadn't followed your advice, if I hadn't gone back to Amanda's that night," Barry shook his head. "I would have never known the truth."

Olivia wondered if it was the same man she saw hanging around Amanda that night at the party. Olivia's thoughts scattered when Barry flashed her an unexpected smile. He should definitely do it more often.

"The way I look at it, you saved me." *Again.* The word was unspoken between them. Like so many things.

Olivia considered his statement but didn't dive too deep. "I haven't heard from her since that night." After Barry's rejection, Amanda didn't need her anymore.

"Good." No matter how confident Barry tried to sound, the cop in him doubted he had seen the last of Dr. Greene.

****

When Mason Deveroux was a no-show at the airport the day before, Silas checked to make sure the FBI agent made his flight. Deveroux had boarded the Las Vegas to San Antonio flight with no stops in between. It meant Deveroux wasn't missing in action. He had purposefully given Agent Sharpe the slip. Since Deveroux had also ditched the fire inspector, there was only one other place Silas could think he would go. Silas had avoided going there. No use upsetting their witness until he had to.

Since losing his bid for re-election, Jim Tennent, the former sheriff of Atascosa County, had become an uncooperative recluse. As the only remaining connection to Andre Roche's operation, Tennent was key to finding any of the other missing girls. Silas had finally convinced the former sheriff the FBI wasn't going away. The interview Deveroux had been pushing for months was scheduled for tomorrow morning. Knowing Deveroux, he probably wanted to get to Tennent first. It wasn't a bad play because Silas wasn't sure Tennent would make the meeting. He was uncooperative for a reason. The former sheriff was afraid, and it had nothing to do with the FBI.

Jon Sharpe had worked with Silas long enough to know his moods, and his boss had grown increasingly broody since their arrival at the Sampson place. The most obvious reason was the missing Agent Deveroux, but Sharpe noticed his change in demeanor even before they found out their visit was a dead end.

"Is the problem with Deveroux or Cruz?" Sharpe finally asked.

The simple answer was both. Deveroux running loose in his city had Silas almost as bothered as Cruz's report. "Cruz knows his paints. I'll give him that," Silas commented, avoiding the question.

"The lead was in the paint on the barn," Sharpe repeated Cruz's explanation.

Cruz was the expert, but that wasn't what concerned Silas. "That could explain the lead found in the dirt, but not the toxicology report. Andre Roche and Ana Lutz also had lead in their systems. The same was true for Lieutenant Bartholomew only in much smaller doses. Since the human body has no known purpose for lead, it had to come from an outside source such as ingestion. In his statement, Lieutenant Bartholomew said Ana Lutz forced him to drink something." Barry maintained that was the reason for the gaps in his memory.

Sharpe was first on the scene. When he found him, the lieutenant was barely able to stand. Sharpe attributed it to the punctured lung, courtesy of Roche. "Why would anyone drink lead?"

"In certain circles, lead represents resurrection and transformation. It's used to communicate with the underworld." All the things Andre Roche was believed to have been doing in the barn.

Sharpe never met the BAU version of Silas Branch. It was easy to forget his boss knew more than most about the occult. Now Sharpe knew what was troubling his boss. "This is about Dr. Osborne, isn't it?"

"It's always been about Dr. Osborne."

Chapter Four

Olivia heard the soft ping of her phone. She peeked and saw it was Jessica Tate. Jessica had plans to join Will in DC for the weekend. Olivia had promised restaurant recommendations.

Barry's phone buzzed too. The scowl on his face told her it was Zavalla again. Barry gulped the last of his iced tea and took the call.

"Where are you?"

The urgency in his captain's voice pushed Barry to his feet. "I'm with Dr. Osborne."

The tone of Barry's voice triggered her senses. Olivia swung her feet off the footstool and planted them on the ground.

"Where? At her house?"

Zavalla didn't sound right. Something was wrong. Fearing Olivia could hear what was on the end of the line, Barry turned his back to her, his thoughts immediately going to Silas. "Yea. Why?"

"Stay there."

The two SAPD cruisers were at her house in minutes. They approached from opposite directions, boxing in Barry's ride. He couldn't leave even if he wanted to.

Olivia rose from her chair, her senses flaring with the wave of urgency coming from the new arrivals. Olivia moved next to Barry, her fingers clutching his forearm, not for support, but to keep him in place. "What's going on?"

"I'm not sure, but maybe you should go inside," Barry whispered, sizing up the four officers heading their way. His biggest fear was they were coming with the kind of notification no one wanted to hear. Except their approach was all wrong.

Olivia shook her head and stood her ground. Barry untangled himself from her grip, his arm sweeping protectively in front of her. Moving forward, Barry shielded her from view.

Captain Zavalla took the lead and approached the house while the other three officers waited in the yard. Next door, Lily had stepped outside on her porch to see what was happening. A lady walking her dog crossed to the other side of the street but slowed long enough to catch a view.

Zavalla noted Olivia peering out from behind Barry. Zavalla gave her a slight nod, his face stony. "Lieutenant, I need you to come with us."

Olivia's fingers gripped Barry's elbow this time. The tension in his arm flowed into her. She stepped from behind him to resume her flanking position.

Her movement drew the attention of the one officer in civilian clothes. "Dr. Osborne, if you could step aside and have a seat."

Lieutenant Renard. The information came from Barry. She wasn't telepathic, but Olivia was learning that given the right dose of energy, she was capable of almost anything. Armed with his name, Olivia shifted her attention, her eyes boring into him.

Under her scrutiny, beads of sweat dotted Renard's brow. The officers next to him began to fidget. "Since you are the one on my lawn, I respectfully request you tell me what you want before you start telling me what to do," Olivia told Renard.

Zavalla shook his head, signaling Renard to keep quiet. "We need to talk to Lieutenant Bartholomew, that's all, Dr. Osborne."

"Has something happened to Agent Branch?" Barry asked. He knew it was the wrong question, but any other explanation made no sense.

"Silas is fine. It's you they want," Olivia whispered. Her phone pinged. She glanced over her shoulder in response. Silas' name flashed on the screen, confirming what she already knew.

Barry focused on the four officers, noticing the two next to Renard had moved their hands to their hips, fingertips away from their service weapons.

Barry took Olivia by the arm and steered her back to the chair. "I'm supposed to protect you. The only way I can do that is if you stay calm. Not like in the barn."

"I did that. That was all me," Olivia admitted. It felt good to finally say it.

"I know you did. Now, this, whatever this is, isn't me."

She looked him in the eyes. "I believe you."

As Olivia sank back in her chair, Barry saw movement across the lawn. Lily had left her porch and was heading their way. Barry looked her way, giving her a slow nod of his head, stopping her at the driveway. Confident his message was received, Barry turned back to Olivia, kneeling to be on her level so she would see him. "Lily's here so you won't be alone. Call Silas." He watched one tear slide down her face. It was all he could do not to reach out and catch it.

Steeling himself for what was to come, Barry stood. With a squeeze on her shoulder, he turned and headed straight for Zavalla. "You better have a good fucking reason for doing this," Barry said under his breath.

"I wouldn't do it without one." Zavalla held out his hand. "Now, I'm going to need you to turn over your service weapon," he said loud enough for those behind him to hear.

"What's this about?"

Zavalla took a step closer. "You really want to do this, in front of her?"

Barry's jaw clenched as he slowly unholstered his gun. He slid the lock and unchambered the round. He held it so Zavalla could see all was clear. With Zavalla in agreement, Barry slid the lock back in place. Barrel down, he handed over his weapon.

Zavalla passed the gun to the patrol officer closest to him. With his free hand, Zavalla gripped Barry's arm and stepped in close. "Keep your temper, answer the questions and maybe you'll get through this." Zavalla gestured toward the patrol car he had driven. "That's our ride. Give me your keys so Renard can take yours back to the station."

Barry dug the keys out of his pocket, staring down his captain as he did. He palmed him the keys, and Zavalla tossed them to the other lieutenant. "Now head for the car and don't look back. I'll check on Dr. Osborne."

"I would tread lightly if I were you," Barry warned him.

Zavalla approached the porch, but the blaze of the

doctor's eyes stopped him. They were the greenest eyes Anthony Zavalla had ever seen. They were unnerving, reminding him of a predator tracking their prey. Under their scrutiny, he answered questions she didn't ask.

"We have questions only he can answer. It might take a while. He's not under arrest. He doesn't need a lawyer."

"The cruiser and the officers on my lawn tell me otherwise. So, try again and don't forget who you're talking to."

Zavalla felt the sweat shedding beneath his uniform even though it was a cool day. They'd worked some horrific cases together. Dr. Osborne always held her shit together better than most, but where he was walking right now felt like a tightrope or a plank. He was wading into the eye of the storm. Things were calm on the surface, but one wrong move, and she would sweep him out to sea. The tone in her voice scared him as much as any suspect he had ever faced.

"You know how tricky it can be between cops and local attorneys." Zavalla tried to sound lighthearted, but his voice didn't sound like his own.

Olivia heard the words as she struggled against the anger raging inside her. She had admitted what she did in the barn. What she didn't tell Barry was how good it felt. What she wouldn't give to tap that energy and alter whatever was happening here. The only things keeping her grounded were the budding lives inside of her. Even now, she had to set an example and forage the path they would follow. Control was the only thing that would set them apart from a place they might never recover. She wanted them to live in a place full of light and life, not one filled with shadows and darkness.

Thoughts of her daughters calmed her. Her serenity leaked into Zavalla.

The tension in his shoulders eased, and the captain dared venture up the steps of her porch. He leaned forward and kept his voice low, just as Barry had. "If you want to help him, pick up when Frank Tobias calls." Zavalla had called his head of forensics on his way over. It's why he made Renard ride with the patrol guys. He would answer for his actions later if need be, but right now, he needed to do things his way.

Zavalla was trying to communicate but couldn't say what he wanted because others were listening. Somehow, he found his words. "When we're done, he's going to need someplace to go. He can't go back home. With Will gone, you're his only hope."

****

"You shouldn't have done that. It didn't have to be that way. You could have asked me to come in," Barry raged as they pulled away from the curb. The tension from before was gone, but he was left feeling tired, drained, and this was only the beginning.

"You done?" Zavalla clapped back.

"You could have done this somewhere else. Telling me to stay with her was wrong."

"I needed you to prove to me you weren't lying." The cruiser was equipped with a low jack. Zavalla knew where Barry was even before he asked.

Zavalla's response told Barry whatever this was, was way beyond the captain, but it didn't ease his rage. Barry shook his head. "Still. It didn't have to be that way. You know you made her think something happened to Silas."

"You were the one thinking of Agent Branch."

Zavalla wondered if it was some Freudian thing. Even he could see the lieutenant was in love with her.

Zavalla's words hit home, but it was Silas Barry heard in his head. *"I know you love her. It has to be you."* Those were Silas' instructions if anything ever happened to him. He and Silas were adversaries from the beginning, but one conversation changed everything. Barry had almost convinced himself the conversation never happened. Except when he woke in the middle of the night and remembered the day Silas asked him the unthinkable.

Inside the car, Zavalla spoke freely. "By telling you to stay with her I knew you wouldn't leave."

Barry shook himself free of the memory. It was his and Silas' private moment. Silas wouldn't have shared it with Olivia. "Still, it was an asshole move."

"Maybe you can thank me later," Zavalla snapped. Whether Barry thought so or not, one day Zavalla would make it right, but not today. "There's a protocol that has to be followed. You know that."

"I don't know shit."

"I can't discuss it." Barry's reactions to the news waiting for him had to be real. "My ass is probably already going to be in the fire as it is." Requesting help from Dr. Osborne was one of the reasons, but it was a risk he was willing to take. Regardless of the doctor's feelings for the lieutenant, she would be honest.

"This is the last bit of advice I can give you. So, listen up," Zavalla said.

Barry glared at him.

"You made it about Agent Branch because you were worried about her. Dump your feelings. It's Dr. Osborne from now on. Agent Branch and his FBI buddies are going to be all over this, so screw your head on straight. Dig deep and think before you speak. You know you're not the only one."

****

Silas had the phone in his hand but had taken it off speaker. "Dammit, pick up." It was his third time calling. In between no answers, Silas also called Lily, but she wasn't answering either. Was it too much to hope they were off somewhere having lunch?

"Silas." Olivia's voice told him she already knew something. "They took Barry," she said.

"Who's they?"

"SAPD. Zavalla was here. They didn't cuff him, but they took his weapon."

"Do you know why?"

"No. You don't?" Olivia sounded more panicked than when she answered the phone. "I thought that's why you were calling."

"I got a call from Deveroux. He told me to meet him at SAPD headquarters. It's about Barry, but what, I don't know."

"There's a crime scene. Zavalla told me to expect a call from forensics."

Lily reached over and pressed a fresh glass of iced tea into Olivia's hand. At that moment, Olivia had never been more grateful to have someone she could call a friend.

Olivia held the cool glass against her cheeks instead of drinking. They were burning up. "Now Deveroux shows up. Where's he been?"

"Don't know, but if Barry's caught up in something SAPD is going to look to the FBI for assistance."

"Are you sure about that?"

"You think Deveroux is somehow involved?" Silas and Sharpe never made it to Jim Tennent's house, but after talking to Deveroux, Silas was convinced neither had he.

"Ask yourself, how did Deveroux know about this before you? Before me?"

Silas saw they were approaching police headquarters. "Before I see Zavalla, tell me, why was Barry at the house?"

"It wasn't a planned thing. I had emailed him with some questions on my new client. I didn't expect him to drop by today."

"How did he look? Do you know where he was before?"

"You sound like you're asking me to describe a suspect." The protest in her voice was palpable.

"Livie, it sounds like he is. Give me your interpretation because you're the last one he was with. I need you to be my eyes if we're going to help him," Silas said, trying to sound reassuring.

Olivia centered herself and took a sip of her tea. "He was dressed for work, yet he said he hadn't checked in for the day. He was relaxed. He ate four cookies."

It didn't sound like Barry was a man with something to hide. "We're heading into the parking garage so I'm probably going to lose you."

"I'm pretty sure Zavalla was trying to tell me Barry is going to need a lawyer."

Shit. It was worse than Silas thought.

They both heard the ping of her phone. Olivia knew who it was without looking.

"Got to go, duty calls," she told him.

Chapter Five

Silas was annoyed Deveroux wasn't there, but happy for the private audience with Zavalla. The captain was eager to talk.

"We have a witness who saw her hit the ground, but not what happened before. I had a less-than-experienced lieutenant on the scene, and some work that should have been done wasn't. It made Meeks nervous, and he decided we needed an ID sooner rather than later. Turns out it was the game changer. Once he turned the body, he knew who she was. So did half the guys there."

Silas leaned back in his chair. "Meeks doesn't think she jumped?"

"Meeks says she landed too far from the building. Once we knew who she was, there was only one place to look. We gained access and found her purse and shoes inside. The balcony door was open."

"How did she get inside?"

"According to the doorman she came in flashing keys."

Silas refused to believe Bartholomew was involved. He had entrusted Barry with the most precious things in his life. "If she came in with keys, she must have thought no one was home."

Sharpe was surprised at how quickly Silas leaped to the lieutenant's defense. "It doesn't mean she was right."

With Sharpe's words, the realization of Barry's predicament took hold. "How can we help?" Silas asked, referring to the FBI.

"I got a call from the DA reminding me my guys were to be on a short leash. Followed by another one from the mayor telling me he doesn't want any screw-ups." Zavalla felt his promotion to the assistant chief position was on the line, possibly even his current job. "We obviously can't investigate this thing ourselves."

Silas did not look forward to working with Kurt Preston again. There was no love lost between the DA and the FBI. Publicly Preston blasted the BAU for using a profiler who offered him no verifiable evidence. Privately he all but said Olivia and Silas should have killed Smythe when they had the chance. Given what Smythe had done to one of their own, Preston might have kept the public sentiment, but he fell from grace when it was Dr. Osborne and not his own team who led forensics to the knife Smythe used to kill Mark Austin. Preston's reputation was tarnished, and his future political career hung in limbo.

"Preston is on his way over here," Zavalla explained.

Supposedly so was Deveroux. Silas wondered if they were together and what that meant. Currently, it meant he had the advantage. "What does Bartholomew know?"

"Not a damn thing."

"You think letting him stew in an interrogation room is a good idea?" Silas suggested. "He could start yelling any minute. Probably the only reason he hasn't is that he's one of yours and knows how this works.

Silence doesn't foster cooperation, especially not in this situation. If Bartholomew didn't do this, holding him under the circumstances could be construed as cruel and unusual."

Agent Branch had a law degree but never used it. Zavalla wondered if he might have missed his calling. "If you were his lawyer, is that what you would do?"

"You bet your ass I would," Silas said, knowing he wouldn't be the only one. Considering he knew what the captain told Livie, Silas decided to use the information to get him what he wanted. "If this goes south, you, the DA, and the mayor will be dealing with someone far worse than me. I'm a bad dream. Anyone else could be a nightmare."

****

Olivia assured the officer who greeted her she knew the way. She rode the elevator she had only taken once in her life alone. She stepped off and headed to the end of the hall where Frank Tobias was waiting with booties in hand.

"Thanks for doing this." His voice was quiet.

"Who else is here?" Olivia asked.

"No one."

From the police presence in the lobby, she had guessed as much. She didn't want an audience. Maybe Tobias didn't either.

"After you," Frank said, holding the door.

Stepping into the living room, Olivia was immediately drawn to the open patio doors. The streaming sunshine was in direct contrast to the heaviness she felt inside. The curtains billowed at her arrival. A cool wind rose to greet her, stirring smells of rich tobacco even though she knew the owner didn't smoke. Her hands moved instinctively to her babies willing them to sleep as she moved further inside.

The room was neat and tidy. Identical to the last time she saw it. There were no obvious signs of a struggle. But there had been. Something feral and untamed had ripped through here, shredding the veil between this world and another. Wild magic still clung to the air causing pinpricks across her skin. Static crackled inside her head like a radio looking for a receiver. Olivia flipped the switch and tuned it out. At any other time in her life, she wasn't sure she could have done it, but her skills were growing.

Olivia knew where she was going, and the other side was waiting. Shattered magic particles scattered at her feet. Wisps of gray beckoned her forward, leading the way. "It's on the patio, isn't it?"

Olivia watched the weight of what Frank had asked to settle on his face. It was one thing to request her assistance, it was another to know he was right to call her. The Bureau had struggled with the same paradox. Olivia was tired of stepping around their feelings.

"I know the way." Olivia slipped past him, ignoring the little yellow sandwich boards that littered the area. They were placeholders, waiting for their turn. They would still be there when she was done.

The wind blew her hair back as she stepped outside on the balcony. In front of her was the centerpiece. The placeholder this time was a glass giving a clear view of what someone didn't want to blow away. To some, it might seem ominous. To her, the iridescent coil glistened in the sun like an endless kaleidoscope.

She headed for the glass, but she came to an unexpected stop. A jolt pierced her as if some unseen force had intervened. Olivia looked down to see what had blocked her. Her path was clear, but the toes of her booties had ended at the point drawn on the cement. The drawing was an upside-down triangle with the base following the balcony railing. She felt an overwhelming urge to cross over, except she wouldn't be going alone. It was the lives inside of her that made her stop.

"Any idea what it means?" Frank asked.

The look on her face told him she hadn't heard him. "I collected samples already. It looks like a combination of salt and maybe sand," he told her.

"A salt circle protects the summoner from whatever they are conjuring." But this was no circle, and they weren't searching for protection. This was a summons. "As for this, I'm not familiar, but triangles are used in many rituals." Since this one resulted in death, it couldn't be anything good.

Firmly rooted in place, Olivia studied the markings at her feet. "The lines in front of the balcony are undisturbed. It means whoever drew them wasn't the one who climbed over the edge. If that's what they did." Olivia glanced over at Frank.

His face had paled at her assessment.

"The coroner doesn't think this was an accident," Frank said, confirming her own realization.

This was no suicide.

Frank led Olivia back inside to retrace their steps. "We found one shoe inside and the other on a balcony three floors down. A purse was sitting on the first couch inside," he said, pointing to the yellow cards.

Olivia concentrated on Frank's assessment, her mind racing to the end. She felt sick inside.

"The purse was unzipped. We have to assume a set

of keys is missing. The way the door works, you can't lock yourself out. You have to have a key. First responders found the door locked. The doorman had to let them in. Also, there is no sign of the owner's car in the parking lot."

Those were all police matters that didn't require her attention.

"What's under the glass?" Olivia heard herself ask.

She could see the revulsion on Frank's face.

"It's a snakeskin. After Atascosa County I hoped to never see another one of those. At least I know a snake wrangler. I'm hoping he can tell me what kind."

Her skin prickled at the familiarity. "That's why you called me. Because what's here reminds you of what was there."

Frank's reluctance gave way to desperation. "Please tell me you know what this means."

"A snake shedding its skin is a classic symbol of rebirth or a new beginning. It doesn't matter what kind it is. When you're finished gathering your samples, cleanse the area with salt water. You need to wash away whatever was done here," Olivia told him.

"How can death be considered a new beginning?" Frank asked.

"That would depend on intent and purpose. This was a murder."

****

"If you're the friendliest face they could find, I must be in deep shit," Barry said.

Silas pulled out a chair and gestured for him to do the same. "Eyes and ears."

Barry barely heard him, but he could read lips no one on the other side of the mirror could see. He did as he was told.

Silas took a long look at the man across from him. They were adversaries the moment they met, like some predestined role. Then Livie had a vision of his death, and Silas knew his world had to change. Barry Bartholomew could not have anything to do with this if he was supposed to take his place with Livie and their girls.

"Tell me about your morning."

"Tell me why I'm here."

Silas smiled. "You know how this works. You show me yours, and I'll show you mine."

"I woke up."

"What time?"

"I don't know. I don't set an alarm. It just happens."

"Guess," Silas told him.

"The sun wasn't up, but it was getting there."

"Were you alone?"

"What?"

"It's a simple question, Lieutenant. Were. You. Alone?"

An idea started to form, but Barry didn't like where it took him. The captain tried to warn him in the car. "Yea, I was alone."

"Then what?"

"I went for a run around IW."

"Incarnate Word, the university, or the high school?"

Barry was finally following along. Silas was trying to establish a verifiable timeline. He really was a friendly face. "The U. Traffic was starting to stack up on the highway. I could see taillights."

"How long?"

"Long enough. Probably thirty minutes, forty tops. I hit the shower, grabbed coffee, and left."

"That's the second time you left your building. How do you exit? Front door or parking garage?"

Whatever happened must have been at the condo. Barry recalled hearing a chopper buzzing around when he got to Olivia's but that didn't mean much, not in a city the size of San Antonio. "Residents use the parking garage."

"When you left the second time, what was your mode of transportation?"

More verifiable information. "My city ride."

"Where did you go?"

Barry stalled. "Since I wasn't on city time that's private. I'm going to need more information before I share that with you." The city could always pull the low-jack information off his car, but that would take time. Until then, Barry would keep his secrets.

Silas didn't like it, but Barry was well within his rights.

"I'll tell you what the ones who put me in this box already know. I ended up at your house. To see Dr. Osborne," Barry offered.

"Why?"

Low-jack information wouldn't tell the others why Barry made that stop, but Silas already knew the answer. He was calling Olivia before Zavalla could haul him away. Silas and Olivia had already compared notes. They would do it again after. Still, Barry wanted her cleared of whatever this was sooner rather than later.

"She asked for my help with some information.

Considering what she's done for SAPD I figured we all owe her one."

Silas liked the answer. "How long were you there?"

"I don't know. If I'd known we were going to be having this little chat, I would have paid more attention." It was a standard fuck you statement. Barry had heard it plenty of times when he was sitting where Silas was now. He had never had a chance to use it until now.

"Is that all? Do you want to add anything?" Silas asked.

"I had some iced tea and cookies. Now, your turn."

"How would you describe your relationship with Dr. Amanda Greene?"

Barry let out a long breath. "Over. Why?"

"But you did have one, correct?"

"Relationship is a strong word."

"What would you call it?" Silas asked.

Barry's jaw tightened. "A one-night stand that lasted a year."

His words were callous. Silas hoped they didn't come back to haunt him. "Are you still sleeping with her?"

Any other time Barry would have told Silas to go fuck himself, but Zavalla warned him to keep his temper in check. "I already told you. It's over. That means no."

"When did it end?" Silas asked.

"Just after she bought her house. Four months ago."

"Was that the last time you saw her?"

The look on Silas' face told Barry this was as

important as his whereabouts this morning. "No. It's been a month, maybe more."

"Where was the last time you saw her?"

"My condo. She was there one night when I got home. She wasn't invited."

"So, she was waiting for you?"

"Yea. She was sitting outside my door. Like I said, uninvited."

"Why didn't she use her key?"

Damn. Something must be really wrong. Silas establishing a timeline involving Amanda couldn't be a good thing. "It was easier to change the locks than ask for the key back. After that visit, I let the doorman know she is not allowed upstairs. I haven't seen her since."

"So, what happened?"

"I asked her to leave."

"You want to tell me what this is about?" Barry asked.

"I'm sorry to inform you, Lieutenant, but earlier this morning Dr. Amanda Greene was found dead outside your condo. My condolences on your loss." Silas got up and headed for the door.

It took Barry a moment to collect himself, but he had to make Silas stop. "You can't possibly think I had something to do with this."

Silas slowly walked back to the table. "Did you?"

"No." Barry leaned forward. His stare was unwavering.

Satisfied, Silas turned to go.

"Amanda wouldn't either."

Silas turned back around. "Amanda wouldn't what?"

"Kill herself."

It was a bold confession.

"I wouldn't be in here if you thought it was suicide," Barry told him.

Bartholomew had a point.

Silas turned around and headed back towards the door.

"Ask Meeks," Barry shouted. "He'll know why."

Chapter Six

Jessica was packing up to leave when she noticed a white SUV exit the barricade. She left Reggie behind and drove the news van herself. It was a ten-minute drive. Reaching her destination, Jessica pulled into the driveway, hoping to be as non-conspicuous as possible. She was relieved to find Olivia's vehicle parked ahead of her. Thank goodness Olivia went home and not downtown.

To Jessica's surprise, Lily answered the door. Behind her, Jessica saw Olivia on the couch with her feet up.

"I can't talk to you," Olivia told her reluctantly, even though talking was exactly what she wanted.

"I know who it is," Jessica revealed. "Soon everyone else will too; pending notification of next of kin," Jessica repeated the press statement. She thought it was curious none of the police brass from earlier were there. "I need to know what I should tell Kim."

Olivia caved at the mention of Kim. Of course. The young girl's therapist was dead. The last thing Kim needed was to read it on the internet. "Don't tell her anything. I'll do it."

Jessica nodded in agreement. Maybe seeing Kim and baby Addy would get Olivia's mind off things. If nothing else, they could provide a distraction Olivia looked like she needed. "I'm worried about the lieutenant. It's his building, but I didn't see him."

"You haven't talked to Will?" Olivia asked carefully.

"I can't get in touch with him. He's in interviews all day."

On lockdown at Quantico, access to his cell phone would be restricted. "Zavalla and three other officers tracked Barry to my house. They came here and took him away." Olivia decided to tell her. Jessica would find out eventually.

"Took him away? What does that even mean?" Surely, they don't think…"

"He's not under arrest," Olivia said. *Yet.* The unspoken word hung in the air. No wonder Zavalla didn't stick around. Jessica tried to piece together the story. "Barry was here? How long?"

Once again, Olivia felt like a witness. "Less than an hour."

Not long enough for an alibi. Jessica kept the comment to herself, but Olivia knew what she was thinking.

"He didn't do it," Olivia assured her.

****

Lily followed Jessica outside to the porch.

"I'm glad you're here," Jessica said. "She looks like she needs someone."

"I threatened to call her doctor if she even thought about asking me to leave," Lily confessed.

Jessica looked alarmed. She meant moral support. "Is she okay, physically? Is it the babies?"

"Her blood pressure was pretty high when she got back. She wanted to go upstairs and have a bath. That's when I told her to lay down instead."

"Given what happened and in her state," Jessica stopped talking. She wasn't the expert. "You're a nurse, right?"

"Yea. For preemies. I told her I didn't want to be seeing her little ones anytime soon." Lily tried to smile, but Jessica could see she was worried.

"Should we call someone?"

"She isn't complaining of a headache. I told her I would take her blood pressure again when she woke up. If it's not down by then…" The look on Jessica's face told Lily she should stop talking and take action. "I have nurse brain. I'm sure it's the situation."

"It's bad," Jessica said, drifting back to the scene outside Barry's condo.

"It's more than that, isn't it? They found something worse than a dead body." Lily didn't have the words to describe what she was trying to say. She knew she was doing a terrible job of it. "It's why they called her, isn't it?"

Jessica hadn't even thought of that. Lily was right. Bad didn't begin to cover it. "Will says no one calls her for normal."

Lily decided she had finally unlocked one of Olivia's superpowers. She was good at blending in. "Olivia says she explains things no one else can. She made it sound so benign." It had been easy to separate Olivia from her family history. Until now.

"That's a pretty safe description," Jessica agreed. "There's a whole other world out there, and she's the go-between."

"And that's a gift?" Lily sounded unsure.

"My answer would be yes. Since I'm not the one gifted. She found my niece when no one else could.

And she's the only one to ever understand Kim. That means a lot."

"And the lieutenant? They're close, right?" After today, Lily felt the need to know.

The question seemed personal, then again, the lieutenant was a memorable guy.

"Olivia and the lieutenant have been through a lot together. Losing Mark, Barry's partner, was hard on both of them. Then there was the incident out in Atascosa County. From what Will told me, Barry's not exaggerating when he says Olivia saved his life."

****

Kurt Preston arrived outside the interrogation room without notice. "What is he doing in there?" Preston asked, watching Silas through the glass. "I told you to wait before you turned the case over to the FBI."

"I got tired of waiting." Zavalla had been complacent before, talking to Silas convinced him he had to act before things spun even more out of control.

While Zavalla was tied up with the DA, Agent Sharpe saddled up to the man who accompanied him. "I waited for you at the airport. You couldn't make a courtesy call to let me know you weren't coming?"

"I had something I had to take care of." Mason Deveroux's tone was dismissive. "Looks like it's a good thing I did." Deveroux stared past the agent to land on Lieutenant Bartholomew.

Sharpe didn't like the cryptic response.

"You shouldn't have let the FBI talk to him," Preston said, watching Silas and Barry through the glass. With the raised voices in the room, no one heard what they were saying. Now, it was over.

"You didn't want SAPD's help, remember?"

Zavalla snapped.

Sharpe stepped up to join Zavalla, leaving Deveroux to linger in the corner. "Our own guy called us and here we are."

"The FBI can't be involved in this. There's a conflict of interest," Preston said.

****

The procession to Zavalla's office was tension-filled, but mercifully quiet, given Preston's announcement. Any further discussion was put on hold by the incessant ringing of Zavalla's desk phone. He grabbed it, hoping Silas and Preston could keep quiet long enough for him to hear what was on the other line.

The coroner spoke first. "Are you alone?"

"No," Zavalla answered.

"Then for God's sake don't put me on speaker. You should know Dr. Greene was pregnant. The DA wanted me to call him first, but I must have forgotten that part."

Zavalla took a breath. "The DA and the FBI are in my office now," Zavalla told him.

"Ask them who is going to be here for the cut," Meeks sighed.

"Dr. Meeks, who is going to be present for the autopsy," Zavalla relayed.

Preston snapped his fingers at Zavalla. "Put me on speaker."

"It's a simple damn question," Meeks grumbled while Zavalla connected them.

"I'll have to get back to you," Preston spoke up, "but I want it done today. Anything you can tell me?"

"I did the usual, scrapped the fingernails and a toxicology panel was drawn and sent. Photos are in process."

"Are there defensive wounds?" Preston asked.

"The body's natural reaction is to break a fall. Having said that, it's going to take time to make that determination. Now, I need to get back to work." Meeks hung up without saying goodbye.

Silas turned on Kurt Preston. "What conflict of interest?" Deveroux showing up with the DA had set off all kinds of alarms in Silas' head.

"Your agent here," Preston said, referring to Deveroux. "He came forward with some information that could taint the FBI's investigation of Lieutenant Bartholomew."

"He came forward? How? He just got here," Silas said as if Deveroux wasn't there.

Deveroux, who had been leaning against Zavalla's bookcase, finally joined the conversation. "I had a last-minute change of plans. An offer, as they say, I couldn't refuse."

Silas held his tongue. He didn't want an internal squabble in front of outsiders. He and Deveroux would settle their differences on their own time.

"Actually, I was the one who contacted Agent Deveroux," Preston said. "Once Dr. Greene's phone was located, we went through her calls and found the agent's number. As it just so happened, he was already in town."

Deveroux didn't wait to be asked. "She reached out to me with information in the Atascosa County case."

Deveroux wouldn't have been able to resist. Silas wondered if that was the point. "The investigation is officially closed," Silas reminded him.

What Silas said was true. Still, the whole purpose of his visit was to interview the former Atascosa

County sheriff. Deveroux counted himself lucky there were others still as curious as he was about what the sheriff knew. "Some of us still have questions," Deveroux countered.

Zavalla stiffened at the suggestion. "You might want to voice your concerns to the Texas Rangers. They were the ones who closed the case," Zavalla pointed out.

Silas smiled at the notion of Deveroux questioning Herschel Gaines' investigative prowess. The Texas lawman was one of the longest-serving officers of the elite force. If Silas was lucky, maybe he could be privy to the conversation.

Deveroux ignored the captain. "I altered my arrival plans to meet with Dr. Greene yesterday. She expressed concerns about Lieutenant Bartholomew."

Now Silas knew why Deveroux cut him out of the loop. "According to the lieutenant, they had gone their separate ways. It didn't sound like she was onboard with the decision. Her motivation could have been personal," Silas told him. "If you talked to some of us locals, you might have known that."

"I can assure you that was not the case. The lieutenant wasn't the only one Dr. Greene mentioned. Her information included Dr. Osborne as well," Deveroux revealed.

"And you were planning on telling me this when?" Silas snapped.

"I'm telling you now. I called your office. I was on my way to catch up with you in Atascosa County when the DA's office called. Considering Dr. Greene's allegations involve not only the lieutenant, but your wife," Deveroux emphasized, "I recommended the

Bureau steer clear of this situation," Deveroux explained.

"After speaking with Agent Deveroux, I have to agree," Preston said. "It's no secret Agent Branch, you and the lieutenant aren't exactly friendly. I wouldn't want anyone to think he was being treated unfairly by a man who has, shall we say, a contentious personal history especially given that history involves Dr. Osborne. Things could get messy."

Sharpe knew from working with Silas that mentioning Dr. Osborne was like entering a minefield. He decided to intervene. "Why not turn this case over to the Texas Rangers?" Sharpe suggested.

Zavalla was quick to agree. "It only makes sense."

"I have it on good authority Herschel Gaines happens to be in the area," Sharpe added.

The DA looked like he wanted to protest, but Preston had no valid reason to refuse.

"I'll make the call," Zavalla said before anyone could find a reason to object.

"I'll inform the lieutenant," Silas announced.

"Given Agent Deveroux's concerns, maybe Agent Sharpe should do that," Preston suggested. "Now, Agent Deveroux, you should come back with me so we can finish your statement."

****

Not trusting what he might say, Silas plopped himself in a chair across from Zavalla's desk and waited until he and the captain were alone before speaking.

"You want to tell me what Meeks said to you on the phone before everyone else?"

"Was I that obvious?"

"I was a profiler long before I was a station chief," Silas reminded him. "In my time here, I've also gathered the ME has a soft spot for the lieutenant. So, do you."

"According to Meeks, Dr. Greene was pregnant."

Dammit, Bartholomew. "Barry said she wouldn't hurt herself. Now I know why. He also said he didn't hurt her. I believe him," Silas said.

"It doesn't matter what anyone believes. As soon as this gets out, Preston will be able to hold him as long as legally possible."

"I didn't see wounds on his hands or his face. Maybe some pics would help."

"If he doesn't refuse," Zavalla said. "The fastest way he can get out of here is to give up where he was this morning. You did good getting him to talk, but it's going to take time to verify. They're still pulling camera footage from the building."

"Barry said he changed the locks since the breakup. Check with building security to confirm his story. He also said the doorman knew she wasn't allowed upstairs. Preston has her phone. If she and Bartholomew were in contact, it will be in there. Since Preston didn't mention it, that tells me it's not there."

Silas grew quiet as he considered his next move. Of all the times for Will Ibarra to be gone. Barry needed all the friends he could get right now. Silas could use Will's help.

Zavalla hated to lose the agent in an official capacity. He saw it as a good time for an apology. "We tracked Barry down by his car. I had no way of knowing we would find him at your house. I'm sorry this went down the way it did," Zavalla confessed.

"You can make it up to me by telling me why you called my wife."

"There were symbols drawn on the balcony. They looked straight out of those pictures from Atascosa County. And a goddamn snakeskin." It was a relief to share. Zavalla was glad for it to be out of his own head. "It's like the Roche brothers had been reincarnated."

The flesh on Silas' neck tingled at Zavalla's words. It was a familiar feeling from his BAU days.

"When I saw that I kicked out the crew. I knew Dr. Osborne was the only one to call."

"I'm assuming your superiors know nothing about that?" Silas confirmed. Zavalla was circling the wagons. Tightening the flow of information. Keeping only those he could trust not to talk.

"It would be a conflict of interest according to the DA," Zavalla repeated.

Satisfied, Silas pushed himself out of the chair he'd been sitting in too long. "I'll be back before the end of the day. Someone will need to let me into Bartholomew's place."

Zavalla couldn't mask his surprise.

"He can't go home once he's out of here," Silas clarified the unspoken offer.

"I'll make it happen," Zavalla assured him. It also meant he didn't have to worry that Barry was on his own and unsupervised.

"You do that. Livie told me you tried to warn her about the need for legal representation. Who do you think she's going to call?"

Zavalla was surprised. "She knows we're on the same team, right?"

"She does," Silas assured him.

"It's still early. Who would she call? What would she even say?"

"Doesn't matter. The man on the other end will listen. I wasn't lying when I used the word nightmare. Deveroux may have the DA's ear right now but trust me when I tell you Deveroux is obsessed and not in a good way. Now, I'm going to get Bartholomew's permission to enter his domicile. Then I need to go check on my wife. I'll be on my cell."

Chapter Seven

Sharpe was waiting for his boss outside Zavalla's office.

"How did Bartholomew take the news?" Silas asked.

"I told him about the change, but nothing else. Preston and Deveroux were outside."

Sharpe headed for the parking garage, but Silas had other plans. "Where are you going? We're out."

"The FBI is out," Silas corrected him. "Pull the car around front. I won't be long.

****

Barry had given up pacing. He was sitting in the chair watching the door when Silas entered. Barry was surprised to see him, but not enough to say. He wasn't sure who was listening.

Silas took his seat across the table.

"I thought the Rangers were up."

"The photographer is next, if you consent."

Barry ignored him. "Why's the FBI out?"

"Dr. Greene spoke to your old friend Agent Deveroux yesterday. Whatever she said convinced the DA that he doesn't want me interviewing you. Any idea why?"

Barry shook his head. It was beginning to spin.

"I need your permission to enter your residence."

Barry looked suspicious. "Why?"

"It's a crime scene and I'm a private citizen who thinks you might need a change of clothes before they let you back in. It's called a favor."

"Thank you."

"Don't thank me yet, there's more." Silas leaned forward and stared Bartholomew in the eyes. "Did you know?"

"I told you. I didn't do it."

Silas shook his head. "That's not what I'm talking about."

Silas' tone was stern. It was a good dad voice. With daughters, he was going to need it. Barry rubbed his face, trying to focus. The day was catching up to him.

"Will I find anything interesting in your nightstand. Weapon? Protective gear?" Silas' face was a question. "Did. You. Know?" Silas enunciated every word.

Barry finally realized what Silas was asking. "It's how I knew Amanda didn't hurt herself. For what it's worth, it isn't mine."

"You're sure about that?"

For the first time, Silas looked like he didn't believe him. "Absolutely."

Barry's face hardened. He was shutting down, but Silas wouldn't let him.

"In case you've forgotten I have a vested interest in you. What could Amanda possibly have to tell Mason Deveroux?"

Barry shook his head. "Nothing. She wasn't there."

"My wife was. She was also there this morning when they dragged you away. And after." Silas could see that got his attention.

"After? What do you mean?"

"Zavalla sent her over to your condo. The DA doesn't know that. Not yet."

"What? Why?"

Silas stared harder, but Barry didn't flinch. "Don't know. I'm on my way to see her now." Looking pissed, Silas vacated the chair. He turned back for one more try. "You're sure that baby wasn't yours?"

"Same answer as before. Absolutely."

"Absolution is a tough sell," Silas warned.

"That's not what the bishop keeps telling me."

****

Sharpe stayed in the suburban, fielding calls while Silas checked on Olivia. He found Lily in the kitchen cleaning up from lunch. "Thai?" he asked.

Lily smiled. "She said you wouldn't mind if we ate your leftovers."

"You have no idea," Silas told her. Thai had been Olivia's food craving for months. Silas wondered if their children would come out hating it or loving it. It could go either way.

"She said you'd say that."

Silas smiled. "Where is she?"

Lily nodded toward the backyard, her eyes sliding away from his. "Out back with the dogs."

Something inside Silas stirred. "Is everything okay?"

"She needs some rest." Lily saw concern streak his face and rushed to soothe him without giving away Olivia's trust. "Growing babies is hard work, and she's doing double time. It's been a hard day. I watched it from my yard. It was scary."

"I'm sorry you had to see that, but I'm glad you're here for Livie."

"Me too."

"Has she been on the phone?"

"As a matter of fact, she has. She seemed better after if that's any consolation."

Silas nodded, digesting. He had been right to warn Zavalla. "Will you be around this evening? I could be home late."

"Sure. Whatever you need."

Silas came up behind his wife and reached down to knead her shoulders. Daisy looked up expectantly. The lanky greyhound was stretched beside Olivia's lounge chair while Alvin fought for space in her lap, losing the battle against the unwavering baby bump. He was half-in, half-out, but hanging in there. The pose didn't look comfortable, but it was the closest the little Schnauzer could get to cuddling with his mistress these days.

Olivia reached behind, her hands covering Silas'. "You should come home during the day more often."

"Don't tempt me." Silas kneaded harder as he bent down to kiss the top of her head. "What are you doing out here?"

"Thinking how I should maybe crack open my great, great grandmother's book on herbs and expand the garden." Until recently, the books were tucked away in the outside shed. Larry Wayne Pittman convinced her she needed to pull her head out of the sand and explore the world around her, a world that now included more than just her. Olivia wanted her daughters prepared for the life they had no choice but to lead.

"I was also thinking the yard's big enough for a pool. I think it would be good for the girls. I want this to be the house where their friends gather."

Her comments were bittersweet. While Silas liked hearing her talk about their future, he knew it was a defense mechanism to distance herself from whatever she had seen.

"A pool sounds nice," Silas agreed. "And a garden."

"It means teaching our daughters about their family history, on their mother's side," she warned.

For years Olivia tried to deny her heritage. Since her pregnancy, she had embraced it. Silas was glad to see she had made peace with her family's past. No matter what that might entail. He'd known since he met her, she was an evolution of the senses.

"They are survivors, descendants of some very powerful women."

"I can't argue with that."

"I intend to see that tradition continues."

The conviction in her voice told him it was worse than he thought. Silas sidestepped the greyhound and took a seat at the end of Olivia's chair, shifting her bare feet into his lap to make room. Her ankles were puffy, and her toes looked like little smokies.

They had a scare during the first few weeks of pregnancy, and Silas had remained on edge. He wouldn't rest until the babies were free from the womb and all three of his girls were safe and healthy. Silas could see Olivia struggling with the pregnancy as much as she had the conception. They were about to give up when it happened.

Silas reached for her hand, noticing she was missing her wedding ring. He rubbed his thumb over the empty space.

"You read the book." *Exceptional Expectations:*

The New Mom's Guide to Pregnancy lived on Silas' nightstand. He read it more than she did.

"How do you always know what I'm thinking?"

"Not always," Olivia assured him.

But more since her pregnancy.

"Swelling isn't uncommon."

"Seems a little early. Are you okay?"

"I will be," Olivia told him. "Once you tell me what you know."

Silas hadn't expected to go first, but he had put her off as long as possible. "Bartholomew won't give up where he was this morning." Silas watched for a reaction but got none. "Did you know about Amanda?"

"They broke up."

"Not that." Silas wondered how she would take the news Amanda was pregnant with Barry's child. As usual, she surprised him.

"Barry told me this morning. It was idle conversation. I told you I thought I saw her at the OB office."

"How long has he known?" Meeks would know once the autopsy was complete, but Silas was hoping to get a jump on the dates. They could be crucial.

"A couple of months; maybe. He didn't know it at the time of the break up."

"What was he going to do about it?"

"It didn't change his mind if that's what you're asking. It wasn't his."

Silas was pissed again at the whole discussion. It was one thing for Bartholomew to lie to him. It was another to lie to her. "Livie, that's a pretty tight time frame to be so sure. Maybe it was a convenient way of saying he didn't want it." Bartholomew was the stupidest smart guy Silas knew.

"Are you speaking from experience?"

"Of course not. I took precautions."

"Not with me you didn't."

"I think we've already established you were different." With Olivia, it wasn't about consequences but possibilities. Silas reached across Alvin to lay his hand on her abdomen. He liked feeling the babies move. He was rewarded with a soft kick in response to his touch. He looked disappointed when he didn't get one from the other side.

"That's our little night owl."

"Aw, like her mother."

Olivia moved his hand back to where it was before. "This is our little sun lover."

"Which is which?"

"Genevieve is our little sun baby." Olivia patted her right side, where Silas felt the kick and got one of her own. She'd been active all afternoon.

"She's going to like the pool."

Olivia moved his hand back to her left side. "Gwendolyn will too, if we add a heater," she suggested.

"I take it you didn't believe him?" Olivia asked when it was clear they weren't going to get a response. Her night owl had been quieter than usual since they left the condo. Olivia wondered what she felt. Whatever it was didn't have the same effect on her sister.

"And you do?"

"When he and wife number two couldn't make it happen, they found out it was him."

Barry's confession surprised even Silas. "Why do you know this?"

"It was the weekend I came home from Florida, the night of Amanda's party. I was with Lily while the paramedics stitched up her feet. I got nauseous at the sight of the blood. Barry and Agent Sharpe showed up in time to see me almost lose my dinner. They thought I was sick, and I explained I wasn't. Barry wished us well and told me his story."

Silas wondered how the news of their pregnancy made Bartholomew feel but quickly discarded the idea. No use pondering what he already knew. This was about Amanda. "What about Amanda? Did she know?" That was the question that begged an answer.

"No."

Of course not. Barry Bartholomew wasn't in love with Amanda.

"Did he know there was someone else?"

"We didn't discuss that part. Amanda made such a production out of how much she loved him. I was surprised she slept with someone else."

His wife possessed many gifts, but personal relationships with her were different than most people. "I hate to point out the obvious, but sex and love are two different things. People have sex for a whole lot of reasons." He should know. He had done it for years.

"Attention," Olivia answered her own question.

Silas couldn't argue with her logic. Amanda knew she didn't have Barry's, so she went elsewhere.

"I don't think anyone truly knew her. She was a mirage." Amanda was hiding something from the beginning. Whether it was suspicion or deception, Olivia was never sure. Either one was enough for Olivia to keep her guard up no matter how hard Amanda tried to slip past it.

Olivia reached over to squeeze Silas' hand. "We're very lucky."

He brought her fingers to his lips. "We are."

"This is different, isn't it?" Olivia didn't have the same experiences as her husband, but she didn't need them to know. She could feel it.

"It is. There are layers I never knew existed." Their emotional relationship began as coworkers long before they consummated the physical one. After that, there was no turning back. "This need to be together is deep-seated; like something outside ourselves."

Olivia warmed at the description. He typically left the mystical to her. "Darwin believed pheromones play an important part in mate selection."

Silas smiled. Leave it to Livie to put a logical spin on it. Balancing the paranormal with the scientific was how she kept her world in check. "Darwin aside, I think it's all you, babe. Another one of your many gifts."

"My gifts aren't enough. Not this time. What I found today is something I don't understand. This was magic like I've never seen before."

The conviction in her voice earlier had returned. But this time, she wasn't talking about her ancestors. She was talking about their daughters and the world they would live in.

"Amanda was murdered by magic?" Silas heard the uncertainty in his voice. She had told him about the revelations Pittman revealed about others out there. Silas didn't want to believe him, but he did see what Olivia did at the prison. She stopped the guards in their tracks. She said she harnessed the energy of the place. Silas knew what he saw, but still he couldn't understand a world where that was possible.

"I believe Amanda was lured to Barry's condo," Olivia said, bringing Silas back to the present.

Lured. In the eyes of the law, that equated to premeditation. "How do you know this?" DA Preston would settle for nothing less than verifiable evidence.

"There was someone else there," Olivia told him. Someone who knows magic."

Silas heard her, but he had to reach for the familiar. "Who would want to kill Amanda? And why at Barry's condo?" Silas asked.

"Not the most obvious suspect," Olivia said what they both knew. Barry checked all the boxes, a personal relationship gone bad and suspected father of the baby, but this time the boxes were wrong. "The kill was specific," Olivia said, mulling over what she had seen.

Silas noted her word choice. Where was she going with this? "What do you mean?"

"I don't know. I need more information. Someone has to know more than me."

"Meeks thinks she was pushed," Silas offered. "If that's true, then Amanda was murdered. Barry said the same thing."

"That's not the kind of information I need. They're both wrong. It wasn't a murder. It was a sacrifice."

Chapter Eight

Silas knew he couldn't give Olivia the answers she wanted, but he could tell her what he knew. She would get there. She always did.

"The DA has pulled the FBI. Preston, doesn't want us involved."

Olivia couldn't believe what she was hearing. "What? Why?"

"Deveroux. He came to town yesterday after all. Apparently, Amanda called him with information regarding Bartholomew and the Atascosa County incident," Silas revealed.

"That's why the FBI is off the case?"

"Given the circumstances, Preston believes FBI involvement could be construed as a conflict of interest. I plan on getting the full details later when I see Deveroux," Silas told her.

Olivia let go of Silas' hand to reach up and finger the cross Gran gave her.

Despite the comfort Livie sought from the ancient symbol, Silas saw the sparks start to dance in her eyes. "Would Bartholomew have talked to Amanda about what happened in the barn?" Silas suggested more to keep her there with him and not off in some dark corner of her mind.

Olivia rejected the idea immediately. "Absolutely not."

Her tone told Silas to dial it back a notch. "Okay, so not intentionally. What about pillow talk?" he proposed.

"Do they strike you as the pillow talk type?"

On second thought, no. "Not really." Bartholomew seemed pretty closed-mouthed, except apparently when it came to Livie. She had that way about her. Over time, Silas learned the ones that didn't talk to her were the ones with something to hide. "Then who?"

"No one else was at the barn." *At least no one alive.*

"Except for Kimmy. She wasn't in the barn, but she knew Roche. She knew Ana Lutz. She knew Amanda. Maybe Kimmy said something during one of their therapy sessions," Silas suggested.

Olivia shook her head. "As her therapist, Amanda would have been breaking patient confidentiality."

"Would that stop her? If it was to get back at Bartholomew. Or even you?" Silas stopped short of telling her Amanda had included her in her discussion with Deveroux. Livie had enough to deal with today.

"Kim's stopping by later," Olivia told him. "I'll feel her out. She said no one in nursing school should be called Kimmy. So, from now on, it's Kim."

"Sounds like your pupil's growing up." The title didn't cover it, but Silas wasn't sure how else to describe the relationship between his wife and the young girl she rescued. Kim had gifts too, not as powerful as Livie's, but enough to catch the attention of Andre Roche.

"Just so you know, I'm calling our girls Evie and Winnie and they can't stop me."

Silas was fond of pet names. "We'll see about that,

tough guy." Olivia wondered how long it would take for their baby girls to wrap him around their little fingers. Silas didn't stand a chance.

"So, who is handling Amanda's death?" Olivia wanted to know.

"Sharpe suggested the Texas Rangers. The DA had no choice but to agree. With the Bureau out, they are the next best thing."

"Herschel Gaines," Olivia mused. She had yet to meet the lawman, but his slow Texas drawl conjured thoughts of Sam Elliott. "At least Barry will be in good hands."

"It also means I can talk freely with the lieutenant. I'm assuming you made a phone call," Silas hedged, hoping she confirmed his suspicions.

Olivia wondered how long the question had been on Silas' mind. "I did. Brennon will be on a plane first thing tomorrow."

Livie had her powers of persuasion, and Brennon Kaine was not immune. He was the type of attorney Olivia worked for back in her days as an expert witness. Kaine specialized in high-profile, not-so-ordinary murder cases. Olivia and Kaine never worked together, at least not on the same side. Kaine would never have ever let her get away if they had. Instead, he and Livie met during an FBI investigation when they were on opposing sides. Silas spent a long eight months watching her relationship with Kaine turn personal.

"Brennon claimed he needed to come for a visit."

"You don't believe him?" They worked together long enough for Silas to know when she was suspicious.

"Why now? The break-in at Smythe's house was

months ago," Olivia remembered.

"If that's the reason, then you're right, Kaine should have been here by now," Silas agreed.

"Unless Barry found something. He believes Jamie broke into his own house."

It took Silas a moment to realize what Olivia was suggesting. "You think Brennon and Barry are working together?" It wasn't something Silas would have considered. The history between the two men was complicated.

Jamie Smythe killed Barry's partner and friend, SAPD Sergeant Mark Austin. Smythe used his one phone call to contact an attorney he couldn't afford. If Barry and Kaine were working together there could only be one reason—*Olivia.* Nothing else could persuade them both to color so far outside the lines.

"Barry didn't tell you anything about what he did this morning?" Olivia asked.

What she meant was to walk her through it like a crime scene. Together they could search for clues that may have been overlooked in the heat of the moment. "I asked about his morning routine and what he did after he left the condo. He said he took his city ride, but because he wasn't on city time he said where he went was nobody's business," Silas told her.

Olivia looked hopeful. "Barry was dressed for work. By using his city car, he could have been using his influence as a cop to get what he needed," she theorized. If Barry and Kaine were working together, and if their collaboration ever got out it could get Brennon Kaine disbarred. It was more than enough motivation for Barry to keep their alliance a secret.

"Or maybe he did something for himself," Silas

suggested.

Olivia refused to give up. There had to be something about today Barry wanted to keep hidden. "Start again. You've told me what you asked him, but what did he say without you asking. What did he give up voluntarily?"

"That he came to see you."

"Barry knew we would have this conversation" Olivia mused. "Maybe he told you something, hoping I would know what it meant."

Of course, he would. Silas had been so focused on their first conversation, he had forgotten the second one, the more personal one. "The only time he was chatty, if you could call it that, was when I called him out when he claimed the baby wasn't his. He said he was absolutely sure. I told him absolution was a tough sell. He said, 'That's not what the bishop keeps telling me.'"

Shit. "What does that mean?"

Olivia knew there was only one reason Barry would turn to the Church. Events in the barn changed them both. For Olivia, that night started her down a path of acceptance of who and what she was. Once she'd believed her extra senses were a burden, but she realized they were gifts and used them accordingly. Barry wasn't so lucky. Ana Lutz first called him a *Watcher* that night in the barn, but neither he nor Olivia knew what that meant.

Then came Pittman.

According to Pittman, her gifts were so seductive and so dangerous, that she needed someone to keep her from straying so far into the darkness she would never find her way out. A watcher was bound to her, not the same as a lover. That's how Pittman knew that person wasn't Silas. A watcher's role was to kill or die to protect her from the darkness. With no one to guide him, there was only one place for Barry to turn to for answers.

"I think I know where he went. I'll handle it," Olivia assured Silas.

The tone of her voice told Silas not to ask. "Do it quickly. When Preston learns Amanda was pregnant, the tide will turn."

"Barry will not be spending the night in a holding cell, I promise you," Olivia assured him, sparks of light swarmed her eyes like fireflies.

It was the second boldest statement he'd heard that day. Silas didn't know how she would do it, only faith that she would.

"Once Barry is free, then what?" Olivia asked. "He won't be allowed back in the condo."

Silas tensed. He had been considering it all morning. "I was thinking he could stay here."

Olivia couldn't hide her surprise.

"We can't leave him on his own. Here is the best place for him," Silas admitted.

Olivia leaned over and kissed his cheek. She felt better already. "Thank you."

Silas flashed her a smile, the mischievous one she liked. "Not what you expected, huh?"

"Not in the least." The relationship between the two men in her life had never been easy. It was dislike at first sight, both vying for her attention.

Silas flashed her another smile. "Consider it payback. For quitting your FBI job and not telling me first."

****

Sharpe was still in the Suburban where Silas left him.

"You should have come inside," Silas said, not for the first time.

Sharpe stopped thumbing through his phone long enough to look up. "How was Dr. Osborne?" he asked.

"She's fine now. After interviewing me, Livie says she knows where Bartholomew was this morning. She promises he'll be out by nightfall, and I said he could stay with us."

Sharpe wasn't sure what he was more surprised about, the promise or the invitation. His boss and the lieutenant had always been at odds, with Olivia in the middle.

"You're right I should have come in. I would have loved to hear that. It sounds like a miracle. Maybe the guys at the station were right. While I was waiting on you to finish with Zavalla, I heard whispers in the hall that Bartholomew found religion." Sharpe dropped his phone in the cup holder and slid the key into the ignition.

Silas didn't know what to make of it, so he didn't. "Did you make your phone call?"

"I wanted to confirm tomorrow's meeting with Sheriff Tennent."

"For all we know, Deveroux could have gone there this morning before Preston got a hold of him."

"Maybe he did," Sharpe suggested. "Tennent's not answering. I hope Deveroux's meddling didn't fuck things up."

"Or he's dodging our calls," Silas pointed out. "Wouldn't be the first time." Silas had always suspected Jim Tennent knew more about what happened in Atascosa County than he was saying. The sheriff's reluctance to talk told Silas he was afraid of something more than the FBI. Silas wondered what had changed.

****

They began by watching Adelyn chase Daisy around. The mild-mannered greyhound enjoyed having a playmate that didn't bark or nip at her heels. She kept her pace to a leisurely walk, looking behind her frequently to see if the chubby-faced toddler was still following. Watching her, Olivia was amazed at how fast sixteen months passed. Both Mom and baby had come a long way.

"She's quick," Olivia observed. "It seemed like yesterday she was barely able to stand on her own two feet."

"I can't take my eyes off her," Kim confessed. "She's fast and mischievous."

Olivia smiled. "Is it true what they say, 'if it's quiet you should be worried'?" Watching Addy, she was already rethinking the pool or at least delaying it.

"Absolutely."

Addy trotted over to wind down in Olivia's lap, but like Alvin, she quickly discovered the cuddles she was hoping for weren't as accessible as they used to be. After a few failed attempts at a comfortable position, she went back to chasing Daisy.

"How old were you when you knew?" Kim began.

It was a familiar topic. Kim liked hearing the stories again. She had no one else to ask. But once she became pregnant Olivia knew it was due to concern for her daughter. The gene was strong among females. In all likelihood, Addy would have her own gifts, but they had yet to reveal themselves.

"Four. It's one of the few memories I have of living with my mother." Sarah, like Kim, had been a young mother, giving birth to Olivia soon after her seventeenth birthday. They lived with Gran until Sarah turned twenty-one, but being on their own didn't last long.

"It happened in our little apartment. I remember the bathroom had a pink bathtub. That's where I saw the lady. She was crying and then she dropped the hair dryer in the water with her. There was a pop, and she was gone." The part of the story Olivia didn't tell, then or now, was the blackness looked back at her and she had been enchanted that she could see it.

"So, no one warned you about how you were?" Kim asked.

Olivia shook her head. "No. I told them."

"Is that what made your mother run away? Was she scared?"

"I don't really know what she was." Olivia watched as tears filled Kim's eyes. She reached for the girl's hand. "You don't have to worry about Addy. I'll be here for her. And for you."

"Like I should have been for Dr. Greene," Kim blurted out.

Olivia's skin prickled. "What do you mean?"

"I knew something was wrong, and I should have told you," Kim said.

Chapter Nine

"You kept me waiting long enough," Deveroux greeted Silas.

"That's ballsy coming from you."

Silas first met Mason Deveroux during the clean-up of the Bureau office post Katrina where Deveroux served as station chief. Silas had been impressed by the former Coast Guard officer. Now all that remained was the military buzz cut, replaced by a man who sported a spreading paunch and a roadmap of broken blood vessels across his face. It was his newfound solace in the bottle that earned Deveroux some time on the sidelines after the Roche case.

"Remember yesterday, at the airport? Agent Sharpe had better things to do than be your driver. The courteous thing to do would have been to give one of us a call."

"I needed to keep my visit under wraps, at the request of Dr. Greene."

"Well, I hope that was helpful."

Settling in, Silas noticed the picture frame on his desk had been moved. He only had one, and it was strategically placed for his viewing only. It was a candid photo of him and Olivia on their wedding day. The exchange of nuptials was an impromptu affair in the garden behind his parent's house. Olivia wore a beautiful cream-colored cocktail dress with her hair pulled back and done up on her head. She was more beautiful than usual, and for once Silas didn't look like an FBI agent. They looked happy. Silas hoped to be that happy for the rest of his life because that was their commitment—for life. With the babies on board, their promise to each other had become something bigger than themselves. It was a step toward the future. Deveroux handling the picture felt like an invasion.

Silas righted the photo. "I need to know what you hope to accomplish here." Deveroux's visit more than a year after Andre Roche and Ana Lutz's death seemed like an exercise in futility. Nonetheless, Silas had been asked to indulge the agent.

Deveroux was back at work on the Human Trafficking task force that got him out of New Orleans, while the Bureau was counting him down to his twenty so he could check out and move on. Silas wondered how much of Deveroux's reduced role was due to past indulgences. From his inflamed eyes and single-mindedness Silas theorized the wayward agent was back to digging holes and chasing lost causes from the bottom of a bottle.

"I want the truth. Not some watered-down version that makes the Bureau and SAPD happy. It's a feel-good story for sure. Your wife, the infamous Dr. Osborne, saved two girls and an SAPD officer's life. I want the details of how she did that."

Silas wondered how it felt to be Deveroux. A once renowned agent, done in by his quest for the truth. Did he realize how close he was? Silas had read Barry's report of what happened. Even Silas knew the lieutenant was skipping details, hiding behind his own compromised condition. In his present state, Deveroux would never get to the truth. Silas wondered if maybe it was time for a reality check.

"You are questioning the statement of a police lieutenant with a stellar career and a former FBI agent with an unblemished record of putting away some of the most heinous killers of the last decade." Silas' tone was terse. "Not to mention the witness you're here to see is the disgraced sheriff of Atascosa County. I'm not wasting my time hauling his ass in here tomorrow if you're chasing rabbits."

Deveroux appeared unconcerned. "I think the lieutenant lost some of his shine today. As for Dr. Osborne, I heard she quit her lucrative Bureau job right about the time the Department of Justice had some very uncomfortable questions for her. And yes, I still plan on questioning the sheriff tomorrow. Since he didn't run for reelection, I hear he has plenty of time on his hands."

"Dr. Osborne's contract was up for renewal," Silas told him. "She chose not to reup in favor of a much more lucrative consulting business of her own. According to the BAU, the DOJ, along with Marc Singer, they impeded an investigation that left behind two families who will never bury their murdered daughters because now there is no one left to question. The DOJ has nothing. If they did, someone else would be here." It was a dig at how far Deveroux had fallen from grace.

"It seems like everyone got wiped off the board. Kind of like in the Roche case."

Larry Wayne Pittman died of surgical complications, and Marc Singer dropped dead of a ruptured blood vessel in his brain. Silas wondered at the insinuation but thought better of it. Mason Deveroux could become his own personal rabbit hole.

"Like any good detective, I seek the truth. The sheriff was involved so deep with Roche he was forced from his job. I want to know what he knows," Deveroux demanded.

Secretly, Silas agreed with Deveroux, but would never encourage him enough to say it. "Sheriff Tennent has been questioned, repeatedly. What makes you think he will talk to you?"

"Maybe he's not been properly stimulated," Deveroux suggested. "As for Lieutenant Bartholomew and Dr. Osborne, they were never questioned by me."

"Their previous statements satisfied those investigating the case."

Deveroux's worn eyes narrowed. "Working with Dr. Osborne changed you. You used to be a by the book Bureau boy."

"I still am."

"As for Bartholomew, he was your biggest opponent in the Smythe investigation," Deveroux pointed out. "Now, here you are towing his line. The DA recommended against it."

"I don't answer to the DA. As for Bartholomew, our differences were territorial. Nothing more."

"Which territory are you referring to?" Deveroux quizzed, a gleam in his eye.

Silas leaned forward his hands clenched in front of him. "If you'd like to be more specific proceed at your own risk." Deveroux was quiet as expected. "As for 'towing the line', the only line I'm towing is the blue one. SAPD spilled blood thanks to Smythe."

"I heard Bartholomew blamed you."

Silas took a stab in the dark. "Is that some wisdom given to you by Dr. Greene?"

"She was a wealth of information. Considering one of my biggest questions, one not answered in those so-called statements, was how exactly did Dr. Osborne and Lieutenant Bartholomew escape when two other able-bodied adults remained inside to burn to death."

"They are both professionals who followed their training. I consider it a win they both walked out alive. Why not take it?" Silas suggested.

"Because there's more to the story. If she followed her training, Dr. Osborne would never have gone inside that barn to begin with. She would have taken her car and not left it to a pregnant teenage girl to get help."

"She was unwilling to let the likes of Roche and Ana Lutz get away."

"How did she plan to stop them? She left her gun in the same vehicle she gave to the teenager. Instead, she went in armed with a snake? I don't know about you, but I never received that kind of training at the academy."

"Maybe she improvised. She's clever like that," Silas suggested, realizing he was stooping to Deveroux's level, but he couldn't let Deveroux go at Livie like that.

"She is clever," Deveroux agreed, but it didn't sound like a compliment. "The snake wrangler said it was one of the biggest rattlesnake dens he had ever seen. Weren't you curious how she escaped without a bite? I know I was. So was the snake wrangler."

Silas stayed quiet. He had already convinced himself he didn't want to know.

"The devil is in the details, Agent Branch. Dr.

Osborne claimed the snake was dead, but according to the autopsy report, if the fire hadn't killed Roche and Lutz the snake venom would have."

"Maybe she was wrong," Silas suggested.

"How often have you known Dr. Osborne to be wrong? I think she never intended for Andre Roche to walk out of there alive. Marc Singer told me how he got a real rise out of her when he mentioned Roche. You know what I think?"

Deveroux was going to tell him whether Silas wanted to know or not.

"I think she is what they say she is." Deveroux finally said what he'd been dying to say all along.

Silas was close enough to reach out and choke Deveroux. Something he wouldn't mind doing. "They? You mean the FBI or the monsters she catches?"

Deveroux was animated by the question. "Both."

"Well, they say many things."

"Don't you see, Agent Branch. This isn't just about girls and sex. It's bigger than that. This is about good and evil. And what they say is true. It's time you and everyone else realize what your wife truly is."

****

Olivia broke the news of Amanda's death as soon as Kim arrived, giving Kim the time, and space she needed, letting Kim guide the conversation wherever she needed. First to Addy and now finally back to Amanda.

"Is it bad that all I feel is relief?"

"Feelings are feelings, Kim. You are entitled to have them," Olivia assured her.

"Why relief?" Olivia asked when all she wanted to know was what Kim hadn't told her.

"No longer having to dodge her calls."

"Was she trying to get you to come back to counseling?" Olivia knew Kim had stopped her sessions with Amanda months ago. What Olivia didn't know was why.

"It was no longer counseling," Kim said. "My sessions weren't about me. Dr. Greene was more interested in you and me and you and Lieutenant Bartholomew."

Olivia felt queasy at the confession.

"What you and I share isn't for everyone. I learned that the hard way."

Olivia and Kim were both raised to keep their gifts to themselves. They both rebelled against their family's wishes and followed their nature. Olivia's quiet defiance led her to join the FBI and hunt killers. Kim's response was more typical, hanging with the wrong crowd, keeping a secret boyfriend, and running away once they broke up. When Kim was looking for a way out, Andre Roche and Ana Lutz were there to provide her with one. They promised her everything she wanted—understanding and acceptance. Before she knew it, Kim was pregnant, with no escape. Luckily, Adelyn wasn't Roche's. A DNA test confirmed it. Thinking he was the father, Roche's endgame was to sacrifice the newborn in exchange for some kind of unholy power.

"Remember Rose?"

How could she forget?

The snake snuck out of the cellar, tucking itself inside her blouse. It coiled in protest as she freed it. Instead of fear, Olivia felt anger. She flung the snake across the room as she hissed Latin commands she didn't realize she was speaking.

Only then did the girl reveal herself. "You asked it if it was afraid. I think it was."

"It should have been. You should be, too," Olivia warned.

In eight months of captivity, Kim had seen girls come and go. Rose had only been there a couple of days, but Roche already had big plans for her.

"I never told you but when we left in your car Rose said we should keep going. Ana told her about a place in Vegas where we would be safe. She said it was a place where we could be ourselves. No one was like Rose. She liked to play with dead things. She said she could bring them back to life."

Kim's words unlocked a moment Olivia had chosen to forget. Like so many other things from the time she spent in Roche's cellar.

Rose bent over the snake. Olivia couldn't make out the words, but the girl's chant was familiar. Olivia had heard it before. When she used to tip-toe down the hallway in the middle of the night, drawn to the flicker of candlelight beneath Gran's bedroom door.

"You can't bring it back," Olivia warned.

Rose beamed up at her. "Andre says he can teach me."

"Necromancy is forbidden."

"Rose could also be manipulative. She reconnected with Dr. Greene and not in a good way. Dr. Greene called and wanted me to participate in group therapy. With Rose. I just couldn't do it. It made me feel like an experiment, like a specimen. It sounded creepy."

It was a valid reaction, considering that's how Kim had been treated. "Roche and Ana were predators, Kim.

Never forget that. They weren't gifted." Olivia offered her hand. Kim took it, looking as small and fragile as Adelyn.

Kim sniffed away any tears she might have had. She sat up straight and retrieved her hand, returning to the young woman she was becoming. "I met someone."

The change in subject caught Olivia off guard. "What do you mean?"

"I got a job. Only twelve hours a week. I can do more on the weekends as long as I keep up with my classes."

"That's wonderful. Where?"

"I applied at some nursing homes and got hired as a personal care attendant. I just passed my test."

Olivia had done the same thing during nursing school. She wondered if that's where Kim got the idea. "Congratulations. That's exciting and smart. So, who is this person you met?" A work mentor would be good for her.

"He's a nurse."

A silent alarm rang inside Olivia's head. While Kim's gifts weren't as evolved as hers, they were strong enough to make her different and lead her straight into the arms of a predator. "How old is this nurse?" Olivia did her own calculations and wasn't happy with the results.

Kim made a face. "He's not like that."

Olivia struggled to say something that didn't sound parental.

"He said I could learn a lot on the night shift."

Kim saw the look of disapproval. "He knows what I am."

History was full of reminders of why their kind

remained in the shadows. "What does he know?"

"I told him nothing. You taught me better than that." Guarding her gifts had been their first lesson. "He knows things, like you. He called me a listener."

Kim's senses were heightened by places and objects. She had an internal receiver, her frequency tuned into what Olivia liked to think of as echoes of the past. Listener was a perfect description.

"He told me it wasn't to be confused with a reader."

Olivia's senses spiked. Did that mean he also knew about her?

"I didn't tell him I knew the difference."

Olivia's fight or flight senses stirred making her feel vulnerable and alone. Soon there would be more than Kim to protect. "How does he know these things?"

"He's gifted, too. He called himself a hunter. It's why he works at the nursing home. There's something dark there. I felt it before he said anything." Kim reached for Olivia's hand this time. She gave it a comforting squeeze. "He makes me feel safe, like you do. His name is Rogan Poe. He said he is looking forward to meeting you."

Chapter Ten

Jon Sharpe was right about Herschel Gaines being in town. It didn't take the veteran Texas Ranger long to get there and interview Bartholomew. Gaines sequestered himself in Captain Zavalla's office to report back to him and the DA. Kurt Preston was not pleased with the results.

"The questions were asked and answered, counselor," Herschel Gaines said not for the first time. "According to the lieutenant, he hasn't seen Dr. Greene in months. He wasn't there when she arrived. And he didn't invite her."

"Preliminary reports from the condo indicate she wasn't there alone." The DA trained his eyes on Nathan Renard. The DA insisted on pulling the new lieutenant away from the ongoing investigation so he could get answers from someone other than Zavalla. Bartholomew was a twenty-year veteran with a loyal following. The captain was one of them. Zavalla's men were on site. So were Preston's, but his had gone radio silent. He could feel the swell of blue closing in around him. Renard was the weak link. His time on the force was short, yet he was newly promoted.

Lieutenant Renard cleared his throat. "We've obtained camera footage from the pertinent areas. Dr. Greene was alone when she exited the elevator to Lieutenant Bartholomew's condo."

Preston wasn't satisfied with that answer any more than the ones he got from Gaines. "Who answered the door?"

"The view from the elevator is limited. It doesn't extend to the resident entry ways. They are entitled to privacy."

"What about security?" Preston insisted. "Aren't they entitled to that as well?"

"That's why they have the doorman," Renard told him.

"A hell of a lot of good he did," Preston snapped.

"We confirmed Lieutenant Bartholomew requested a change of locks, and the work order was completed. There was also a formal request Dr. Greene not be allowed past the front desk," Zavalla interrupted.

"Doesn't it mean he didn't give her another key," Preston muttered. "Someone had to let her in."

"Why don't we stick to what we can verify?" Gaines suggested. "The elevator isn't the only entrance and exit." The ranger turned to Renard. "What about the stairwell?"

"There is no coverage of that area. It requires a key card which is only available to residents or employees of the building, maintenance, cleaning crew, etcetera," Renard explained.

"When did Bartholomew last use his?" Preston wanted to know.

"That information is maintained off-site and not readily available. We're working on obtaining it," Renard told him.

"What about other camera footage?" Gaines asked. Like Silas before him, he was into establishing facts, not supposition.

"Dr. Greene arrived at 9:03. Exactly as the doorman described, she flashed him keys and he waved her on by."

"By Bartholomew's account he was out the door between 8:15 and 8:30," Gaines said.

"Can we verify that?" Preston asked.

The ranger shook his head. Preston was so determined Bartholomew was involved that he refused to consider another possibility. "I hate to break it to you, but Bartholomew isn't the only one who could have let Dr. Greene inside. Lieutenant Renard already raised that possibility. Check the elevator footage for Bartholomew. He estimated he returned from his jog around 7:30. He took the stairs down, but not back up. He went inside, made coffee, showered, and left via the elevator some forty-five minutes later."

"One time he takes the stairs, the next the elevator. Why?" Preston sounded desperate.

"Maybe after a forty-five-minute jog he didn't feel like climbing thirteen flights of stairs," Gaines suggested. "Who knows?"

"You have Dr. Greene's phone. You used it to contact Agent Deveroux. Is there proof in there of recent contact with Lieutenant Bartholomew?" Zavalla asked even though he already knew the answer. If so, Preston would have moved forward with what to do with Bartholomew. They were still debating because the DA had nothing.

Preston stopped his pacing. "No. But it doesn't mean he didn't. He has a work phone. So does she. As for his departure, it doesn't mean he didn't take the stairs back up. You can't tell me he doesn't know where the cameras are," Preston said without looking at

Gaines.

"No, it doesn't, but it is verifiable," Gaines reminded him. "Everything he told me so far is. He admitted to giving her a key. He admitted to not getting it back. He submitted a work order to maintenance, and they changed the locks. The front desk has it on record Dr. Greene wasn't allowed upstairs," Gaines recited from memory. "There's a paper trail for all of it."

"Yet we don't know where Bartholomew was this morning," Preston reminded them. "Where are we with the surveillance footage?'

Renard shook his head. "There is more than one exit from the resident parking garage. One camera is non-functioning. We're combing through what we have."

Preston wondered what Zavalla knew that he wasn't telling. "I take it they still haven't found Dr. Greene's car."

"Not yet. There's a BOLO out, but that's about it."

Preston was growing more frustrated the longer they talked. "We have to show we did our due diligence."

Zavalla sat up straight in his chair. Preston wasn't the only one frustrated. "Don't tell me how to do my job."

"Dr. Greene knew a lot of guys on the force," Preston said. "A young, professional woman dead. She was well-liked. Public sentiment will be high."

"What about my lieutenant with more than twenty years of exemplary service?" Zavalla asked. "Take your blinders off. This is about all of us."

"Then why don't you remind Bartholomew of that? He could make this easier on all of us if he would tell us where he was this morning," Preston suggested.

"Lieutenant Bartholomew has been forthright with his answers," Gaines chimed in.

"As long as they are verifiable within that building. You said so yourself," Preston reminded the ranger.

"And we haven't caught him in a lie yet. Bottom line is, he didn't have to tell us anything at all. He knows his rights. He doesn't have to sit in that room. From the looks of him, he's about done. What are you going to do when he gets up and walks out? I think you're lucky he hasn't already," Gaines said.

"He has nowhere else to go," Preston said. "He's a loner."

"Don't be so sure about that," Zavalla warned. "Agent Branch is making a visit to the lieutenant's place later."

"I explicitly said the FBI is not to be involved. That's what I have him for." Preston pointed his finger at Gaines.

"Because of your decision, Silas Branch is now just another citizen who is getting some personal items for the lieutenant, which is allowed since we're occupying his residence." Zavalla pointed a stubby finger back at him. "You did that."

"Kind of shoots a hole in your theory about some beef between the station chief and the lieutenant," Gaines mumbled.

"You should know Lieutenant Bartholomew has legal counsel at his disposal," Zavalla said.

Preston showed an equal amount of shock and fear at the suggestion. "Legal counsel? When did he make a phone call?" Which of his city colleagues would dare challenge him?

"I doubt he had to," Gaines said.

"He was with Dr. Osborne," Zavalla reminded the DA.

Preston drug a hand over his face. He was considering the ramifications of who she would call when Ida, the gatekeeper of Zavalla's private sanctuary, rushed in without waiting for an invitation. She looked out of sorts. "I'm sorry, but I just got a call from downstairs. There is someone on his way up to see you."

****

Zavalla paled at the news.

Preston was the only one to speak. "How the hell, does he know?"

His soon-to-be visitor's legal name was Nicefero Saldaña Mendoza. His close friends called him Chaffee. Anthony Zavalla's parents were part of that select group. When serving as their parish priest, the Archbishop spent many Sunday dinners at the Zavalla house.

He was no longer a small parish priest. He had ascended the ranks of the Church and now served under a title bestowed upon him by the Pope. Nicefero Saldaña Mendoza tended a flock of over half a million parishioners. To them, he was known as Archbishop.

****

The man standing on her front porch was first, and foremost a servant of God. As an Archbishop, he was both a leader and a politician. Today he had dressed carefully to embody all of his roles. He wore a simple servant's robe made of black. The belt holding it together was fashioned after the towel Jesus used to wash the feet of his disciples. The belt and the skull cap were purple, signifying his position in the Church. A large wooden cross around his neck served as a reminder of the ultimate sacrifice.

He was the holiest-looking man Lily had ever seen. When he asked for privacy, she steered him toward the back garden. Fortunately, Olivia appeared in time to redirect him to the front porch. She didn't need the Archbishop and *Alleracsap* sharing the same space.

"Your Grace," Olivia greeted him. She dipped her head and kissed the Archbishop's ring before they sat.

"Your friend said you were sleeping," Archbishop Mendoza began.

"I was awake." His presence alerted her even before he knocked on the door.

"Still, I'm sorry if I disturbed you. I know it has been a trying day, but I bring news I hope will lessen those burdens."

Their conversation paused while Lily stepped outside to bring the hot tea Olivia requested. It was one of her great-grandmother's recipes.

"I did as you asked," he revealed once they were alone again.

"I asked you for nothing," Olivia clarified.

"Then let me rephrase. Your intent was implied and received."

Olivia didn't correct him. She took a moment as they sipped together.

"What I did was for you. Not him."

"He didn't do it," Olivia insisted, not for the first time.

"You said as much."

"It was dark magic that no one can prove."

"Except you," he pointed out. "But those are

secular matters. What we have between us is something else. Tell me, is Bartholomew the target or you?"

"I have no idea. Other than it wasn't murder. It was a sacrifice."

"For what gain?"

Olivia shook her head. "I don't know." All she knew was death had greeted Amanda Greene before she hit the ground.

"The sacrifice was not to bring one closer to God," the Archbishop mused.

Olivia nodded. It went without saying.

"You and I have not discussed Mr. Pittman, but from what the lieutenant has told me, I can confirm everything the dead man said is true."

The confession surprised her.

"What you should ask yourself is, who sent him and why."

The mysterious Samael Knight, the Collector, was the who. As for why, Olivia was still trying to work it out.

"What I've asked myself is why you didn't tell me." Olivia had already decided her old friend Father Dominic didn't know. If he had, he would have told her. The Archbishop was a secret keeper. It was why he sent Dominic back to Rome.

"It was not my place. You had to find your own way. Perhaps that was why you were sent the message. Now that you know, you must allow the lieutenant to take his place in your life. Your actions today prove to me you trust him implicitly. In doing so, it is now time to listen to his counsel. Let him guide you. Dark ones are watching."

The Archbishop drained his cup and stood,

signaling his departure. The staff he gripped in his right hand was similar to the one carried by Moses. Since his hip surgery last year, the cane was a necessity, not an adornment. Still, he made a striking figure, the embodiment of a servant and leader. That was the point.

"Thank you," Olivia whispered.

His time as Archbishop was coming to an end. If his trespasses today were uncovered, they would destroy his legacy. If ever asked, he would say his memory failed him. He had confirmed nothing. The implication, as Olivia reminded him, was a tricky thing.

"I did it for the future," the Archbishop confessed. "You are a gatekeeper between this world and the next. My eternal prayer is that you choose wisely. Others will be watching you. One day, they may even follow the path you set."

Chapter Eleven

"So, that was Dr. Osborne's doing?" Preston asked once the man in the frock left the room.

"She seems like a pretty good friend to have," Gaines commented, mainly because the DA was an asshole.

Preston wasn't convinced. "She can just call up the Archbishop and get him to come all the way down here?"

"He personally blessed her house as a wedding gift," Zavalla informed him. "So, yeah, I guess she can."

"Bartholomew doesn't strike me as the religious type," Preston said.

Zavalla opened his email and found the video file the Archbishop had promised. It was a grainy image, but it was one of Barry Bartholomew entering the archdiocese. Zavalla clicked the file closed. "I've seen enough. I'm cutting him loose."

"That hasn't been authenticated," Preston protested.

"Are you going to seriously accuse the Archbishop of lying?" Zavalla asked.

The DA tried again. "Meeks hasn't done the cut yet."

"Meeks already told us it was going to be hard to determine defensive wounds. Bartholomew consented to photos. According to the photographer, there's nothing. I'm hearing the same from my forensics team at his place. If it wasn't for the shoes, and purse she left, it doesn't look like Dr. Greene or any other woman has ever been in his place."

"What about the inconsistencies at the scene?" Preston finally confessed. It was the last thing he heard from his people before they went silent.

Zavalla knew the DA was keeping things to himself, but so was he. "My head of forensics suggested we bring in another set of eyes," Zavalla confirmed. "I already authorized it." It was his cover for the visit Olivia had already made.

The DA considered the offer. An outside investigator might be the way to go. "Do it."

"In the meantime, I'm letting my guy go," Zavalla announced. Preston looked like he wanted to protest, but Zavalla cut him off. "Given what the Archbishop gave us, there's not enough to hold him. Anybody else would have called a lawyer by now."

"Yet he didn't." Preston doubted the previous threats about Bartholomew calling one in the first place.

"He didn't have to," Zavalla said, exiting his desk before he said anything else.

"Dr. Osborne probably did it for him." Gaines couldn't resist.

"Really?" Preston glared, hands on his hips. "Who else does she have on speed-dial?"

"Brennon Kaine. I'll be sure and refer him to your office when he calls," Zavalla promised.

****

The view was stunning. Thirteen stories up the green of the city was unobstructed. The scene reminded

Silas of Virginia. He could only imagine what it looked like at night when nature was replaced with a blanket of stars. He couldn't help but think how much Livie would like it here. The first description that came to mind for her was safe. Maybe because that was the word Silas needed for her and his children. Bartholomew had promised to be their protector.

Silas shoved aside the dark thoughts, reminding himself that Livie's visions of the future were merely glimpses inside an ever-changing kaleidoscope of alternate endings. Silas shifted his focus back to the here and now where it belonged. He was surprised at what he found. Away from work, Barry Bartholomew existed in a separate world. His home was neat and orderly, a sanctuary of sorts. The peace and tranquility he sought reminded Silas of himself. He and Bartholomew weren't so different after all. Perhaps, they were different versions of what could have been Livie's future.

Silas headed down the hallway that was bound to lead him to the bedrooms. The door to his right was open. Curtains blocked the stunning view outside. Silas nudged the door open wondering what had captured Bartholomew's attention instead. Inside the room, Silas found the lieutenant he knew. To his left was a desk littered with folders reminiscent of Barry's office downtown. Competing for space were two open laptops. Where the desk ended, a patchwork of newspaper dotted the wall. From the looks of it, Bartholomew was chasing something old. Silas was so distracted he didn't realize the room was already occupied. In the far corner was a forensics tech studying the collection. Silas backed out of the room and moved on. He wasn't going to find what he was looking for in there. From the looks of things, neither had Bartholomew.

Next was the main bedroom. There were no window coverings. Like most cops, Bartholomew probably didn't sleep much. Silas wondered if staring at the stars offered comfort in the dead of night. Out of place with the rest of the room was the unmade bed. Silas recognized the head of SAPD's forensics, Frank Tobias. He was standing over the bed, surveying the linens. A hand-held light would confirm if Bartholomew had indeed been sleeping alone.

"I thought the FBI was out," Frank said, ending his sweep.

"I'm here to pick up some personal items for the lieutenant," Silas explained.

Frank caught the eye of the tech working in the bathroom, dismissing him with a nod. "Can you believe this shit?" Frank asked once they were alone.

Silas shrugged.

Frank gestured to the rumpled bedsheets. "I can say nothing has been going on here. No girlie stuff in the bathroom either, no obligatory drawer, no female friendly snacks in the kitchen. If it weren't for the hefty supply of liquor bottles, I'd say a monk lived here."

When he was single, Silas also had a robust collection of whiskey, mostly gifts from colleagues that he kept on hand for special occasions. His sheets too would have been clean. He preferred to indulge in his extracurricular activities elsewhere. The only key he ever gave away was to Livie. Barry admitted the one he gave to Amanda Greene was a lapse in judgment.

"The lieutenant had nothing to do with this," Frank

said what Silas was thinking.

The only thing keeping this investigation alive was Bartholomew's own stonewalling and a hard-on by the DA for reasons unknown.

Frank stayed while Silas grabbed what he came for. For good measure, he checked the bedside table. Just as Bartholomew said, no protective gear.

Frank walked him down the hall, but Silas couldn't resist another peek inside the room he bypassed earlier. The tech from before was still there. Silas stepped forward to introduce himself.

She met him halfway. "Katie Morgan. I know who you are."

Her admission triggered a memory Silas had from the Smythe murders.

Frank slid over to check out the wall. "What's all this?"

"Something Sergeant Austin was working on. The lieutenant's following up," Katie explained.

His interest was immediately piqued, and Silas leaned in to get a better look, bumping one of the laptops in the process. The screen saver came to life, and Silas was distracted for a whole other reason.

"That's a good picture of her," Katie said tracking Silas' gaze.

The man on the screen looked a lot like him, but what captured Silas' attention was the familiar way the man's arm dangled around Livie's neck. They were looking at each other, their eyes locked, their mouths wearing matching smiles.

"That's Jason Austin, Mark's brother," Katie explained. She redirected Silas' attention by tapping one of the clippings on the wall, redirecting his attention. "All the murders leading to Jason's started there, *The Divide*. It's a dive bar in Old Town Alexandria." Katie knew Silas would know the location. "Mark was working the case for Dr. Osborne."

Silas stared at the tech, wondering what else she knew about his wife.

"Tell her, thank you, from me, for coming here for Barry," Katie said.

"Katie is the one who insisted we call Dr. Osborne." Frank had specifically avoided the topic. "Tell her we took the pictures she requested and scrubbed the patio with salt water," Frank said, his voice lowered.

Silas nodded his affirmation, his eyes straying back to the computer with the picture of Jason Austin and his wife. "The lieutenant is going to have some time on his hands."

Katie closed the lid and handed the laptop over.

Silas stuffed it in the duffle bag he was carrying.

"I heard about the babies. Congratulations," Katie added.

Silas smiled politely. "Thank you," he said, wanting to be anywhere but here.

"Do you think she'd mind if I gave her a call? There's someone I'd really like her to meet."

****

At first, when Silas suggested she and Lily meet him downtown for dinner, Olivia wondered if it was some elaborate plan to get her out of the house. Her perspective changed when Silas requested they meet at *Mi Corazón*. Authentic Mexican cuisine was one of their favorites, full of memorable meals and happy memories. It also happened to be located in the heart of the downtown market, a short walk from SAPD headquarters. The Archbishop's visit must have gone as anticipated.

Olivia requested a table outside, away from the noise inside, and a view of the open market. While they waited, she encouraged Lily to order the margarita Olivia knew she wanted.

After the day's events, Olivia craved a return to normalcy. "Now that I've completely monopolized your day, why don't we start over. You weren't coming over just to discuss my family history. You said you had something to tell me."

"Who says I didn't come over for the cookies?"

The way Lily clutched the stem of her margarita glass said otherwise. Neglecting her own needs was a familiar pattern, cultivated no doubt during her marriage. Olivia understood the natural give and take in a relationship, but the more she learned about Ross, the more Olivia believed Lily gave more than she received. Olivia would be happy when Lily found her voice again. Until then, she would be happy to help her do it.

"I do," Olivia smiled. "I'm psychic, remember?" She disliked the word, but it seemed like a good way to break the ice and get her friend to open up.

Lily took a hefty gulp of her drink. "I heard from my lawyer."

"Another delay?" Ross moving out of the house and immediately in with another woman was the wake-up call Lily needed to start her own new life. Returning to work was the first step, but dissolving a decades-old marriage was more time-consuming than she imagined. Lily's patience was wearing thin.

"The financials are back." Ross was a successful

financial consultant and the breadwinner of the marriage. While Lily relished her role as a stay-at-home mom, it left her financially dependent on Ross and in the dark where their finances were concerned. Once divorce proceedings began, it was revealed her husband had planned his financial exit well in advance.

Lily grabbed her glass again. "I'm not going to be able to keep the house." She took a gulp to keep the tears from falling.

Eventually, she forced a smile. "Luckily, with the upgrades and the neighborhood, I won't be destitute, but we won't be neighbors anymore."

"But we'll still be friends," Olivia assured her.

Tears returned for both of them, but for different reasons.

"If you really want to pay me back for today, make sure I get to see more of that handsome lieutenant," Lily requested with a sly smile.

"I think that can be arranged," Olivia told her, choking on her own emotions as she saw Silas approach with Barry by his side.

****

Barry couldn't remember the last time he had shared a meal with someone. Dinner with friends seemed so normal. Silas briefed him before they arrived that there was no work talk at the table. It seemed like a good rule. One that people who focused on each other made.

Olivia and Lily chatted about the baby cribs they saw on their stroll through the market. So far, Olivia hadn't found anything she liked. It was the precursor she needed to drag Silas away to see them as soon as the meal was over.

Barry was content to keep eating. The cookies he shared with Olivia felt like a lifetime ago. Before departing, Silas took the liberty of ordering Barry another beer with the promise of liquor at the house. Barry wasn't in the mood to say no.

"Can I ask you a personal question, Lieutenant Bartholomew?"

The request caught him off guard. Lily was so quiet during dinner, Barry almost forgot she was there, not to mention he was tangled in his own world. He looked up to find Lily staring back at him. No one had looked at him like that in a long time, at least no one sane.

Feeling the intense gaze of her eyes, Barry sat up straighter. "Sure," he said, recalling the night they met.

Lily had just gotten her feet stitched up in the back of an ambulance, and he was helping her find her way next door to Olivia's. Lily was under the influence of drugs, but Barry did remember her telling him she was alone for the weekend because she suspected her husband was spending time with his "new" girlfriend. The way she said it made Barry think her husband must have had more than one. Today, Barry noticed she was missing the wedding ring. Women always knew when there was someone else. Even the crazy ones.

Lily leaned in closer and lowered her voice. "You and Olivia never, you know?"

Barry froze. He had expected something simple. "Did we ever, what?"

"You know, date?"

Barry let out the breath he was holding. "Uh, no, we did not."

Lily's cheeks flushed red, realizing how her

question must have sounded. She blamed it on the tequila. She was on her second margarita. "I'm sorry, that was too forward of me. And way out of line."

Barry pushed his plate aside, his food forgotten. Thoughts of Mark Austin ran through his mind, not to mention how he was sitting here now rather than in some holding cell. "Olivia saved my life."

His words brought tears to Lily's eyes.

Barry flashed Lily a smile. She looked like she needed it. "It's okay. I saved her dog once, so we're even."

Chapter Twelve

Silas and Olivia held hands as they made their way back to the restaurant.

"Any particular reason we needed to do this tonight?" Silas asked. Despite all their time together, he still didn't know all of Olivia's quirks. Sometimes she packed things away so tightly that it took her time to unpack them. It's what she'd done with him for years. Other times she moved with swift purpose.

"I want to be prepared," Olivia told him. She felt a change was coming, more swiftly than expected, but she couldn't say those words to him. Instead, she squeezed his hand, looking for her own sense of calm.

"I thought you might be avoiding talking about today," Silas suggested.

"I'm still processing," Olivia told him. She wasn't ready to discuss the crime scene. There was a lot Olivia still didn't know. What she did know scared her.

"I wondered how you knew Barry visited the Archbishop."

Olivia chose her words carefully. "He needed someone. After the barn."

Luckily her answer satisfied him.

Crossing the courtyard back to their table, Olivia caught a glimpse of Lily and Barry. They were smiling. A feeling of comfort washed over her. "Maybe this is why we needed to be here tonight. Things can change before we know it."

Silas saw it too. The beginning of something else. "You're a good friend." He snaked his arm around her waist. Olivia leaned into him, soaking it all in. Past, present, and future.

"Bartholomew and I still need to talk," Silas said with a kiss on her forehead. "It could be late."

"Do what you need to do. Say what you need to say."

****

Barry watched the waitress bring Silas another beer. By Barry's count, it was number three, maybe four. He had stopped at two.

Silas dug around in his pocket while looking at his phone. He came up with a set of car keys and tossed them to Barry. "Meeks is estimating Amanda was at least four months along. By my count, that doesn't put you in the clear, buddy." With Olivia and Lily gone, Barry's reprieve was over.

"It ended the night of Amanda's housewarming party. When I left your house after the incident with your next-door neighbor, I drove back to Amanda's. That's when I saw someone else was there. Things between us had been strained for a couple of months. I was pulling away, trying to find the exit. I thought she was busy buying the house. Guess I was wrong."

"Why?" Silas knew the real reason was his wife, regardless of what Bartholomew was about to tell him.

Barry looked away, not wanting to answer a question Silas already knew. Just like him, Silas knew the truth, deep down, but just like Barry, he would never say it. He and Silas might be mending fences, but at the end of the day, Olivia was still Silas' wife.

"It was never anything. When it became obvious Amanda wanted something I couldn't give, I was done."

"Was it a kid?" Silas might be inebriated, but not so much that he didn't see another answer that had nothing to do with Livie.

"No. Amanda didn't know I couldn't until the night she showed up to tell me she was pregnant. That's how she knew that I knew I wasn't the only one. I told you I was looking for a way out, but I knew it was going to be tricky. She was beyond possessive. I was willing to let it ride until the night we picked up the dogs from your house."

Silas looked lost.

"Remember the night when Olivia came back from DC. When your dad passed."

Silas nodded, halting the flood of memories both good and bad. It was a change of love. He gained Livie and lost his father all at the same time.

"What does that have to do with that other night when you picked up the dogs?" Silas was starting to think he might have had too much alcohol for this conversation, but he pressed on.

"I had to take Daisy with me because Amanda's car was too cramped. Watching Amanda take the turn down the street, something about the way her headlights reflected in my rearview told me I'd seen it before. It was Amanda. She was the one who drove by Olivia's house the night Daisy got sick, and I had to call you."

It was then Barry knew Olivia had made her choice, and he wasn't it. Silas also remembered the night. He had been awake, missing Livie after spending a week with her. He came back that same day and never looked back. He had also discounted Bartholomew's concern over the drive-by.

"Remember I told you the car had dealer tags. I checked with the DMV. They confirmed Amanda bought the car the week before. I already suspected something wasn't right with her. Her obsession with me wasn't healthy, but once I learned she was also fixated on Olivia, I couldn't let that slide." Barry had seen what the results of an Olivia obsession could do. It drove Madeline Austin to poison Daisy in revenge for the death of her brothers. While under the same spell, Andre Roche took her hostage with plans Barry couldn't bring himself to think about. Then there was Jamie Smythe. No one knew his endgame.

The Archbishop had warned him watching over Olivia was a full-time job.

Silas pushed the half-empty beer bottle away. "Livie saw Kim Burleson this afternoon. She confirmed Amanda's preoccupation with Olivia. It's why Kim stopped going to therapy."

The two men sat in silence, the facts settling over them.

"You remember the doctor who told you about, you know, your condition?" Silas finally asked.

It was one of the least forgettable days of Barry's life. "I do."

"Dig out his info. You're going to need it." Silas flagged down the waitress, and Barry reached for his wallet. "I got this," Silas told him despite Barry's protest. "Don't worry, if it makes you feel better, I'll give it to your attorney, and he can reimburse me for baby-sitting services." Silas smiled. It was the first sign he was not himself.

Barry was confused. "My attorney?"

"Brennon Kaine. He'll be here tomorrow, or hell, maybe he's here now. I can't really remember what Livie said." Silas reached for the rest of his beer and downed it. "To be honest, I tend to block out thoughts of him."

"I didn't call him," Barry told him.

"I know you didn't. I know he wouldn't be your first choice." Silas wondered what bothered Barry more, the fact Brennon Kaine's client was Jamie Smythe or that Kaine and Olivia had once been involved. Silas decided he didn't want to think about it, either.

"Calling Kaine was all Livie's doing. After today, buddy, you've gotta watch your back. I saw people crawling all over your place. There were murmurs about how you could afford to live there. There will be more if someone doesn't put a stop to it. Kaine is good at that sort of thing. It's why Livie called him. I've seen him in court. Let him off the leash. They deserve it, especially the DA."

"Is that what you would do if you were representing me?" Barry wanted to know.

"You bet your ass. I would throw the book at them. They showed you no respect today. Remember I told you Deveroux was coming for you. What I didn't know is he would have help. I can help you with Deveroux, but the DA is the driving force behind this case. To me, his vengeance feels personal." The waitress came back with Silas' card.

"So, there was no big blow up when you found out Amanda was sleeping with someone else?" Silas asked as he signed his name and tucked his wallet away.

Barry shrugged. He wasn't going to admit to Silas Branch that Amanda wasn't the first woman to leave his bed for someone else's. "No. I figured whoever it was gave me a way out." All Barry had felt at the time was relief and gratefulness. If Olivia hadn't sent him back that night, he would never have discovered Amanda's secret.

"Did you recognize the car? I heard Dr. Greene had a type. Do you know which cop?"

"Yea, she had a type, but not that night. The car didn't belong to a cop."

****

With Lily safely tucked in at home, Olivia could relax. She trudged upstairs with the dogs trailing behind her. She indulged in a nice long soak in the bath while Daisy and Alvin lounged on the bathroom floor with their favorite, *Doggie Delights*. It was the bribe for the walk they didn't get.

Olivia dosed the warm water with lavender oil and sea salt. The oil soothed her tired muscles, and the salt cleansed her. Made from the earth and the sea, salt was a pure substance. It could provide protection as it did at Barry's condo. Or purification, which was what Olivia sought. Cleansing with salt water restored innocence. It was one of the first lessons Gran taught her.

Olivia watched the movement of her belly as her babies squirmed in response to the water. They enjoyed the retreat as much as she did. Water had always been therapy for her. Maybe that's where the pool idea came from. If tonight was any indication, the babies were in agreement. They were so much alike, yet different. It was the differences she needed to learn. It was enormous responsibility knowing they were totally dependent on her to guide them through life. This was probably one of the only times Olivia yearned for a traditional mother-daughter bond. Olivia was grateful for Gran, but she was not the teacher Olivia once believed her to be. Driven by fear, Gran didn't prepare her. She hid her away to exist in the shadows. Her daughters deserved better.

Done with her purge, Olivia headed downstairs, seeking answers Gran didn't give. She propped her feet on the stool beneath her desk and logged into the account she used exclusively for exchanges with Kevin Branch. There were two messages.

The first one had multiple files attached, along with an apology from Kevin for the time it took him to compile it. It was the topic that launched their joint venture, background on Larry Wayne Pittman. During their jailhouse interview, Pittman told her he had been seeing evil since his teens, at least two decades before he killed his cousin's children.

Olivia's finger hovered over the attachments. Did she need proof of something she already knew? A swift kick in the ribs on her left side was a reminder from her moon baby they depended on her.

Inside the files was enough evidence to convince her Pittman was what he claimed. Threads of his story lead her straight to Oak Hollow with interesting facts on one resident in particular and Barry's favorite suspect, Rogan Poe. The traveling nurse had also piqued Kevin Branch's attention. He went so far as to describe Poe with a line from Winston Churchill, saying he was *a riddle, wrapped in a mystery, inside an enigma.*

Poe wasn't his original name. From the look of it, Olivia could see why he changed it. She wondered if there was some significance behind his new choice. Was he a fan of the author? Or the raven? A quick search of the meaning of the raven told her the appearance of a raven in one's life signaled transmutation—meaning a change or an awakening. It was a conclusion she had reached on her own.

Feeling full of devilish thoughts despite her cleansing, Olivia sent Kevin one final request. This one was for Lily. Olivia asked Kevin to look into Ross Forester's financials. She didn't want Lily to give up on the house if there was another way.

****

Silas spent the ride to the house in silence, still on his phone texting instead of talking, when Barry pulled the car into the driveway. "It isn't Olivia on the other end," Silas mentioned.

Barry nodded, and wondered how fatherhood would change the man's work schedule. He sat, letting the car idle. It was late, and he was tired, but not enough for bed. He needed to unwind. Any other night he would have wandered his empty condo, only to end up on his balcony where he'd sit with his feet up. He'd cut back on his nightly alcohol habit, but after today, he needed something to take the edge off. Tonight's weather was perfect outside, hinting of cooler nights and a promise of a harvest moon in time for Halloween. Thoughts of the future reminded Barry this wasn't his car or his house. He killed the engine, but Silas made no move to get out.

Silas pocketed his phone. "Sharpe's got a bee in his bonnet about Sheriff Tennent and our sit-down tomorrow." Silas heard what he thought was a chuckle. "What's so funny?'

"You don't sound like you. Are you drunk?"

"Used to be four beers wouldn't do it, but those days are gone. So, probably."

"They did go down pretty fast," Barry said, trying to give Silas an out.

"Maybe," Silas conceded, staring up at the house, wondering if Livie was awake.

Barry was hopeful he was going to get out.

"I saw a picture of my wife with someone today. I had no idea who he was. It was on an old laptop at your place. It's back there in that bag. A girl named Katie Morgan told me it was Jason Austin."

Barry looked for a way out, but there was none. He lowered the windows instead glad the trees overhead blanketed the moon. He preferred the dark for this conversation. "You should talk to Olivia."

"Do you know? Was she in love with him?"

Barry knew what Alan Austin had told him about his son Jason and Liv, that's what Jason had called her. "I know how he died. She told me the story the night before Mark was killed."

"When we were at the haunted hotel?" It was the same night Silas and Livie ended up staying together. It's when he knew what would eventually happen between them. She knew it too, but she waited. Once they blurred the lines between work and personal, there was no going back for either of them. That's how it worked with her.

"What was Jason chasing?" Silas knew the public details, but not the private ones. He was hoping Barry could enlighten him. The case predated Olivia's time with the FBI.

"A string of murders all originating from the same bar in a place called Old Town."

Silas knew the place well. He and Livie had eaten at several restaurants in the area.

"Jason pulled Olivia in for a psychological profile. She agreed with him that it was a serial killer. She insisted it was a female."

"It was a girl that killed Jason," Silas confirmed.

"Yea. The cops shot her several times, but she wouldn't stop. She died a few days later in the hospital. Knowing what I know now, the girl was like Smythe. A demon was behind the killings," Barry summarized.

"Did Olivia know?" Silas asked.

"In the end that's when *It* first spoke to her."

"A demon?" Silas asked.

The more he revealed, the more Barry realized Olivia had not told Silas the story. "I think Jason knew before she did. Whether he told Olivia or not, only she can say. Jason might have been following a crime, but his real interest was in the paranormal. If he hadn't been killed, he probably would have ended up with his own haunted reality show or podcast or something."

"Was he special too, like Livie?"

The question sounded almost like a moan. "Not like her. There is no one like her," Barry corrected him.

"Everyone around her has some kind of something."

"Don't say it," Barry stopped him. He couldn't listen to Silas Branch whine about his lot in life. "You are the father of her children. It doesn't get any more special than that. You ensured her bloodline would continue."

Silas accepted the rebuke. "I never would have taken you for the philosophical type."

"My father was a philosophy professor. Now I spend my off time learning about good and evil with priests and bishops. It's not a fairytale."

"No. It's history. One no one wants to believe, except for Agent Mason Deveroux. He claims my wife is a witch."

Chapter Thirteen

Barry watched a sliver of light pierce the darkness as someone slipped from the house next door. It was too late for people-watching, but this was the perfect neighborhood for a nightcap outside if that's what Lily had in mind. Barry saw the soft red glow of a cigarette. He hadn't figured her as the smoking type. Maybe she only did it with a side of alcohol.

"You never talked to Deveroux, did you?" Silas asked.

"You're asking me this now?" If they had this conversation, things would never be the same.

"In here, it's just us," Silas encouraged him.

From the soft glow upstairs, Barry saw that Olivia was still up, yet Silas was still here with him. There was nothing Barry could do but appease him. "He tried to talk to me, but I'm pretty good at avoiding people," Barry admitted.

Silas couldn't argue with that. "What did Deveroux want to know?"

"What do you think? Deveroux wanted to know about that night in the barn. Mainly, what Ana Lutz said. I told him he could read my statement."

"I read your statement, and I know that's not all." Silas saw Barry cut his eyes toward him. "We're on the same team you know."

"Which team is that?"

"Olivia's." Silas chose to call her by her full name, not his shortened version. He had picked up on the fact Barry never abbreviated it. The gesture seemed almost reverent. "She's always between us."

Barry finally turned to face him. Silas took it to mean they were getting somewhere. "Your agent is after Olivia's mother. I never heard the name Sarah Larsin until that night. That's the truth."

"But you heard something or saw something," Silas suggested. He couldn't take Deveroux's word for it, even that was second-hand. Deveroux was so hell-bent on connecting Sarah Larsin to missing girls that he would stitch together any story, forcing the pieces to match if necessary. Silas needed to know if the agent was right, and Barry was his only source of information.

For the first time, Barry looked uncomfortable. He glanced down the street and finally back to Silas.

"You and Olivia must have talked about this," Silas prompted.

"When were we supposed to do that?" Barry wanted to know.

Days after the incident in the barn, Silas whisked her away to Virginia so he could tidy things up at Quantico before moving to San Antonio. When they returned, Olivia had a big fat diamond on her finger, and Branch was her last name. With Jamie Smythe in the wind, they all went back to leading their lives. Barry and Olivia were still navigating their new normal when today's shit storm hit.

"There has to be more," Silas insisted. "If you didn't talk to my wife, then what made you go to the Archbishop?"

The statement caught Barry off guard. "The Archbishop? How do you know about him?"

"It was his alibi that set you free."

Barry didn't know until now. Silas didn't say, and Barry didn't ask. All he had wanted was out. Dinner was a pleasant happenstance. Barry didn't have time to consider what that meant because Silas was still talking.

"You don't strike me as the religious type. You tell me, and I'll tell you what Deveroux said because frankly, I can't keep it to myself anymore. If I'm going to talk to anyone, it has to be you," Silas insisted.

Did Barry hear that right? Silas Branch needed a friend? "Why not your wife?" Barry asked the obvious. Where was Will Ibarra when Barry needed him?

"I don't want the cleaned-up, sanitized version she'll give me. She holds back because she doesn't want me to see what she truly is or maybe she doesn't want to see herself. Sometimes seeing things from another person's perspective helps you accept what you already know. I used to think of myself as someone who got things done. Livie was the only one brave enough to tell me I was also an asshole about it."

"I think the word she used was prick," Barry reminded him of their first meeting when Silas had blown into town in full FBI agent mode. Silas took not only the Good Samaritan case but Olivia, too.

"She saw me for who and what I was. She didn't turn away. She accepted me," Silas acknowledged with humility Barry didn't know he had.

"These are things you should be saying to her," Barry told him.

"I will, but I need you to say them first. I need some of those words to get her to open up." Silas could see Barry was still locked down. Tight. Apparently, Barry needed someone else to start, something to convince Barry that he knew what he was asking. "Olivia told me Roche was looking for a demon."

Demon. It was the magic word that lifted the cloak of secrets. "Olivia was the bait. Roche believed by sacrificing her he could broker some kind of deal for unholy power. Olivia might not mix potions in a cauldron, but she is gifted. The Church considers those abilities to be a source of witchcraft. In her profile, Olivia described Roche as a dabbler. He had no idea what he was doing. That was his big mistake. He didn't respect the power he so desperately sought," Barry explained. He let it all out at once so he couldn't take it back.

"Since Roche didn't sacrifice her, where did the power to destroy the barn come from?" Silas asked. "The fire inspector said it was kerosene and dried hay, but I know it was more. There was a demon, wasn't there?"

"There was," Barry conceded, knowing he sounded cagey.

"If Roche couldn't conjure one, how did it get there?"

Barry hesitated, but only for a moment. Once unleashed the secret could never be put back. Silas would learn the same truth he had lived with since that night. "Either Olivia brought it with her, or it was waiting for her all along."

"You're saying it chose to spare her and take Roche instead," Silas summarized.

Barry nodded, not trusting himself to speak. Silas' version was neater. The implication Olivia was more valuable to a demon alive than dead was something Barry didn't want to consider. He also wasn't sure if Silas' rendition was correct, but he wasn't going there either. He and Olivia both survived, and that was all that mattered.

"Tell me about the fire in the barn."

The memory stirred the hairs on Barry's arms. "When Olivia saw me on the altar and Roche threatened me, the air suddenly became *charged*. It felt electric. Like a thunderstorm just before lightning strikes." Barry shook his head at the memory. He should have been afraid for his life, but his fear had melted away. "I've never seen her eyes so green."

Silas witnessed a similar demonstration at the prison when they visited Pittman when she stopped the guards from attacking him. He remembered the sound of their Billy clubs as they fell to the ground. The sound still haunted him.

"Do you know how the fire started?" Silas asked.

"The fire marshal was right about the kerosene. I heard the lanterns breaking, but Olivia never touched them. She just stood there with that bag in her hand, looking at Roche."

"The one with the snake she said was dead? The tox screen said there were hallucinogens in all of your systems. Is that why Roche and Ana Lutz stayed on the altar? Were they under the influence too?"

"I don't think they could leave," Barry said carefully. "Olivia was communicating with Roche without ever saying a word. When Ana Lutz cut me free, Olivia's voice was very clear. She told me to get out. I did." For a split second, Barry considered stopping, but he had come too far. He had to finish it. "I saw *It* come out of the fire. The fire Olivia started."

"By *It,* you mean the demon, *Alleracsap?*"

Barry gave him a cold stare. "You're not supposed to say *It*s name."

"Livie told me she was the one with the power. Not *It*," Silas explained

Barry nodded, trying to come to grips with his thoughts. He couldn't argue the point.

"So, Olivia told you *Its* name?" Olivia never told him. It just came to him, like the thoughts in the barn—the ones that didn't belong to him.

Silas nodded. "Deveroux also knew. He said Amanda told him."

Barry shook his head, confused. "How?"

"According to Amanda, you talk in your sleep," Silas explained.

Barry shook his head again. "That's a lie. Tell me, why is Deveroux fixated on Sarah Larsin?" Barry might have been holding back, but so was the FBI. It was clear Roche was a suspected serial rapist linked to missing girls long before Atascosa County. Where Sarah Larsin fit in that scenario was never clear. Barry would very much like to talk about something else.

Silas was happy to share. "It started with Ana Lutz. She was a sixteen-year-old runaway working the streets in Vegas." Her story was similar to the girls Roche targeted. "Eventually Ana ended up employed by Sarah Larsin."

"Ana was a witch," Barry interrupted. They might as well get straight to the point. Ana Lutz might have touted herself as a Wiccan priestess, but Barry knew it wasn't nature she was interested in.

"As far as Deveroux is concerned, there's nothing

Wiccan about her. He's involved because he thinks Ana and Roche were recruiting girls for Sara Larsin. Having worked for her, Ana would know the kind of skills she was looking for. From all accounts, Ms. Larsin is protective of her merchandise. Ana's first pimp ended up dead in the desert, missing his head and his hands. It's ancient history, but it piqued the FBI's attention because that's the exact same way the Atascosa sheriff deputy wound up."

Barry remembered him well. He found him splayed on Roche's dinner table.

"What started as sex trafficking has now become about witchcraft and the occult. Deveroux's next move is to go to Vegas and confront Sarah Larsin."

"No matter what we think of Deveroux, he's not wrong," Barry told him. "What does it mean to behead someone anyway?"

"Decapitation is the ultimate form of intimidation. It was common practice in ancient times."

Barry suspected even in the witchy world, there was no coming back from that. "According to Ana, Roche killed the deputy to appease their mistress. From what you just told me, I think that would be Sarah Larsin." And the connection Deveroux was looking for.

"You heard her say that?"

"Not in so many words. To be honest, I'm not sure what was actually said or what popped into my head all on its own," Barry confessed. He wondered if that was how it worked for Olivia.

"You were drugged." It was the default phrase Barry used when asked for specifics. "That's what you need to remind Deveroux," Silas told him.

"I'm not telling Deveroux shit," Barry assured him.

"You need to know Roche and Ana's objective was to obtain the asset and assess," Barry repeated. "Those were Ana's exact words."

Silas' mouth went dry. "By asset, you mean Olivia?" Those were cold, calculating terms.

"They pushed her. The incense subdued me, but it was really for her. I think they wanted to see what she could do. They were goading her."

Silas went quiet, looking out the car window, trying to summarize all that he had learned. "So, Deveroux and the Church are right. My wife is a witch." Silas tried to make the words sound normal— like a joke between friends.

Barry pulled him back from the edge he was staring over. "You told me yourself she was an evolution of the senses. Maybe working and living with her, you've become numb to her talents. The Church believes she carries ancestral traits handed down through the ages. Sarah Larsin wanted to know what her little girl grew up to be. Whatever Olivia can do, doesn't involve incense and teas, an unfortunate mistake for Ana. She was afraid in the end. Like she unleashed something she couldn't put back."

Silas looked to Barry. "Olivia told me what happened that night made her realize she wasn't cursed. She told me saving someone's life could be nothing short of a gift. Saving you was what she needed to accept whatever she is."

Barry didn't want Silas dwelling on that thought either. Pull at it too long and it could unravel the peace they were making between them.

"According to that killer, Pittman, and the Archbishop, I'm Olivia's *Watcher*. It's exactly as the word implies. I'm supposed to watch over her. Apparently, that road goes both ways." Barry hoped the explanation helped soothe whatever Silas was feeling.

Silas understood, although he wouldn't confess it to Barry. His explanation mirrored what Olivia told him when she said she needed both of them in her life. They were a trifecta. "And Sarah Larsin?" Silas asked instead. "Where does she fit?" Given the fact she had left her daughter at a young age, Silas never considered having to deal with her. Neither had Livie.

Barry shrugged. "If she's the kind of woman you say she is, then maybe Roche's end would have been the same as in the barn. No matter what, I don't think sacrificing Olivia was part of the deal."

Olivia grew up believing her mother left because she was afraid of her, but Sarah Larsin had almost forty years to reconsider. Had her four-year-old daughter become something unexpected? Was she an asset? And if so, to who, or what?

"In my opinion, Sarah Larsin might not be the only one you need to worry about," Barry warned.

"The way Deveroux made it sound the whole notion of gifted ones sounds like some secret society," Silas agreed.

"In the eyes of the Church, it is," Barry confirmed.

"So, that crazy bastard Deveroux is right again." Silas let out a sigh. "Who else do I need to look out for?"

"Olivia's father. No one seems to know who he is, including her mother. According to Ana, he's the reason Olivia is the way she is."

"Another gifted?" Silas asked.

Barry hesitated. "My gut says more than that.

Darker. Like that thing that came out of the fire."

It grew quiet between them, both absorbing the story they had exchanged.

"I don't know how to tell you how much I appreciate you letting me stay here," Barry said, eager to change the subject. That was enough discussion for one night.

The conversation dredged up unpleasant memories and gave him perspective. Maybe it was acceptance of everything he had learned over the past year, but it hit him all at once. Olivia loved Silas. She always had. Olivia didn't spend her time thinking about what might have been. She cared about him, of that Barry had no doubt. What Olivia felt for him was more than friends, but less than lovers. She wanted his approval, his acceptance, and his support. What Silas gave her, he never could.

"I know you think Olivia needs someone to take care of her, but you didn't see her in the barn. From what I saw, she can take care of herself. What she really needs…"

"Is someone to teach her about her world. For her and our daughters," Silas interrupted. As much as he hated to consider it, was Sarah Larsin that person?

"That's neither one of us," Barry told him. "What she needs is an anchor to this world. To this place. And that's you."

Chapter Fourteen

"You up for that drink I promised you?" Silas asked. "I think there's a bottle of the stuff you like somewhere in the kitchen."

"Maybe later. I'm going to take a walk. Don't wait up, and don't lock me out," Barry told him.

"Will do." Silas saw the light next door the same as Barry. "Try to be home before sunup. I don't want to have to explain to my wife how I let you get away already."

As Silas made his way inside, Barry crossed the grass to Lily's house. The porch was dark, telling him she was still there. If she had gone in for the night she would have turned the light on.

"It's late. What are you doing out?" Barry asked.

"Are you on neighborhood watch now?" Lily asked him. The cigarette was gone, but there was still some liquid left in her glass.

"Is that a job? I might need one," Barry told her, enjoying the sound of her girlish giggle. It was a welcome respite from the events of the day.

Lily had been watching him and Silas. It was a long conversation. She hadn't guessed they were friends. "Can I offer you a nightcap?"

Barry hesitated, his foot resting tentatively on the first step of her porch.

"You shouldn't leave me to drink alone,

Lieutenant. I know you're not on duty, so you can't use that as an excuse."

Barry smiled. She had been out here a while. Maybe waiting for this. "No excuses," he conceded. After talking to Silas all Barry wanted was to forget. And maybe he wanted the same thing Lily did. Not to be alone.

"I have wine or bourbon." Neither seemed to get his attention. "Canadian whiskey?" she ventured.

Barry was pleasantly surprised. "That would be excellent, thank you."

Barry was still standing when she returned. Lily pointed him to a chair as she handed him his drink. She refilled her wine glass from the bottle she brought with her. They sipped together. Barry savored the familiar taste, glad he said yes.

"I take it that's your preferred poison?" Lily asked.

"How did you know?"

"I didn't until now. Olivia gave me the bottle. It had barely been touched. She said she had it for a while; got it for a friend. It was for you, wasn't it?"

Silence was her answer.

"Is it weird that I offered it to you?"

They both smirked at the comment. Barry took another sip in a show of goodwill. "No, not at all. It's been a weird night."

Before Barry knew it, Lily had emptied the wine bottle, and he agreed to a refill. They had a good time, talking about anything other than their day. As the night grew cooler, Barry considered offering her warmth when a sound interrupted the moment.

It came from the direction of Olivia's house. Barry whipped around, straining to see what it was, but all he found was darkness.

"It's probably an opossum or a raccoon," Lily assured him. "The neighborhood is full of them."

Barry remained standing, waiting for the sound to return. "I thought I heard glass."

"That clanking sound is old Mrs. Welch discarding her empties. Tomorrow is recycle day. She drinks more than I do," Lily whispered and pointed to the house on the other side of Olivia. "She uses one of the little open bins. The animals like to get in there and rummage around because it smells sweet. She drinks those fruity beers. That's probably what you heard."

She could be right. It was the right direction. If it was something sinister, like a window there would have been a house alarm blaring, confirming his own paranoia. Maybe Lily's heavy-handed pours had caught up with him. "Did you notice the porch light? I thought it was on earlier," Barry said, still staring next door.

"It faded out a few minutes ago. Better remember to change it in the morning."

"Good idea." Barry turned to find Lily standing next to him. Before he knew it, she wrapped her arms around his neck and pulled him into her. She didn't feel cold, just the opposite in fact.

"Thanks for not letting me drink alone," Lily whispered. Her breath smelled sweet. Her lips teased him with hints of the wine she had been drinking.

Lily stopped before he did, backing away slowly, looking shy. "Goodnight, Lieutenant."

Barry wandered back to Olivia's in a daze, wondering what just happened. He almost tripped over the chair in the middle of the dark. He grabbed the table to break his fall and almost knocked over the beer bottle. Luckily, he grabbed it before it could slide off the table. The wildflower stuck inside of it caught him off guard. Must have been Silas. It didn't seem like the agent's style, but who was he to judge? Silas had been a little tipsy. Maybe so was he.

Barry slipped inside and set the house alarm behind him. Luckily, Olivia had never changed the code. He was staying in the downstairs bedroom, the one with her grandmother's bed. He had stayed there before. Someone had turned the covers down for him. He bet it wasn't Silas.

****

Silas left without breakfast. He had a showdown to get to. Olivia slept in and woke up feeling refreshed. It was amazing what several hours of sleep could do. Seeing the door to the downstairs bedroom still closed, Olivia gathered the dogs and slipped out the gate in the back.

The morning was cool and crisp. All around her, lawns were prepped with pumpkins and scarecrows. Olivia loved Halloween. It was the preamble to the more important day that came after. The day of the dead. It was a time of remembrance for those who had passed beyond this world and into the next. Gran taught her to honor her ancestors rather than mourn them. It was a time to celebrate what came before.

Her family had lived on this land for over a century. Even as the city grew around them, their quiet little neighborhood still managed to cling to a small-town feel where kids played outside and walked home from school. It was an idyllic place to raise her daughters. In a week, the streets would be clogged with trick-or-treaters, all feeling safe and secure to roam free and visit the neighborhood houses where the porch lights remained lit, and treats were handed out to kids and dogs alike.

Despite the cool morning, Olivia soon found herself out of breath. She wanted to blame it on the dogs' clipped pace, having missed their walk last night, but it was most likely due to her advancing pregnancy. Her body was changing and nothing was as it used to be.

Olivia stopped at the corner to catch her breath and noticed the post littered with paper signs. She had seen them piling up but never stopped to read them. There were a few announcements for Fall Festivals, but they were choked out by missing pet posters. Her curiosity took over, and she began profiling them like people. The disappearances started after the kids returned to school. An elder gray tabby cat named Shadow was the first to go. His picture was still up but barely visible for the succession of others that came to join him. What started out as a cry for help now looked like a memorial.

One of her neighbors stopped to join her. Olivia thought his name was Judd. She and Silas often saw him on their nightly strolls.

"I think it could be opossums or maybe raccoons." Judd stooped down to offer his hand to Daisy as a greeting. It wasn't the first time he had stopped to admire the sleek greyhound. Females of the breed were slim compared to their male counterparts. With Daisy's light golden coloring and the traditional slender greyhound snout, she had the look of dog royalty.

"It could be why it's only the small ones," Olivia agreed, relieved to see Alvin and Daisy didn't fit the profile. "The majority are kittens or older cats, a few puppies, but no adult dogs."

The vulnerable ones.

"We've lost two cats in eight months," Judd said.

"Greyhounds are gentle, and loyal, not guard dogs," Olivia told him. "They don't bark." Judd was seeking protection, not companionship.

Judd withdrew his hand and moved on. He didn't say anything about being afraid. How did she know his regular walks were really a patrol, looking for anything that didn't belong?

Olivia headed home. Her eyes roamed the streets like an apex predator surveying her kingdom. A prickle inched its way down her neck. It was a subtle signal wildlife lurked among them. The thing stalking her neighborhood did so on two legs, not four.

****

Barry woke up to a quiet house. He glanced outside to see the empty driveway. In the corner sat the bag Silas brought from the condo. The last time he saw it was in the backseat of Silas' ride. Glad for its arrival, Barry snuck into the shower and emerged to the smell of breakfast.

"Bacon and biscuits are on the menu this morning. Don't get used to it," Olivia greeted him. Silas was the one who usually did the cooking. She made do with half a grapefruit and a scrambled egg earlier. They were merely an appetizer before now.

With a tilt of her head, Olivia directed Barry toward the coffee. He was glad to see she looked rested. The baby bump hidden under the folds of her dress yesterday was on full display this morning with her tee shirt and yoga pants. Barry wondered how much babies could grow overnight.

"Do I have time for a quick chore?"

"We're not asking you to earn your keep or anything like that," Olivia quipped.

"Last night I noticed the porch light was out. I want to change it before I forget."

"Is that why the chair was in front of the door? Did you try and change it in the dark?"

Barry looked confused.

"Silas almost tripped over the chair in his hurry to get out the door this morning. He felt the need to text me about it," Olivia explained. "Silas just changed it." She scooped up crispy strips of bacon and piled them on the plate next to her.

"Are you sure?"

"Of course. I have a schedule for those things. The outside lights are changed at the beginning of October, the same as the time change, whether they need it or not."

Barry had never known anyone so methodical.

Olivia saw the look he was giving her. "It was my defense against getting caught coming home in the dark."

Before marrying Silas, she traveled a lot and lived alone. Given what she did during the day any number of things could have been lurking in the night. The thought made Barry's gut clench.

"Indulge me."

"Suit yourself but hurry it up. You have a busy day ahead. Brennon will be here in a little over an hour. Before that, you should enjoy some breakfast." The oven buzzed, and she pulled out a tray of biscuits. "I know I am."

On the porch, Barry found the chair back in its place. He pulled it back out and used it to reach inside the decorative glass. He twisted the bulb and it lit up in his hand. From this new vantage point, Barry surveyed his surroundings. A blanket of realization settled over him as he looked ahead and saw Lily's porch in full view. He pondered who stood here last. It certainly hadn't been Silas.

Replaying the events Barry recalled the clanking noises he heard, the ones Lily attributed to animals. Relinquishing his vantage point, Barry stepped down from the chair. Pushing it back to the table, he saw the beer bottle with the flowers still in it. They were the same as the ones growing in front of the porch. He brought the bottle inside and sat it on the kitchen counter like the offering they were.

Olivia looked up from the laptop angled next to her plate. "Are those for me?"

Barry concentrated on pouring himself the cup of coffee he deserved. "Not unless they're from Silas. I found them outside on the table." It was the only excuse he could come up with.

Olivia dismissed the suggestion. "Not likely." Silas was a big production kind of guy. Wildflowers seemed more like something Barry would do. Olivia studied the label on the bottle. "Not to mention that's a fruity beer. Silas wouldn't be caught dead drinking that stuff."

Barry slid into the chair across from her, wondering if he was taking Silas' spot. "Then whoever unscrewed your porchlight last night must have left them."

****

For the second time in two days Silas found

himself on the way to Atascosa County. Deveroux was in the back looking out the window while Sharpe rode shotgun, working his phone. He'd called the sheriff no less than three times since they left the office.

"There's something wrong," Sharpe said. By now, it had become a mantra.

Sharpe's gut was talking. It was instinct, something Silas couldn't argue against. He checked Deveroux in the rearview.

"I haven't been out here, if that's what you're thinking."

Deveroux never said where he was yesterday before the DA found him. If Silas had to guess, he was probably sleeping one off.

The house was set back off the road. Jim Tennent's pick-up was parked in the circular drive. Silas rolled up behind it, wondering why it wasn't in the garage. Maybe the man had dipped out for a few minutes without his phone. Silas remained behind the wheel, waiting to see if the sheriff would step out on the porch to greet them.

"When was the last time you talked to him?" Silas asked Sharpe when the scenario didn't play out.

"Three days ago," Sharpe said, sounding grim. "He never answered any of my messages yesterday."

Silas surveyed the house. The curtains were pulled. The place looked locked up tight. "Does he have another vehicle?" Silas asked.

"A refurbished cruiser he bought at auction." Sharpe exited their vehicle but made no move for the house. He was waiting on something.

Silas followed next but kept the car between himself and the house. He swept his jacket aside and unsnapped the holster of his gun. His gut was talking now, too.

Sharpe let out a loud whistle.

"What the fuck are you doing?" It was Deveroux. He, too, was out of the car but remained behind the open car door.

"Calling the dog." Sharpe said. "I thought he would be here already."

Chapter Fifteen

The lines to the shadow world were still there. They called to her from the other side. Olivia reached for the ever-present silver cross that hung around her neck, grounding her to the here and now. The life inside her stirred, reacting to the blanket of energy surrounding them. She placed a hand protectively on her abdomen, shielding her offspring from those eager to make their acquaintance.

Graham Banks wasn't there to guide her today. Olivia assured him she could find her way to the resident dining hall alone. At this time, it was empty, except for the two women she had come to see. Kevin Branch could untangle the data provided by the facility, but Olivia knew the women in front of her were the keepers of the real secrets.

In a show of solidarity, the nurses sat next to each other. Olivia took the seat across from the one in scrubs. The badge clipped to her uniform said Kacey Shultz. Uncertainty rolled off her in waves. People who experienced strange occurrences feared disbelief. Working in a science-based profession seeded feelings of doubt.

"I'm here to listen. Not judge," Olivia tried to soothe her.

Kacey looked at her companion who wasn't wearing a uniform. She must have come in on her day off. The name badge clipped to the massive purse next to her read Christie Willis. Christie gave Kacey a nod of encouragement. Christie wasn't without fear, but she hoped finding answers would chase the fear away.

"It started with Miss Inez. Her doctor believed the increased confusion and agitation were a normal part of her condition. He changed her meds, but nothing helped. One day I stayed over to help the next shift when I found her crying in her room. Miss Inez said she was afraid to go to sleep."

"Room 104." The words slipped out before Olivia could stop them. It was the storage closet Banks had shown her.

"How did you know?" Christie interrupted.

Olivia shook her head. It would take too much to explain. "It doesn't matter. Go on."

Kacey cast a quick glance at her coworker. Christie nodded, encouraging her when she needed it. "Miss Inez insisted someone was in her room. She pointed to the corner by the bathroom."

Tapping into Kacey, Olivia saw a frail lady with white hair, her face buried in fingers as gnarled as tree branches. It was her daughter's budding paranormal abilities that were intensifying Olivia's own perceptions. She wondered, not for the first time, how much of these shared abilities she would retain after their birth. Olivia wished there was someone she could ask. Unfortunately, there wasn't a chapter on psychically gifted children in Silas' copy of *Exceptional Expectations.*

"You know that prickly feeling you get on the back of your neck when you know someone's watching you?" Kacey asked.

Olivia nodded. She'd felt it that morning on her walk.

"She made it sound so real. I turned on all the lights. I checked the bathroom and the closet. I even looked under the bed. Right about that time, the door alarm at the end of the hall went off."

Olivia recalled reports of faulty alarms that came up in Barry's investigation. "What would cause the alarm to sound?" she asked out of curiosity.

"A patient elopement," Kacey said.

"The patients who can ambulate on their own are fitted with monitors. When the alarm sounds it flashes across the computer screens at the desk, telling us who tried to make a getaway," Christie explained.

This wasn't mentioned in Barry's information. "So, which patient was it?" Olivia wanted to know, wondering why the facility changed alarm companies if everything was working.

"It was a ghost," Kacey said.

This was not the answer Olivia expected. "What?"

"Instead of a patient name on the screen it was a number," Christie explained. "That was the way we used to do it, but now we assign the monitors by patient name and enter it into the system. When IT tracked down the number, it was assigned to a patient who died two years ago," Christie said. "As you can imagine, once word got out about the IT thing, other nurses came forward with similar stories."

"Everything was fine for about a week. Then Miss Inez started again with the man in the corner story. She claimed he moved closer to her bed every night. She said he made her feel frozen like she couldn't move." Kacey closed her eyes and pinched the bridge of her nose.

"Then she died," Christie chimed in, breaking the tension in the room.

"I never got to say goodbye. I was gone on vacation when it happened. One of the nurses thought she might have been smothered. Her hair was matted. The pillows were rearranged on her bed," Kacey said, eyes still closed.

"Is there any reason to think these deaths could be suspicious?" Olivia asked, choosing her words carefully.

Kacey deflated as tears spilled from her eyes, telling Olivia Kacey had heard these words before. As the money man, Graham Banks made it clear the board members wanted this matter buttoned up quickly and quietly. Now, Olivia knew why. Stories like these would spread and eventually hurt not only their bottom line but also the staff.

Still, Olivia had to pursue all other avenues first. "Considering this is a skilled nursing facility, there are a higher-than-average number of calls to the coroner. Not everyone who goes into healthcare wants to help," Olivia reminded them. "These patients are vulnerable."

"You're talking about Mr. Hughes, aren't you?" Kacey asked. "I thought they didn't find anything."

"Technically, the investigation is ongoing. That's why I'm here." It was a white lie. The Hughes family didn't proceed with an autopsy, but the idea of one helped propel the story forward, where it eventually got to Father Dominic. If Olivia had to guess, it was Christie who went to him.

"Because you're a profiler?" Kacey asked, looking dejected. She was losing faith fast.

"I am," Olivia confirmed. *Of monsters and men.*

"But I was a nurse before I was an FBI agent. Investigating public records is a component of my analysis. Like taking a patient's medical history before beginning an exam," Olivia explained, using a familiar analogy. She needed Kacey to trust her. "I used to work in Alzheimer's Units, just like you," Olivia said what Kacey needed to hear. "I believe you. But I'm not the one who needs convincing."

"The padre trusts her. That's good enough for me," Christie said.

Away from the priesthood, Father Dominic returned to his roots as a social worker. Oak Hollow was one of the facilities he served. Olivia wished, not for the first time, for his counsel, but Dominic was away on Church business, learning to be an exorcist. Olivia could attest to the fact he was already familiar with demons. They fought one together.

"It wasn't Mr. Hughes' family who called the coroner," Christie said with confidence. She looked over at Kacey. "She's on our side. We just had to get her here."

Olivia was grateful for the endorsement. "Who do you think called the coroner and why?" Olivia wanted to know.

"Shelia was a charge nurse on nights," Christie answered. "She kept finding these little bags with more of the worrisome patients, like Mr. Hughes. Shelia complained to management about them. She called them talismans, like they were something bad. When they didn't do anything, she got pissed and quit. Not that it was any great loss."

Talisman was an interesting word choice. "Bags of

what?" Olivia wanted to know.

Christie opened her purse and began to dig.

"They look like those *gris-gris* bags you get in the French Quarter," Kacey told her. "The ones that are supposed to be full of magic herbs to help you catch a lover or scare away the monsters."

Olivia's heart thudded at the description.

"This," Christie said, lobbing one Olivia's way.

Olivia caught it but the sting to her hand caused her to drop it.

Her reaction caught the nurses off-guard.

"I think there's cedar in there. Maybe you're allergic," Kacey offered.

Olivia rubbed the tips of her fingers. The tingling sensation that sent a wave up her arm was already in retreat. The shock had been instantaneous, like touching a live wire. As far as Olivia knew, she wasn't allergic to anything.

Olivia took a closer look at the bag. It looked like it was made of burlap. It was knotted tight at the top with white ribbon or string. Tentatively, Olivia picked it up from the top so as not to touch whatever was inside. She didn't get halfway to her nose before she detected the smell of cedar mixed with probably sage. It was strange she would react to things she herself used.

"Shelia said she found salt and some rust-colored substance on the windowsills of some of the patient rooms," Christie told her.

Olivia suspected the other substance Christie described was cumin. When mixed with salt, it was a ward against evil or thievery. The same person who bound those properties together had also concocted whatever was contained in the bag she was holding.

Olivia flashed back to the crystals she found in the sealed room. The one that she now knew belonged to Miss Inez. There had been salt there, too. She had tasted it. The reaction she had to the bag wasn't an allergy. It was a binding spell, cast by someone skilled in old magic. Her great-grandmother, Abitha the apothecary, would have known how and why.

"If these talismans make the residents feel better, what's the harm?" Kacey lamented. She was thinking about the worrisome patients, the ones like Miss Inez.

Any other time Olivia would agree, but was she too distracted by the bag and its maker to contribute.

"More residents are telling the same story," Christie said. "It's always about the same dark figure in the corner."

"Who?" Olivia asked, her thoughts still wandering.

"It's a feeling, not a lurker," Christie explained.

"Lurker?" Olivia repeated.

"It's a word my mom used. For things that come in the night," Christie admitted.

Olivia nodded. She knew what a lurker was. It meant someone who kept to the shadows for evil deeds. "What I meant was, do you know who made the bags or where they came from?" Olivia clarified.

Kacey looked at Christie, again. This time it was some kind of internal debate and not an ask for permission.

"Poe's a good nurse," Kacey said, taking the lead for the first time. "He knows stuff, sometimes before it happens. He has crazy nurse senses," she said, sounding like part defender, part admirer.

Olivia's face remained passive, but her heart clipped faster at the name. "Poe?"

"Rogan," Christie clarified. "He calls them trinkets."

"Where did he get these trinkets?" Olivia asked.

"He said he made them from an old family recipe," Christie explained.

Free from patient obligations, Christie walked Olivia out the way she came in, through the common room. It was more crowded now than when she arrived.

"Something I didn't ask you was, who was the first resident who complained about the dark figure?" Olivia wanted to know. Patterns were as important in medicine as they were in profiling.

"Mr. Hughes," Christie answered. "The sad part is, whoever talks about it ends up dead, eventually. It's like a plague."

It was a sobering thought.

Christie reached for Olivia's wrist, invading her thoughts. "Father Dominic said you could sense things, but most of all, that you would believe us."

Christie had been strong when Kacey was present, but now it was just the two of them, and Christie sounded as vulnerable as Kacey. Both nurses were looking to her for answers, and for the first time, Olivia felt a trickle of doubt. She only had so many tools in her arsenal.

"As nurses we're privileged to share the most sacred of human experiences. The beginning of life and the end. My gran used to say those are the times when the planes of existence are the thinnest. Because of it, we can sometimes catch a glimpse into another time and place. I've seen those places, and I do believe you."

Olivia saw a spark of hope in Christie's eyes. Before the nurse could ask for more than she could deliver, Olivia turned to go, but something tugged her back. She scanned the room, looking for the familiar that had breached her perimeter. A TV was mounted on the wall, but no one was paying attention to the guy talking about the benefits of longer life. Instead, there were vacant stares, not at the screen, but into the abyss of lives lived and lost. They were waiting for the dark to come. Most were ready. Except for one. He was sitting in the corner talking quietly to a woman slumped over in a wheelchair next to him. The woman was oblivious to what he was saying, but he seemed undeterred. He stopped what he was saying to look up. Their eyes met, and Olivia caught a fleeting glimpse of the flickering light inside him, a lantern swinging in the night.

Olivia nodded toward the man. "Who is he?"

"Everyone calls him Mr. Sunshine," Christie said. "His name is Franklin Pope. He's one of the bright spots in this place. The light against the dark."

Olivia knew he was also something else.

****

What started out as a welfare check quickly turned into something else.

Ranger Herschel Gaines arrived before the Bexar County coroner. Atascosa County didn't have one of its own. "For such a little bitty place they sure know how to cause a ruckus. Am I going to inherit this one too, since the sheriff was pending questioning by the FBI?"

Gaines took a drag on his cigarette, glad to be out of the house. It reminded him of the scene at Andre Roche's place, only worse. Someone left behind a hell of a mess. The crime scene techs had their work cut out for them.

Silas waited with the ranger on the porch, deciding he wanted the FBI to take this one. Silas called Frank Tobias and told him to bring his best team, meaning those who knew how to keep their mouths shut, probably the same ones who worked the scene at Barry's condo.

Deveroux sat quietly on the porch swing. The can of empty cigarette butts beside it said Tennent must have also liked the spot. Agent Sharpe disappeared around the house, trying to walk off what he had seen.

"Before I got the call, I was on my way to your house to speak with the lieutenant. I ran across a familiar name while combing through a list of people who had access to the lieutenant's condo. Rose Corey. Wasn't she one of the girls Dr. Osborne rescued from our friend Roche?" Gaines asked.

"She was," Silas confirmed. "What does she have to do with Bartholomew?"

"That building he lives in provides maid service for a price. Ms. Corey was hired a few weeks ago. She was the last one to clean his place."

Silas knew it couldn't be a coincidence. He was trying to put the pieces together when John Sharpe came around the side of the house.

"Someone killed the dog."

"Smart. Take down the early warning system," Deveroux commented.

"His name was Bentley. He was a good dog." In the last eighteen months, Jon Sharpe had seen three dead bodies and a head in a freezer. His body count before Silas Branch came to town was zero.

"Any circular drawings, like inside?" Silas tried to make it sound like a routine question.

Sharpe paused, trying to pull himself together. "I didn't see any." Because he hadn't looked. "His throat was slit, like the sheriff's. Who the fuck does that to a dog?" Sharpe turned around and disappeared again.

"I guess I'll finally get to meet that wife of yours," Gaines mused.

Silas stuck his hand in his pocket, gripping his phone, waiting for a reply. He had texted her pictures of the scene, wanting to preserve it before the parade began.

"I told you there was more to this than sex and girls," Deveroux reminded him from the corner.

Chapter Sixteen

The parking lot was packed. As Olivia circled, looking for a space within a reasonable walking distance, she wondered how Barry got there. SAPD had taken his city car, and Silas had failed to get keys for whatever Barry drove in his off time. Once inside, the smells pushed out all thoughts of Barry and his transportation needs. She was going to like it here.

Olivia zigzagged across the room through the maze of tables aligned to accommodate as many patrons as possible. She planned on telling Barry what she learned at her meeting, but that would have to wait.

"Is this an ambush?" Olivia asked instead as she wedged herself into the space between the table and chair.

"We took the liberty of ordering you your favorite soda," Brennon said, hoping to soothe her surprise that he was joining them.

"It could have been worse. Ranger Gaines was going to stop by the house. Word is he's looking forward to meeting you," Barry told her.

"So, where is he?" Olivia asked, scanning the room for a cowboy hat. She, too, was eager to make his acquaintance. She had questions for him.

"This is where things get worse. He had to take a detour to Atascosa County. At the request of the FBI," Barry explained.

"Who died?" Olivia dug in her purse for her phone. "Silas was supposed to meet with Sheriff Tennent this morning."

"Sharpe couldn't get ahold of him last night, so the sheriff would be my guess," Barry offered.

Olivia sank a straw into the old-fashioned glass bottle Brennon nudged her way. She indulged in a long sip of much-needed caffeine as she watched her phone screen light up with messages from Silas. Some of them came with attachments.

The arrival of food interrupted her scrolling.

Barry was the first one to finish. "So, was I right? About the sheriff?" he asked.

Olivia offered her phone. "Look at your own risk," she cautioned.

Barry swiped back and forth, widening angles and turning the phone for a closer look. None of it helped explain what he was seeing.

Brennon shielded his eyes while posing a legitimate question. "Is this going to require a special circumstance amendment to your contract with the FBI?" he queried Olivia.

Olivia might have severed her ties with the Bureau, but she would be available for testimony on previously worked cases. New consultation requests were at her discretion. Olivia had employed Isaac Kaine, Brennon's son, to handle those requests.

"Given what the lieutenant has told me about Ranger Gaines and Atascosa County, I'm assuming this will require your expertise," Brennon continued.

"Unless the FBI has acquired someone else fluent in black magic, then your assumption would be correct," Olivia confirmed.

If Brennon didn't know her, the smile she flashed him might have been menacing. Something sparked the darkness inside of her. Hunting it thrilled her. Her desire to unravel mysteries of the dark was one of the things that made her so attractive. It was also something she would never have dared admit when they met years ago.

Brennon pulled out his phone and sent Isaac a text.

Barry passed the phone back to Olivia. He had no rational explanation for what he had just seen. "Those pictures conjure any ideas?"

Olivia smiled. His word choice was on point. "Unfortunately, yes. None of them good."

****

Silas cornered Frank Tobias off to the side of the house. "First impressions, from your gut," Silas encouraged.

Frank was more than happy to take him up on the offer. Frank hoped freeing his thoughts would bring clarity. "Someone cut the sheriff's throat. After which he got up and walked through his own blood. How he did that, I have no idea, but that's my best explanation based on what I just saw."

"Leave the explanation to me," Silas assured him. "What I need to know is the blood on his feet his? Make sure you get prints of his feet before you move him." Proving the prints on the floor belonged to Tennent was key. What happened here would be discussed and debated for years. So would the forensics. This case and Livie's interpretation of it would put her and her career in the crosshairs. For the first time in his career, Silas wished he had someone else he could call. "Forensics has to be by the book.

You're going to be talking about this one for a long time."

Frank nodded as the weight of Silas' words washed over him. Getting the prints was the smart move. "We took samples, but we'll get the prints, too." If the pooled blood on the floor belonged to the victim, then they should also find it on the feet and hands. Footprints were as unique as fingerprints. Given the victim was barefoot confirmation should be easy.

"My blood spatter guy noted the gait seemed off like the sheriff was dragging one foot or shuffling. It's something you would see in a stroke victim or someone with a neurological condition."

"Or someone who should be dead," Silas said for him.

"Yea, that," Frank agreed, realizing how flippant they both sounded, but it was the only way he could keep his head on straight.

"Are the handprints usable?" Silas wanted to know.

Frank shook his head. "Doubt it. They appear to be smeared."

"Ever seen anything like this?"

"Considering your background, I was going to ask you the same thing," Frank countered.

"Go with what you do know," Silas encouraged him. "Start with the original wound. The cut to the throat. Give me your theory." Past experience taught Silas that allowing someone to find an explanation on their own helped them manage the impossible.

"The sheriff was right-handed. Whoever cut his throat was a lefty. I'm not going to say it's not possible for him to cut his own throat, with his non-dominant hand, but nothing I saw in there is possible. Meeks will run a tox screen, but so far, we found no signs of drug paraphernalia. One empty beer bottle on the kitchen counter along with an empty glass of what looks like wine. We didn't find any, but there is a bottle of grape juice sitting on the counter."

"Anything interesting in the sheriff's medicine cabinet?" Silas wanted to know since Frank had taken the drug route.

"A common medication for high blood pressure. We also found the little blue pill for erectile dysfunction. According to the prescription bottles, both of them were filled recently. Other than those, nothing but Ibuprofen. There was an open box of condoms on the bedside table. A used one in the bathroom trash," Frank told him.

The combination prompted Silas to consider a much younger woman. The sheriff was mid-sixties. Condoms for birth control didn't seem like a consideration if the sheriff stayed in his age range.

The tech assigned to the dog came over to join them. "The cut to the neck came from a left-handed individual same as with the sheriff. The dog's been dead for at least two days. There was some vomit near the food bowl. The pooch was probably poisoned first."

"Any markings around the dog?" Silas asked him the same thing he had asked Sharpe.

"Something that looks like salt," the tech confirmed.

"If the same person who killed the dog, did the sheriff, then at least we know he didn't cut his own throat," Frank said once they were alone again.

"So, there was someone else," Silas surmised.

"I can't believe I'm saying this, but God, I hope so.

If I had found bites on the sheriff or the dog, I would be out of here. You know what that looks like in there, don't you?"

Silas nodded, letting Frank vent rather than feeding the paranoia.

Frank took a moment to compose himself. "Are you going to tell me what you think happened in there?"

"I can't." Silas was being honest. "But I did call my expert," Silas reassured him. "She can tell us both." If she couldn't, then God help them all.

Chapter Seventeen

Olivia and Barry parted ways with Brennon in the parking lot. Brennon was meeting with Zavalla and the DA the next day. Barry's presence was optional. Until then, Brennon instructed Barry to keep doing what he was doing and stay off social media.

Olivia connected with Silas and agreed to walk the scene, but it would have to wait. She had another appointment at Oak Hollow, and Silas wanted the forensics team gone before her arrival. Barry was along for the ride because Olivia wanted his input.

Kacey ushered them to a room not much bigger than a med room, which it probably was once. "Dr. Hudson is almost finished with rounds," Kacey told them.

"I didn't see Mr. Pope in the common room," Olivia mentioned.

"You know him?"

"Christie told me about him. I realized I know someone who knows him."

"He doesn't have a lot of visitors."

"You want to tell me what that was all about?" Barry asked once Kacey left them on their own. "Is this Mr. Pope a person of interest?"

"Yes, if he wasn't in his mid-eighties. Kevin Branch sent me some files about this place, resident profiles. Mr. Pope checked some boxes. It seems our friend Ranger Gaines put him away for a long time."

"For what?"

"According to reports, an unprovoked argument with a neighbor led to homicide. Mr. Pope spent more than two decades in prison."

His past reminded her of Larry Wayne Pittman, but she didn't get to share that before the doctor arrived.

"I graduated high school just after I turned seventeen," Dr. Hudson explained, knowing exactly what they were thinking. He looked like a kid.

Barry still felt old despite the explanation.

"Geriatrics is tough," Olivia said. When working with the elderly there was always a delicate line between life and death.

"Somebody's got to do it." Dr. Hudson shrugged. "Kacey told me she talked to you about what's been going on."

If young Dr. Hudson seemed concerned about meeting with a forensic psychologist, he didn't show it. He did take a good long look at Barry, causing Olivia to wonder if he was picking up cop vibes.

"And you are?" Hudson asked.

"Mr. Bartholomew is a colleague of mine. He's in security," Olivia cut in, not giving Barry a chance to respond. "As the physician in charge, I'm eager to hear your thoughts. Kacey described the reported experiences as a shared delusion given several of the residents reported similar experiences. I was curious to know if you had a medical explanation."

Barry was surprised at how accommodating she was. Maybe it was the doctor's age, or Olivia was fostering cooperation. It was different seeing things from her perspective. It was also different sitting across from someone who wasn't a potential perpetrator.

"Kacey is a good nurse, but sometimes she can be overly dramatic." Dr. Hudson stretched his legs and leaned back in a chair that was probably older than he was. "The patient reports sound like delusions. Sundowner's syndrome is my diagnosis. It's the most plausible explanation. More than half of Alzheimer's patients experience it."

Olivia predicted the syndrome would come up in the conversation. She knew because she had heard it all before. It was the easiest and safest assumption.

"I had a grandmother who used to say she could see angels. But only after the sun went down," Hudson said.

"After the sun, darkness always falls," Olivia reminded him. "There can be no angels without demons. No light without dark." It was a mantra she had heard since childhood. It was one thing Gran did teach her that Olivia still believed.

Dr. Hudson sat back up in his chair. "The behavior these patients exhibit is irrational, and illogical. With Sundowner's, rapid changes in mood are expected. They display signs of anger, agitation, fear, paranoia, sometimes even violence."

Hudson had recited everything he had been taught in school, relying on the text for answers. Science was his religion. He hadn't been out of school long enough for his real education to begin. "What's the one thing you're forgetting?" Olivia asked.

Dr. Hudson looked confused, positive he had recited the symptoms verbatim.

"How do you discount the stories they tell?" Olivia prompted him.

Hudson opened his mouth to debate her and realized he had no argument.

"Someone experiencing a paranoid or hallucinogenic event doesn't realize it isn't real. Patients with Sundowner's can't recall their experiences long enough to tell anyone because they don't remember them. That's not true, however, in the patients we're discussing, is it? Because they recall their experiences, thus the stories the nurses are telling. That would lead me to believe they are not hallucinations," Olivia explained.

Barry had no medical expertise, and her response made perfect sense to him. He looked over to find Hudson looking deflated. Maybe even a little scared. Barry decided to halt his trip down that path and steered him back to the familiar.

"You mentioned violence. Any incidents come to mind?" Barry asked, thinking of Mr. Pope.

"Not violence. But we do have one resident who displays a different set of behaviors," Hudson offered. "I would describe what he does as patrolling rather than wandering. Does that make sense?" Hudson asked Barry, while avoiding looking at Olivia.

"Meaning what he is doing is purposeful?" Barry explained what the doctor could not.

"Yeah, that's it," Hudson agreed.

"Which patient?" Olivia wanted to know.

"Mr. Pope."

"What else?" she probed.

"Sometimes the nurses find him standing at the end of his bed at four o'clock rounds. Most of our residents are early risers, but even that's early for them. Once the nurses speak to him, he goes right back to bed."

Olivia looked at Barry. She thought there was some significance to the ritual.

"The nurses have also found him washing his clothes in the toilet," Dr. Hudson continued.

"Prisoner bed check is typically at four in the morning. When you go on lockdown, water in the toilet is the only water available. It would be the only place to clean your clothes or yourself," Barry explained.

It took Hudson a minute to work it out, but he got the reference. "Mr. Pope was a prisoner?"

"He did some time," Barry confirmed.

"It's important to remember that everyone in this place had a life before they came here. They weren't always old," Olivia reminded the young doctor. It was something one of her nursing instructors taught her. She had never forgotten it. "Treat him as the man you know him to be today," Olivia urged.

"Any other residents or staff stand out?" Olivia was curious if Hudson would mention Rogan Poe. When Hudson remained silent, she wondered if maybe the male nurse's charm was lost on the young doctor. "It was suggested that one of the residents may have been suffocated. Do you think that's possible?" she probed.

Dr. Hudson drug a hand over his long face. "I'm guessing you're talking about Miss Inez." His eyes shifted, his thoughts traveling back to a scene he wanted to forget. "Her hands were folded neatly on top of her blanket. They looked just like my grandmother's did in her casket. Isn't that all any of us can ask for?"

Olivia rose to leave, understanding the description was what the young Dr. Hudson had to believe. Otherwise, he might have to rethink what he was doing here. She had no reason to badger him further. He did enough of that to himself. "Thank you for your time, Doctor."

Dr. Hudson looked panicked by her departure. "Wait, what are you trying to say?"

"We're not saying anything. We're just having a conversation," Barry stepped in to assure him.

Dr. Hudson shot to his feet, making the room feel even smaller than before. "No. I want to hear it from her."

Her hand on the door, Olivia turned to face him. "Are you sure? Because once I tell you there will be no going back."

Dr. Hudson appreciated the warning, but he had been repeating the line for too long, and somehow this woman knew it.

It wasn't all a lie. Miss Inez did look peaceful from the doorway. Her hair was neatly arranged on the pillow. Someone had taken the time to tuck her in. Her hands were clasped just like he said, but up close, her fingers looked like claws the way they clutched the blanket. Whoever took her away would have to take the blanket with them or cut it free. But it was the eyes that got him. They were open, the pupils were murky blue with cataracts, but as he peered down at her face, he saw something very different. The pupils blazed green and snapped open like elevator doors. Inside them was a black tunnel that he imagined reached all the way to Hell.

Dr. Hudson clenched his jaw. "I need to know what I'm missing."

Like with the nurses, Olivia spoke to him in familiar terms. "Sundowning is a plausible explanation.

Mild symptoms manifest as confusion. It's the more severe cases you need to watch. They result in a loss of self and transcendence into another world. That's where things go very wrong. In science, this experience is known as the Seven Second Theory. In religion, it is known as possession. I'm familiar with both. Do this long enough and you will be, too."

****

"We're just having a conversation," Olivia did her best impersonation of Barry once they were out of the building and on their way to her car.

"I'm in security?" Barry mocked her.

Olivia tossed Barry the keys. She didn't want to drive. The visit with Dr. Hudson had been taxing. "You prefer chauffeur?"

"I think you scared him," Barry said as he came around to get the door for her.

"That was my intent," Olivia said with the same hard look in her eye that she gave Hudson. She hadn't been aware she was projecting her feelings onto the young doctor. Maybe it was the Teller inside of her. The daughter who could see the past. "Maybe he'll listen to the nurses next time. As for me, I'm done keeping things to myself."

Sometimes Barry forgot how fierce she could be. The monsters should fear her.

****

Back home, the car Silas had promised was waiting. Olivia and Barry were surprised to find Sergeant Will Ibarra behind the wheel.

"I thought you were spending the weekend in DC," Barry said, wondering if he was the reason behind his partner's early return.

"Change of plans. Captain Zavalla had a job for me. Seems the FBI has requested my assistance," Will said with a wink.

"You're not theirs, yet," Barry reminded him.

"Yea, well tell that to the station chief," Will said, watching Olivia come back out of the house to join them. She went inside to change her shoes and grab a bottle of water.

Barry looked across the yard and saw Lily slip out onto her front porch. She gave him a tentative wave only to disappear back inside. It was probably the cop car that did it.

****

"Sorry about the weekend," Olivia echoed Barry's sentiments once she and Will were on their way. "How's Jessica holding up?"

"Hoping she still has a job when this is all over. She's been struggling to take the high road, but you know the media. The dirtier the secrets, the better the story."

"Is Barry's name out there?" Olivia asked. She didn't need Brennon Kaine to tell her to stay away from the news. She learned long ago if it was bad enough, someone would call her.

"Not publicly, but internally that shit spreads like wildfire. I hate to speak ill of the dead, but it didn't help that Dr. Greene slept with half of the force. Sentiment is split down the middle, but there are always pot stirrers. Most of it is coming from her family." Dr. Greene had four brothers, all of them in law enforcement. "It only got worse after it got out she was pregnant."

So much for confidentiality. "Her family didn't know?" Olivia was surprised. She looked down at her lap. The cut of the seatbelt left nothing to the imagination about her condition. She and Amanda were similar in height and build. Olivia wondered how Amanda thought she was going to keep it a secret.

"Apparently, not."

"What about her job?" Olivia wanted to know.

"That is in the lieutenant's favor, for now anyway. She was let go a few months ago due to unprofessional conduct. How's Barry doing, really?" Will asked.

"I'm keeping him busy," Olivia said, thinking she wasn't the only one. She saw him cross her lawn on his way to Lily's. "And he's making new friends."

****

They had to make a pit stop along the way. Luckily, they didn't lose any more time looking for the house. It was the only one on the lonely road with a barricade in front. High grass in the bar ditches was laid down where several trucks had been earlier. The area bore all the signs of a high-crime scene.

An Atascosa County deputy stopped them for identification before they entered the short dirt road leading to the house. While he logged them in on his clipboard, Olivia took note of their surroundings. There were no close neighbors. Great for privacy, unwanted visitors, and murderers. In front of the house was a circular drive, still dotted with cars, the coroner's van being one of them. They left the body for her. Olivia wondered what ritualistic horrors awaited her inside.

A team of Bexar County employees filed out the front door. The deputy must have radioed ahead. Silas followed at the end of the line. He stood waiting to open her car door. He cocked his head at Will to go on ahead. Agent Sharpe was waiting to brief Will on what they knew so far. Silas specifically requested the sergeant, but it wasn't because he was trying to preempt his move to the FBI, he needed someone with paranormal experience. Will's first meeting with Olivia took place in the now burnt-out barn. He'd also been present when Jamie Smythe went full demon mode. Will's introduction to this world was a steep learning curve, but he adapted. Silas needed someone who didn't spook easily, which was more than he could say for Sharpe. The agent had not returned to the house.

"Seems like old times," Olivia said. In an uncharacteristic move, she grabbed Silas' hand, prompting him to step closer. Typically, they never touched when working a scene, but this one was different. Olivia could feel it already. She saw remnants of shock on the faces of those now wandering into the fading evening sun. Beneath her dress, the babies went still.

"It's been a while," Silas agreed. They had not walked a crime scene together since Smythe murdered Travis Hobbs in the shower.

"This is the last one while I'm pregnant," Olivia told him.

Silas searched her eyes. "I wouldn't have called you if I didn't have to."

"I know," she said softly, reading his thoughts. "They will feel it," she told him.

Olivia pressed his hand to her side while she touched the other. She closed her eyes. "Lord, I ask this not for myself, but for our children. I pray You to keep them safe and guard them against any plans that are meant to harm them. Be close and surround them with Your favor within the shield of your wings. Allow them to rest safely between Your shoulders."

Before Silas could stop her, Oliva turned and began a slow trek toward the house, her head down, repeating the same prayer only in Latin this time. *"Domine, non est tibi a me: sed ad liberos meos. Oro te incolumem custodiat et in omni servare consilia et ea quae intelliguntur, ut noceat. Propinqui scuto et circumdabis tibi gratiam in pennis patiuntur inter tuta suis."*

Her posture read as subservience, but not the look on her face. Olivia looked ready for a fight, and Silas realized her words were not a request. They were a warning to whatever was inside waiting for her.

Chapter Eighteen

Olivia flooded her daughters with thoughts of sleep. The barrier between worlds had to be stronger than the one she erected earlier when she visited the Alzheimer's unit. Whatever awaited them across the threshold here was not like the patient deaths at Oak Hollow. This was worse. Oliva brought the silver cross to her lips as she crossed the threshold. Inside, the room felt strange and still. Empty even. As if the energy of death had been sucked into a vacuum, leaving behind a void.

Silas trailed behind her. Walter Meeks was there, with Frank Tobias, and Agent Deveroux. Even though they had never met, Olivia knew who he was. His suit and tie said FBI. The tall man in the cowboy hat had to be Herschel Gaines. No one spoke. The only sound was the howl of the wind outside and the creak of the eaves of the house above them.

Olivia shut out the living and focused on the scene. The couch and coffee table were shoved to the sides, leaving the center of the room open like a stage. This had been a performance. A large area rug was in the middle of the hardwood floor. The body of former Atascosa County Sheriff Jim Tennent was on the floor of his living room. Olivia set her sights on what death left behind.

The sheriff was on his back, his mouth open caught

in an eternal scream. His eyes were open, a strange shade of opaque blue. He was shirtless, revealing a bloody symbol carved in the middle of the chest. Olivia didn't bother to bend down; it was big enough that she could see what it was. The absence of blood told her the artist had at least waited until the heart stopped beating to begin carving. Olivia doubted it had anything to do with mercy and everything to do with ritual.

The sheriff was wearing only jeans. They were missing a belt, the top of them undone. The knees were soaked in blood, smears traveling the length of the legs to the top of his bare feet. Just like his hands, they too were covered in blood. The body was empty, as devoid of life as the room. Even the energy of the murder was absent, its fuel harnessed for something else.

Olivia knew this spot was not where Jim Tennent met his end. He bled out more than six feet away before he rose. The maroon stain on the rug appeared consistent with at least a gallon of blood, the amount contained in a human body. The surrounding area was marked by a circle of white and smaller particles. The white was salt. Olivia assumed the other was sand.

The ring of protection was broken. Dark energy lapped at her feet, the disturbance unseen by anyone but her. Her steps left ripples behind, reminding her of the snakes parting for her in Roche's cellar. She was hit with another wave of familiarity. She was welcome here, yet Olivia gave the space a wide berth. What crawled out of the circle was tainted by a demon and manifested by bloody handprints on the floor.

Streaks of blood trailed behind as the prints made their way to the couch. Smears on the fabric cushions made their way up the side. Olivia realized she was watching the transformation from a crawling corpse to one walking upright. One foot was functional, leaving behind clear prints. The other one lagged behind, a trail of smudges marking its way. Bloody handprints dotted the walls, sweeping aside anything in their way. Bare nails remained embedded in the walls. Splinters of glass littered the floor beneath them, stained with blood. The walker didn't feel pain.

Olivia tracked the trail to the kitchen. Tendrils of blood streaked the door frame on either side as the walker turned and retreated back to the living room, stopping where the sheriff now lay. This time he was truly dead. Olivia didn't need to see it again. She surveyed the kitchen instead. Take-out bags were scattered on the counter. Forensic techs had lined the receipts in date order. The most recent purchase came two days ago from the convenience store down the road where she made Will Ibarra stop. Her bladder needed a break from the soccer match going on inside her uterus.

A beer bottle and an empty glass sat beside the kitchen sink. Inside, the bottle smelled bitter. The rim of the glass had a film of something glittery and pink on one side. The bottom was caked with what looked like blood. Olivia sniffed it too, expecting the smell of copper. Instead, whiffs of pungent fruit filled her nose. That's when she saw the container sitting nearby. Grape juice. It was the only item on the convenience store receipt.

Something was still missing.

Olivia stood on her tiptoes to look out the window above the sink. "Where's the dog?"

The ranger and Silas exchanged looks. "How do you know he has a dog?" Gaines asked. He didn't hear

Silas mention the detail when she called.

Olivia turned around and favored the Texas Ranger with a smile. His voice rivaled that of Sam Elliot, and the physical description wasn't far off, minus the mustache. Herschel Gaines fit the construct she had formed in her head. With his standard-issue cowboy hat, he was even taller than Silas. Beneath it was a healthy mop of snowy white hair racing toward the streaks of black above his collar. With the shiny star pinned to his crisp white shirt, Herschel Gaines was the quintessential portrait of a Texas Ranger. Unfortunately, he didn't ride in on a white horse to save the day. They were all looking for her to do that. Too bad all she had for them was a nightmare.

"This is Texas. In the middle of nowhere. Of course, the sheriff had a dog. Or did. Is it dead, too? Did someone cut its throat like our victim?"

Herschel Gaines nodded, signaling he agreed with her assessment.

"Was there a circle around it?" Olivia asked.

"Yes," Silas confirmed. "If the circle is for protection, why one for the dog?"

"This circle was not for protection. She used this one for magic."

"She?" It was Gaines again. "Not taking anything away from the female gender, but you're telling me a she took down the sheriff and his dog? You can tell all that by looking at all this?" Having never seen her in action, Gaines was intrigued.

Olivia was undeterred. "I see lipstick on the glass, a frosty pink color, which tells me she's young and attention seeking. Dr. Meeks, correct me if I'm wrong, but I would say time of death was at least two days ago.

It matches the date on the receipt for the grape juice. That is what's in the glass, not wine. The store where it was purchased is just down the road. They have a camera above the door. If we're lucky we'll catch a glimpse of her."

"You need no correction from me," Meeks confirmed.

"If she did all this, don't you think she would know enough to avoid the cameras?" Gaines asked again.

"I don't think she's trying to hide a damn thing. At least not from me."

"Why come into the kitchen?" Silas asked. He was asking about Tennent or some version of him. Silas wondered if it meant something. At the same time, his question was intentionally vague, or otherwise, he would be acknowledging that a dead man had walked where they were now standing.

"It was a demonstration. To see if it could be done," Olivia told him. Turning back to Gaines, she continued her assessment. "I didn't see evidence of forced entry or a struggle. The dog, however, would have been a problem. It would have smelled her intent. As for the sheriff, I doubt a young female would have trouble subduing him. The beer smells unusually bitter even for an IPA. It would have been easy to slip something in it. Dr. Meeks, look for belladonna on the tox screen, also known as nightshade. I'm guessing she calls it the devil's cherry."

"Out of curiosity, what does belladonna do?" Gaines asked.

"Before it kills you, it subdues," Olivia explained.

"It also induces delirium or illusion. If I recall my ancient history, some women rubbed ointments made with belladonna on their thighs. Because the alkaloids were easily absorbed through the skin, they used a broom. The hallucinations were so vivid it made them think they were flying. That's why witches are associated with riding broomsticks," Deveroux explained.

The statement earned a glare from Silas.

"What kind of ancient history are you reading?" Frank Tobias asked.

"You have to know where to look," Deveroux said, his eyes on Olivia.

"Belladonna, while deadly, has been used therapeutically for centuries," Olivia clarified. "Venetian women used the extract as a rouge to flush their cheeks, a feature considered attractive at the time. Belladonna means beautiful woman in Italian."

Deveroux smiled at the revelation. "So, Dr. Osborne, are you suggesting a beautiful witch is responsible for this?"

"Witch is too simple a word for her."

"You used the word demonstration," Silas said moving to seize control from Deveroux. "This wasn't just about killing. There was too much ritual."

Frank and Olivia exchanged glances, both reminded of what they found at the condo.

"She needed something warm blooded," Olivia said, adding up everything she had seen.

"You mean something other than the sheriff?" Gaines asked.

"Silas is right. She had intent. She poisoned the dog, too. It was an offering. A sacrifice."

"A sacrifice for what?" It was Meeks this time.

"If you'll excuse me." Olivia rushed out the back

door with Silas on her heels. He got there just in time to grab her hair as she leaned over the porch railing and threw up in the grass.

****

Will chauffeured her back home. Jessica was waiting with dinner on the table.

No matter how exhausted he felt, Silas was glad to see Will and Jessica were still there. He walked into a fully occupied dinner table and a house full of something other than events of the day. Silas knew this was the kind of life Oliva wished for.

She was still soaking in the tub when Silas came in for a shower.

"Is this what it's going to be like with teenagers?" Silas asked.

"I hope so. I want our home full of friends. Ours and our daughters'."

Silas smiled at the thought.

Olivia emerged from the bathroom, the light behind her illuminating the sheer white gown she wore. She watched as her husband watched her. Her breasts had swelled along with her belly, and he could not look away. Olivia slipped the nightgown off her shoulders and shook her damp hair free before crawling into bed.

Olivia reached for his hands, taking them in hers, guiding them, but not to their babies. "I miss couch night. I also feel very fat right now."

"You're pregnant, not fat," Silas corrected her, struggling to control his breathing, drowning in whatever chemical component existed between them, the one that made him commit. "Why did you never tell me about Jason Austin? I had no idea you and he were…."

"Jason? That's what you want to talk about right now?" Olivia asked, her voice throaty and full of promise.

"What can I say, I'm a selfish man. And a jealous one."

Olivia trailed her fingers along Silas' arm, sending a tingle further down. "I had never been in love before. He was my first," she confessed. "He was taking me home to meet his parents. He said they were going to be as shocked as he was." A fleeting smile played across her lips as she relived the memory.

"So, Jason was like me?" Silas interrupted her thoughts.

Olivia did smile this time. "A philanderer?" she asked using the polite euphemism.

"That's putting it nicely."

"Yes, I suppose he was," she told him.

"But you tamed him."

"Yes. I did. Just like you, Silas Branch. I had no illusions about what kind of man you were when I married you. You got the wife you wanted, and I got the babies I asked for."

"I'm afraid of losing the things we have," Silas confessed.

They had a scare right after they found out she was pregnant—bleeding that turned out to be nothing. "You're not going to hurt me. Or them. I'm not made of glass." There was a need in his eyes, but something else, deeper than that, swimming beneath the blue. Her vision. The one where she saw his death. They hadn't spoken about it since the night she had the dream. Yet it was always with him. Now, in this moment, thoughts of not being around to see his daughters grow up hung between them as silent and pregnant as she was. Was it an alternative version of their future lives, or was his time with her drawing to a close?

As her daughters grew within her, Olivia adapted. She learned to block most of the images they shared. She didn't want to see the future. Some things were best left to fate because they could always change.

Olivia took Silas' face in her hands. She looked deep into his tranquil blue eyes and hoped to swim in them for a long time to come.

****

"I have an early debrief in the morning," Will told Barry. He and Jessica took a page out of Silas and Olivia's book and avoided mixing work talk with personal time, especially tonight. Will needed the distance. As for Barry, Will didn't know if talking about work helped or hurt. "Let's grab a beer tomorrow night, just us guys," Will suggested watching Jessica and Lily wrap up their talk about throwing a baby shower for Olivia.

With the driveway empty, Barry walked Lily home. They had discussed her safety that afternoon. Since he probably scared her away from sitting in the dark anytime soon, Barry wondered if she would invite him inside.

Lily stopped him at the door. "Hold on, I have something for you." She returned with a glass with a hefty pour of whiskey inside. "One for the road. And I want my glass back."

Barry took the glass with a smile, slightly disappointed but hoping he didn't show it. Saying goodnight to Will, Barry noticed the lights upstairs had gone out. The house would be sleeping.

"I'm keeping the bottle because I want to make sure you come back," Lily teased.

"You think you have to bribe me?" Barry asked.

Lily smiled and moved into his arms. "I'm not above it," she whispered and raised her head in time to meet his lips.

Like the night before, Lily was the one to end their embrace. "I would let you tuck me in," Lily confessed, placing her hands on his chest, keeping him at bay. "On any other night, but I'm already up way past my bedtime, and I picked up an extra shift at the hospital tomorrow. I have a divorce lawyer to pay."

Barry remained in place but didn't move his free hand from her hip.

Lily flashed him a mischievous smile. "I know I'm way out of practice, but that is an invitation, in case you were wondering," Lily said as she closed the door between them.

Chapter Nineteen

Olivia was still sleeping when Silas tiptoed out of the house. The door to the downstairs bedroom was closed, leading Silas to believe Barry was asleep on the other side. Seeing him and Lily together, Silas wondered how long it would be before he didn't come back.

Silas arrived at the office only to find he was the only one there. Agent Sharpe had taken a personal day. After yesterday, he wondered if Sharpe was done, not only with this case, but with the Bureau itself. Deveroux should have been there but wasn't. Silas decided he didn't care.

He shed his jacket and settled in behind his desk, indulging in the coffee he grabbed on the way to work. He didn't make any before leaving the house, not wanting the aroma to wake Olivia. She had a busy day yesterday, and she wasn't nearly as sleepy as she claimed when they went to bed. Silas smoothed his tie and scanned the document he had just printed.

The FBI had agreed to her terms. Silas wondered if the substantial increase in her fee was her idea or Brennon Kaine's. Given her attitude toward the Bureau lately, probably hers. Either way, they didn't balk at the price.

****

Walter Meeks spoke first. The medical examiner

looked tired and all of his sixty-nine years. Silas heard Meeks had recently put in for retirement. Silas couldn't help but wonder if after this week, Meeks would move up his requested end date.

Meeks' report was short. James Sampson Tennent, age sixty-six, died of exsanguination due to a cut to the throat that severed both his carotid and jugular veins. Meeks described the laceration in enough detail to build a composite of the weapon. It would be easy enough to match if the knife was ever located. A consult with the veterinarian who performed the necropsy on the Labrador retriever known as Bentley concluded the weapon used on the dog was the same one used on the sheriff. Both cuts came from a left-handed individual.

"Based on the decomposition of the body, I'd say death occurred approximately thirty-six hours before discovery. No defensive wounds were found. Slight bruising was noted on either side of the decedent's rib cage. The carving on the torso occurred postmortem.

"A toxicology screen was sent for both the sheriff and the Labrador. On the advice of Dr. Osborne, I added belladonna to the request." Meeks closed the file in front of him, signaling he was done. This was a case he would take to his own grave.

"Belladonna causes hallucinogenic effects as well as a lack of coordination," Olivia explained before Captain Zavalla had to ask. "Both, reasonable explanations why a trained law enforcement officer didn't put up a fight."

Zavalla's eyes strayed to the blank whiteboard where Frank Tobias stood and wondered what horrors Sheriff Tennent met while not putting up a fight.

Frank flipped the board, revealing a scene that

looked like something out of a slasher film. By the time Zavalla's eyes adjusted, he noticed the display was divided into two parts, with Frank Tobias standing in the middle so his audience didn't get ahead of themselves.

"The only blood in this room belongs to Jim Tennent. All the prints, both hands and feet are confirmed to be his." Frank stepped aside, showing the same room with superimposed footprints strategically placed to highlight the trail of bloody prints with a progressive path across the room and back.

In painstaking detail, Frank explained what the pictures told him forensically. "Based on my findings and that of the experts on my staff, we have concluded that after bleeding out Jim Tennent rose to his knees, crawled to the nearest piece of furniture, achieved an upright position, and walked into his kitchen. He then turned around and made his way back to collapse at least six feet away from where he died." It was the simplest story he could tell.

The room was silent as Frank took his seat next to Silas.

Zavalla's face didn't leave the whiteboard for a long time, as if searching for his own answers. When he came up empty, he turned on those surrounding him. "Are you really saying this," Zavalla gestured wildly at the board, "happened post-mortem?"

"That is what the forensic evidence tells me," Frank confirmed.

Zavalla turned to Walker Meeks. He had been a coroner for decades. Surely, he had another answer. "How is this even possible?"

"From a biological standpoint, the body requires

blood to function. How this one continued to do so once it was all over the floor, is beyond my skill set," Meeks told him.

Reluctantly, Zavalla turned to Olivia. "Are you here with the full backing of the FBI?"

"They have retained my services," Olivia assured him. What she had done for him earlier in the week was off the books, but only because it was Barry.

Zavalla spread his hands in surrender. "Then, please, Dr. Osborne, explain."

Olivia felt the weight of the captain's gesture. For once, she was the hope, rather than the alternative. "A dead man walking is the only way to account for this blood pattern," Olivia said what Frank and Meeks would not.

"This looks like some kind of ritual. Why not start there?" Deveroux interrupted.

"Let's stick with the murder, shall we?" Silas redirected. He would not have Deveroux derail this meeting.

"I agree with Agent Branch. Let's start with the why," Zavalla said. "That much I can do. Why the sheriff?" Disgraced and forced to leave office following the events in Atascosa County, the untimely demise of Jim Tennent would not have been surprising, but a year later. What changed? "So, why now? Why this?"

"Every detail of this crime scene was planned. Each step served a purpose."

"Which was?" Silas asked. He and Olivia had worked together long enough they didn't have to rehearse how this would go. Olivia would answer all their questions, spoon-feeding the nonbelievers until they converted. She would break down the details of the homicide just like any other case they worked. Only then would they be ready to follow her into the shadows.

"Sheriff Tennent has been a missing piece to a puzzle the FBI can't solve." Olivia looked at Deveroux as she said it. She was talking about the still missing girls attributed to Andre Roche and Ana Lutz. Somewhere, someone was waiting for them. Kimberly Burleson had said as much. So had the sheriff, but he had refused to name names. That was the reason for Deveroux's visit. The case in Atascosa County was never about drugs. "Maybe someone other than the Bureau wanted to know what the sheriff was going to say before he said it. His death was very personal."

Silas couldn't help but think of the condoms and the blue pills.

"My guess is she straddled him so she could look him in the eye while she slit his throat. You don't do that to a stranger," Olivia said.

"That could account for the marks on either side of the rib cage," Meeks concurred. The bruising told him it occurred while the heart was still beating.

"There's also a more sinister motive. She's seeking attention. She wanted to know if she could do this," Olivia added.

"You mean murder," Silas said, hoping that was all it was. After the events of yesterday, he knew that was a pipe dream.

"Among other things." Olivia confirmed his fear. "She's practicing her skills. From my assessment of the crime scene, I would say she was successful."

"Hold up," Zavalla interrupted, still stuck at the beginning. "Our murderer is female?"

He sounded like Ranger Gaines. "History has proven time and again, that we are not the weaker sex, Captain," Olivia told him. "You're just distracted by the packaging. So was the sheriff. He knew his killer intimately, that is how she gained access. Physically, she was no match for him. That's why she brought the belladonna."

Deveroux cleared his throat, redirecting attention his way. "How does someone acquire this type of knowledge?" he asked.

The agent was asking a question he already knew the answer to. Olivia was sure of it. His knowledge of the occult intrigued her. "It's not a common skill," Olivia acknowledged.

"So, this isn't just about murder?" Zavalla looked back at the whiteboard. "The theatrics of it looks ceremonial."

"There was a circle around the sheriff," Frank confirmed, referring the captain back to the pictures.

For Zavalla, the dusting of white was lost in the blood.

"There was also one around the dog. Both contained salt and sand," Frank said.

"Like with Ferdinand Roche," Herschel Gaines recalled. The death of Andre Roche's brother was the ranger's introduction to Dr. Osborne. He had given her a pretty hard time about her talk of magic. At the time, he didn't know what to make of her. He still didn't, except now he trusted her. She made him a believer in things that had no real-world explanation.

"These are different. A circle made of salt is for protection. Adding sand with the salt gives it magic. And you were right to call it a ceremony," Olivia clarified, her words slowing as she said them. The symbols at Barry's condo flashed inside her head.

"Are we looking for a witch?" Zavalla couldn't believe the question he was asking. Then he remembered who he was asking.

"She is a murderer, and I would consider her a sorceress not a witch." Olivia's admission slipped out as she pulled herself back to the present.

The room went silent waiting for her to continue. Even Silas was at a loss for words. In all the time they had worked together, he had never heard the term.

Deveroux broke the stalemate. "Care to explain the difference?"

Olivia noted Deveroux's role as wingman today. Unlike Silas, his intent wasn't for the locals. It was personal.

"Witches abide by a code. Some might call it a religion. They are in tune with nature and its elements. Centuries ago, apothecaries were considered witches because of their extensive knowledge of plants and herbs." Olivia thought of her great-grandmother, Abitha, who sold healing salves to the locals. "A sorceress, however, is willing to look outside the bounds of nature. It is why she has no code."

It sounded like a decree. The mesmerizing lilt in her voice sent a chill down Silas' spine.

"The circles are ritualistic, and belladonna is a plant. What distinguishes this killer as a sorceress? In your opinion?" Deveroux pressed.

Silas had lost his place as a guide. Deveroux had an agenda. Silas just wasn't sure what it was.

"History. This ceremony," Olivia said, using Zavalla's words, "is a shared phenomenon across multiple cultures. The Catholic Church forbade it centuries ago. Their reasons for doing so were valid," Olivia told him. The conviction in her voice was unwavering.

"I guess the symbol carved into the sheriff's chest was also part of this as well?" Meeks wanted to know.

"You didn't think to mention this earlier?" Zavalla asked.

"I said there was a carving. I knew we would get to the details." Meeks appeared irritated at the interruption. "It's identical to the upside-down pentagram I found on Ferdinand Roche's shoulder. Although, I have to say, whoever left this one has better artistic skills."

"Fuck me," Zavalla murmured, taking a moment to rake his hands over his face. "Don't tell me there are more Roche brothers."

"Or someone else," Frank spoke. His eyes locked on Olivia. He was supposed to keep quiet about her visit to the lieutenant's condo, but he couldn't. "There was sand mixed with salt in the symbols we found drawn on Lieutenant Bartholomew's balcony. Just like those at the sheriff's house."

Olivia felt Silas' eyes on her. They hadn't talked about what she found at Barry's. It had disturbed her, and she didn't want to bring that kind of darkness into their home. They already had a demon lurking in their back garden.

"Are you saying these two cases are connected?" This time it was Ranger Gaines. He and Frank Tobias were the only ones privy to the details of both cases.

Walking the crime scenes, Olivia closed herself off, not allowing the other side to breach her walls. By shielding her daughters, she hampered herself by failing to make the connection. Maybe because it had been even too sinister for her to consider. Either way, they would still be here.

Snakeskin. Roche. Ritualistic magic. Demon.

"What kind of person would do these things?" Zavalla's voice was laced with panic.

"A dangerous one," Olivia answered him.

"Please tell me you know who."

Chapter Twenty

"I speak Latin sometimes, too. You asked it if it was afraid. Those were the words you said before you killed it." Rose was talking about the snake that followed Olivia out of the cellar.

"Who's afraid now is the literal translation," Olivia corrected, staring down at the younger girl.

"I think it was. Just in case you were wondering."

"It should have been." Olivia took a step closer. *"You should be, too."*

Except she wasn't.

"Rose Corey. I met her in the cellar where Andre Roche was keeping Kimberly Burleson. According to Rose, Andre had plans for her." According to Kim, Rose liked to play with dead things.

Will Ibarra was sitting quietly in the corner until Olivia's comments snapped him to attention. He was surrounded by folders of evidence, his presence here was to learn and to supply whatever additional information didn't fit on the whiteboard. He shuffled through the trove in front of him to come up with a snapshot. "Is this her?"

Facial recognition wasn't working on this one. The look on Olivia's face told Will they didn't need it.

"This was pulled from the security camera at the convenience store less than two miles from Sheriff Tennent's residence. The time corresponded with one of the receipts found at the sheriff's house. Based on Dr. Meeks' time of death, the items were purchased after the sheriff was already dead," Will explained while Frank reached for the picture to get a better look.

"The oversized plaid shirt she's wearing looks like the same shirt we found on the sheriff's bedroom floor," Frank said.

Olivia recalled the receipt. It had stuck out to her because it wasn't the red wine everyone expected for a party of two. "The unfermented grape juice would have been part of the ritual. So is wearing the clothes of the deceased," Olivia said.

"I know that girl," Gaines chimed in. He pulled out his phone and held it up for all to see. "This is surveillance footage from the stairs at the end of Lieutenant Bartholomew's hallway taken the morning Dr. Greene was killed." The girl was looking right at the camera. It didn't take an expert to see it was the same face as the one in the convenience store video. "Ms. Corey was hired by Cardinal Towers three weeks ago as part of the cleaning crew. Given the lieutenant employed those services, Ms. Corey would have access to his condo," Gaines suggested.

"Wait a second," Zavalla snapped, struggling to keep up. "Are you saying the death of Dr. Greene and the sheriff are related?"

"Dr. Greene was the crisis counselor on call the night Rose Corey and Kimberly Burleson were rescued from Roche's cellar. Dr. Greene would have offered her counseling services just like she did Kimberly," Will Ibarra explained. His personal relationship with Jessica Tate gave him intimate knowledge of the events that could have put Rose and Dr. Greene together.

"You're saying Ms. Corey was there with Dr. Greene?" Zavalla asked.

"That could be how Dr. Greene gained access to Lieutenant Bartholomew's place," Gaines theorized.

"Ms. Corey is a runaway," Mason Deveroux interrupted. "She was returned to the custody of her grandmother after the barn fire last year, but she didn't stay long. She's a young girl on her own. How dangerous can she be?" Deveroux asked.

Gaines knew when he got the info from Lieutenant Bartholomew's residence, that the name was familiar. "I tried interviewing Ms. Corey after the barn incident, but by the time I got out to her grandmother's house to interview her, she was missing again. Maybe we should consider Ms. Corey was running to something and not away."

"We should listen to the Ranger," Olivia warned. "Rose Corey is a skilled sorceress who violates the natural order of things." Now that she could see clearly, Olivia's emotions were spiraling out of control, but not so much that she didn't wonder what secrets Deveroux was hiding.

"I thought you said she was looking for information," Zavalla said.

"I did. What I didn't say is communing with the dead is most often used to gain knowledge of past events. I would also assume the recent dead are probably the easiest to raise," Olivia theorized.

Sometimes Silas wished she didn't know these things. Especially now.

"That's what killing the sheriff was about?" Zavalla asked. "Talking to the dead?"

"It started out that way. She was looking for

information."

"And a simple conversation wouldn't do?" It was Deveroux.

"Maybe because if she did, the sheriff would know it wasn't Rose who was asking. I also told you she is honing her skills. She's also resourceful. The sheriff had something she could use, and he was easy. There was no love lost there. This wasn't their first rodeo."

"What skills are those?" Deveroux asked. This time he didn't seem so sure about the answer.

"Necromancy." The word earned Olivia a sharp kick in the ribs. She readjusted herself, searching for a comfortable spot. "It is the term for raising the dead."

"Who taught her this? Andre Roche?" Silas asked.

"Andre sees me for what I am." Olivia had heard Rose say those very words. Olivia shook her head. "No. Roche recognized Rose's gifts, but he wasn't skilled enough to teach anything." Roche's incompetence was what got him killed. He also underestimated her. "But his mother, Marceline, was rumored to be many things."

Zavalla turned to Meeks. "Is what she's suggesting even possible? A dead man walking?"

"I did say that was the only way to explain the bloody prints in the sheriff's house," Frank answered instead.

"Going in circles isn't going to get us anywhere," Olivia said gently.

The medical examiner shook his head. "I already told you, I'm out of my depth here."

Zavalla raked his face again. He looked at Silas, but the FBI agent looked like he was struggling with something of his own. Zavalla took a deep breath and began again. "What does this have to do with what happened at Bartholomew's place?"

Aware that the captain was struggling, Olivia fed him smaller bites. "Raising a human is not for the faint of heart."

Zavalla's eyes searched the room, looking for a lifeline. Dr. Osborne was the only one he had.

"You did ask my expert opinion," Olivia reminded Zavalla. "If not me, then turn to your faith, Captain."

Zavalla looked unsure, unhappy that he had to hear any of this.

"Seek out the Archbishop. He'll tell you the same thing. There's a reason the Catholic Church forbids this type of magic. The Church believes resurrection is reserved for God. To proceed without him is considered blasphemy. Without the assistance of God, the only choice is summoning. That's what the symbols on Lieutenant Bartholomew's balcony were for. The only entity, other than God, powerful enough to raise the dead is a demon. I walked the scene at the lieutenant's condo at your request. A demon was there as well as at the sheriff's house."

"So, this girl Rose, killed Dr. Greene and the sheriff?" Zavalla asked.

"A demon's service doesn't come for free. The price for raising the dead requires an offering—specifically, a blood sacrifice. That is what Dr. Greene was for," Olivia explained.

The room went silent. Zavalla was so still Olivia wondered if he was still listening, so she force-fed him her answer again. "Dr. Greene was sacrificed so Rose Corey could raise the sheriff from the dead."

It was a long time before anyone spoke. When they

did, it was Ranger Gaines.

"Agent Deveroux, you were the one investigating these missing girls long before the rest of us got involved. Who do you think could have sent Ms. Corey?"

Silas shifted in his chair. It was the right question. He just didn't want to hear the answer.

"Sarah Eden Larsin. Also known as Lila. She owns strip clubs, massage parlors and a high-end brothel known as *Delilah's Den* located just outside Las Vegas in one of the few counties where prostitution is legal. It has long been the FBI's belief Ana Lutz, a former employee, was supplying Ms. Larsin with girls. She's been on the Bureau's radar for some time now, but we've had no way to get to her. She's the reason I wanted to question Sheriff Tennent," Deveroux explained.

Silas' glare toward Deveroux was interrupted by Olivia shifting in her chair. "Do you need a break?" Silas asked softly. He didn't want her to hear this.

"No," Olivia whispered. She caught Gaines looking at her before his eyes shifted. Having worked the Roche case, Gaines had also heard the name Sarah Larsin. He was thinking how Olivia shouldn't have to hear this. If he had spoken the sentiment aloud, Olivia would have told him she had no illusions about who and what her mother was, but his chivalry was appreciated. Her gran would have said he was a man cut from a different cloth.

"Ms. Corey was also known to spend time in Las Vegas as a guest of Ms. Larsin," Deveroux said.

"These are just girls." Zavalla seemed to snap back to attention. He would take discussing prostitution over raising the dead.

"Not *just*, Captain," Deveroux suggested. "Andre Roche targeted girls for a specific talent or ability."

It was the same theory Olivia proposed. It was how she profiled Roche's victims. They all had something special.

"I believe Ms. Larsin is doing the same. Sex is her business. What she's looking for is seductive in nature. With *Delilah's Den*, she is paying homage to the most famous seductress of all time," Deveroux explained.

For a fleeting moment, Olivia wondered how differently she might have turned out without Gran's guidance. She had seen her family tree. There were as many witches in those branches as there were harlots.

"We all have abilities, Agent Deveroux," Olivia interrupted.

"Yes, that's quite the theory, Agent," Silas said feeling the need to intervene.

"Some of us are more in tune with them than others." Olivia's words sounded like a warning.

"Of course, we won't know that until someone talks to her," Deveroux said. "I think that's where you come in," he suggested. In a room full of people Silas couldn't stop him.

Olivia's gaze slipped from Deveroux to the cell phone buzzing next to her. She read and reread the text from Brennon Kaine trying to come to grips with what he was saying. "Please excuse me."

Olivia scooped up the phone and headed for the door. Outside in the hall, she paced as she listened. "You didn't say yes, did you?

"Not without talking to you first."

Olivia closed her eyes. She pressed her free hand

against her side and breathed slowly.

"Livie, are you okay?"

Olivia opened her eyes and exhaled. "I'm fine, Brennon."

"You sound out of breath."

"I'm pacing and I'm pregnant," Olivia snapped. She stopped her pacing and leaned against the wall. "Tell me what she said."

"She said she knew someone who might be in trouble. It sounded like she was testing the waters, curious to my receptiveness. Anything you would like to add?" Brennon asked.

"I haven't talked to her in thirty-six years so it's kind of hard to know what she's thinking." Olivia heard the door to the conference room open and saw Silas heading her way. She pushed herself off the wall and raised a finger, signaling him to wait. "I'm in the middle of a briefing with SAPD now," she told Brennon.

Silas noted the wince on her face as she said it. It was slight, but he noticed. Behind him, the door swung open again. Footsteps followed as Ranger Gaines joined them.

"We need to talk," Brennon said in her ear.

Olivia leaned forward, her hand going back down to her side as Silas stepped closer. "Who is paying your fee?"

"Since I'm not taking the case, I can tell you. Not her. Although it looks like she could afford it." He had an excellent screening system in his office. His staff checked her out before he called her back.

"Then who?"

"A Samael Knight. Apparently, he's into

collections and acquisitions. He was prepared to pay the retainer."

Silas took the phone. "She's going to have to call you back."

Olivia's free hand joined the other one at her abdomen.

"Everything alright?" Gaines asked as he moved to her other side.

Olivia felt crowded. She finally let go of her abdomen to brush the hair out of her eyes.

"Your cheeks are red," Gaines noted. "You look flushed and out of breath."

"It's hot in here, and I'm pregnant." Olivia's hand went back to her side.

Silas slipped his hand over hers. "That feels really firm."

"There are babies in there."

"You look tired," Gaines told her.

Olivia started to say something, but her brow pinched, and she went silent.

"There's that look again," Silas told her.

"She was doing the same thing in the conference room," Gaines chimed in.

Olivia turned on him.

"You were wincing. I saw it. You kept shifting in your chair. Like you were uncomfortable," Gaines told her.

Olivia sighed heavily. "I am uncomfortable. You two are giving me a headache and these babies feel like they're playing soccer."

****

Olivia rested in a recliner with three belts strapped around her waist. One to monitor each baby and one to check for uterine contractions. With a slow grind, the machine produced paper like a ticker tape while Dr. Tammy Murdoch studied the irregular blips. "You did the right thing coming in."

Olivia concentrated on trying to read her doctor's face, while avoiding Silas' glances. He reminded her more than once on the way over that at least he read *Exceptional Expectations: The New Mom's Guide to Pregnancy.*

"Are you feeling those?" Dr. Murdoch asked, her eyes moving between her patient and the machine next to her. At least Olivia looked better than when she arrived. The absence of the red in her cheeks was a good sign. Now, she seemed more annoyed than in pain.

"Yes and no," Olivia said carefully.

"She was reacting to them," Silas added.

"I've felt like this before," Olivia said. "I thought it was the babies shifting, looking for somewhere else to go. I swear I'm getting bigger every day."

Dr. Murdoch smiled. "Based on the quick scan I did when you came in, those little ones have both turned head up so you're probably right. The pressure and discomfort you felt might have been that."

"Turned up? What does that mean, exactly?" Silas asked.

"They're both breech now," Dr. Murdoch translated.

"That means a c-section," Olivia explained, feeling the prick of tears in her eyes.

Dr. Murdoch reached out to touch her shoulder. She knew how much Olivia wanted a natural delivery. "Hey, we knew this was likely. You're right, they are looking for more room and you don't have a lot," the doctor explained.

Olivia was five feet three and carrying two babies. "Look on the bright side. Their new positions give them more room and your bladder a break. The downside is soon you may start to feel some shortness of breath."

Olivia nodded silently. "So, what's with these?" she asked, wanting nothing more than to rip off the belts and scratch her stretched skin. "Am I having contractions?"

"I'm going to call it uterine irritability. Also, possibly due to the change in positioning, but preterm labor isn't uncommon in multiple gestation. Now that you know what the irritability feels like, you need to give me a call if it becomes regular. Time them if you have to."

"This is way too soon," Silas spoke up. The concern hadn't left his face.

"Correct. Pregnancy is forty weeks. On average twins are typically born somewhere around thirty-five. But we're not quite at twenty-eight yet. These kiddos are roughly two pounds apiece. And their lungs are nowhere near ready. They need to cook a while longer."

"Bedrest," Silas suggested despite the daggers Olivia shot his way.

"I'd like to avoid that if possible. But having said that, I also have to tell you your blood pressure was up a little today as well. I'll have the nurse recheck it when she comes back to unhook you from this contraption and give you some instructions. Preeclampsia is more common in twin pregnancy so we're going to want to keep an eye on it. My recommendation for both would be a nap or some quiet time during the day." Olivia was like a lot of her patients, career-oriented with only one speed—busy. "Are you currently working a case?"

"She just finished one," Silas answered for her.

Dr. Murdoch nodded at the news. "Good. That should make things easier."

"Just so we're clear, you're not telling me to stop working, correct?" Olivia clarified. Silas was clearly shaken, a rare condition for her alpha husband. He was handling it well, so far, but he made no secret about wanting her to stop working altogether. The pregnancy had given him the perfect excuse to revisit the prospect.

"Not at all. Just don't push it. I'll see you back in a week."

"So, the nightly dog walks and pregnancy yoga are okay?" Olivia asked. Silas would stake his claim without a clear set of parameters.

Dr. Murdoch smiled. "Yes, for now. Take it easy. I know you're not a woman accustomed to sitting still, but I'm telling you these babies need to stay right where they are for at least another six weeks. You'll thank me later. That's not a long time for me, but for you..." Dr. Murdoch left the statement unfinished. The couple could work it out. She hated to tell Silas, but he was fighting a losing battle on this one. He might be in charge at work, but definitely not at home.

Chapter Twenty-One

Olivia headed upstairs as soon as they got home to lie down, as Dr. Murdoch suggested. The fact she didn't complain told Silas the pregnancy was catching up with her no matter what she told him or the doctor.

On his way out, Silas noticed Bartholomew at the dining table with the old laptop open. He must have missed him the first time.

"Is everything okay?" Barry asked.

"We had an unscheduled doctor visit. A reminder Livie needs to slow down."

"Good luck with that," Barry mused. "I'm not supposed to enforce that rule while you're out, am I? Because I'm not sure I'm cut out for that."

"I'm taking her car. Mine's still downtown," Silas smiled.

Enforcement by default.

They were interrupted by a beep from the kitchen, signaling the oven was ready. It was a reminder to Silas that Barry was stranded and was eating whatever he could find. "Are there car keys somewhere you want me to bring to you? So at least you have a ride?"

"Thanks, but Brennon's meeting with SAPD today about releasing my place. He's going to drop by and grab them."

Silas nodded. "Don't say anything to Livie, but I could be leaving town the first of next week. Just for a few days."

"You'll be the one breaking the news, right?" Barry clarified. They had yet to go over the house rules, but he didn't want to be in the middle.

"Unless you care to volunteer."

Barry shook his head. "Uh, negative."

"I haven't worked out the logistics, yet." Silas' plan was to spend the weekend in San Antonio with Livie. He would discuss the rest with Deveroux when he returned to the office.

"I'll stay here," Barry offered without being asked. "She shouldn't be alone." He wasn't sure if Olivia had a chance to tell Silas about Smythe or not. He wasn't sure how much talking they did last night, or if there was some rule about work talk in the bedroom. Barry felt like he was living back home with his parents.

"Did Amanda ever talk to you about work?" Silas asked.

"Not really. She was more interested in my work."

"You're absolutely sure you didn't tell her anything about that night in the barn?"

If Silas had asked the question at any other time in their relationship, Barry would have told him to mind his own business, but those days were gone. It felt like circling the wagons. Barry wasn't sure what was coming, but something was. Things were changing between all of them.

"Any case information I ever gave her was the glossy PR version," Barry conceded. You and Olivia don't talk work at the dinner table. I don't discuss work with people I don't work with. In my sleep or otherwise. I never told anyone the real story about that night in the barn except you. Not the bishop, not Father

Dominic, or even Olivia."

Silas nodded. He believed him the first time. "Did Amanda ever mention patient specifics?"

"Only what I told you before. She was concerned when Kimmy stopped coming to therapy. What that really meant is Amanda was jealous Kimmy chose to spend her time with Olivia and not her."

"Did she ever mention Rose Corey?" Silas wanted a look at Dr. Greene's patient files, but getting them was going to take time, if it was even possible. There were still patient confidentiality rights in play.

Barry considered the name. "No, but I know that name from Roche's case file. Wasn't she the other girl Olivia rescued? The one no one reported missing?"

"Same one. No one reported her missing because she seems to be a professional runaway. Olivia thinks she killed Sheriff Tennent." Silas held back on the part about Rose working in Barry's building.

"Then there you have it. Deveroux's specifics may have come from Amanda, but there's a pretty short list of who could have given them to her. I'd say Rose is the top contender."

"Rose could have an unhealthy interest in Livie," Silas said, even though it wasn't something he and Livie had discussed. They left everything back at SAPD while they concentrated on their daughters.

"Define unhealthy," Barry asked.

"The scene at the sheriff's house was intense. Real old-world stuff."

"Stuff that would be sure to catch Olivia's attention," Barry translated.

"Something like that," Silas admitted. "Livie described Rose as attention-seeking."

"She described Andre Roche the same way," Barry felt compelled to remind him.

"Deveroux is trying to connect Rose to Sarah Larsin."

The admission settled deep in Barry's gut. It would nest in there until someone confronted that bitch or took her off the board. Barry just wanted to be there when they did.

"Livie told me about the flowers someone left on the porch and your theory. I think we should consider it could have just as easily been Rose who put them there and not Smythe," Silas suggested.

"What's the distinction?" Barry wanted to know.

"Olivia was bothered by the choice of flowers. They're snapdragons."

"I hate to point out the obvious, but they were convenient. They came from your front yard," Barry said.

"They have a special meaning," Silas told him.

Of course, they did. Everything in Olivia's world had meaning. She called them talismans. He and Will had gone looking for them when they interviewed the families of the missing girls in Atascosa County. The ones thought to be "gifted". Now Barry knew she meant witches. Olivia described how they could identify them by objects placed outside their homes. Wind chimes to keep spirits away, a wreath of rosemary for protection from unwanted entities, floating balls in the trees, or a mirror hung outside the door were all common decorative pieces. In Olivia's world, they had a more important purpose. They were forms of protection.

She was right—about all of it.

"According to Olivia, historically, plants are a way

of conveying feelings and sending messages. Plants buried on a property represent the family and serve as a warning to others. Her great grandmother selected the flowers when this house was built. Snapdragons symbolize strength, grace, and deviousness."

Barry couldn't argue with the depiction. Olivia embodied all of those traits. He witnessed the deviousness that night in the barn with Roche. It's what saved both their lives. Silas probably hadn't seen that side of her yet. What happened at the prison was different. She was protecting Silas like she had protected him. She just didn't have to feed anyone to a demon to do it.

"The snapdragons we have are known as night and day. The dark red petals growing alongside the white ones is a nod toward twilight. Olivia says it's the most magical time of the day when the light and the dark swim together as equals. That dichotomy appealed to her great grandmother Abitha as much as it does to Rose."

The buzzer sounded again, and Barry got up from his chair and headed for the kitchen. Silas pulled out his phone and sent Barry the surveillance photo of Rose from the convenience store. With Barry gone, Silas stole a glance at the laptop. He reached over and angled the screen in his direction watching the pictures scroll past. Most were nighttime scenes, glints of starlight through the trees, or abandoned buildings. Maybe Jason was ghost-hunting. The only ones in the light of day contained Olivia. Most were of her and Jason together, always smiling, but there was one photo Jason must have taken when she wasn't looking. She appeared relaxed, almost dreamlike, no worry lines creasing her brow, no million-mile stare. Perhaps at that moment, her monsters were only figments of her imagination before the real one showed up to take Jason away.

Barry came back carrying an overdone pizza. They had been Olivia's obsession early in her pregnancy before switching to Thai. There must have been one still in the freezer.

"I'll text on my way home so I can pick up dinner," Silas told him.

"I saw steaks in the fridge. I thought I might throw them on the grill tonight. If that's okay?" Barry missed grilling. He couldn't have one at the condo. It was the only time he wished for a yard. He bought one for Mark as a housewarming gift. They only used it once. There hadn't been enough time. "Got to earn my keep."

Silas had forgotten all about the food and whatever their plans had been for the week. "Sure, go ahead."

Barry noted the shift in Silas' attention. "You haven't talked to her?"

"She didn't have much to say." But it was enough. Jason was her first.

The man didn't sound like the same confident FBI agent in charge that Barry first met. He felt compelled to say something. "Maybe because it was a long time ago. Either way you're here, he's not. The dead don't come back."

"Tell that to the former sheriff."

****

"I think you should consider what your life would look like if you didn't go back."

Barry and Brennon were meeting outside. It was warm in the sunlight and Barry hadn't heard Olivia stir. If she was sleeping, he didn't want to wake her.

"If I leave, won't that look like an admission of guilt?" Barry had never walked away from anything in his life. He didn't count the marriages, because he wasn't the one to throw in the towel first.

"You're not guilty of Dr. Greene's death. That much everyone knows. Surveillance from the Archbishop gave you an ironclad alibi. I heard he even made an appearance in Zavalla's office. Quite the statement. Did Livie have something to do with that?"

Barry gave a shrug, obviously uncomfortable by the show of support.

"Smooth move on her part. Then again, she's a very persuasive woman. Even with men of faith." Brennon cleared his throat and continued.

"No charges will be filed." Captain Zavalla and the DA went out of their way to say it, pretending ignorance as to why they were talking with a lawyer in the first place. Brennon had been more than happy to remind them.

"You were being blamed for Dr. Greene's unfortunate choice. Yet we both know she made that decision on her own. Your trial was one of public opinion where the jurors change on a whim. What I discussed today were facts about how your captain and the DA handled the situation. Perception is reality, and there is no getting around it. By coming to the home of your pregnant friend and engaging in a stand-off on her lawn, they gave the impression you were guilty of 'something'. That is what you told me bothered you the most. I painted them a pretty clear picture of how that might have looked through Livie's eyes."

Barry was still bothered by the image. It now included Lily. She had seen it, too.

"You've put in more than your twenty, so your retirement is secure, for now. After this incident, you will never make captain whether you wanted to or not, despite scoring in the top percentile. Go back and you run the risk of someone, at any given time, finding something else that could place your retirement in jeopardy. I did some background on Dr. Greene, and she for various reasons, some of them not flattering, has the sympathy of many of your peers. That puts a target on your back that will never go away. Agent Deveroux working with the DA also did you no favors. Judging from my brief interaction with DA Preston today, I would say his issues with you are personal. Any idea why?"

Barry stewed for a moment, trying to take it all in. The first answer was an obvious one—the other was only now coming into focus. "Olivia exposed Preston's inability to investigate when she told SAPD where to look for the weapon used to kill Mark Austin. My protege, Will Ibarra, helped, and it made Preston look every bit as incompetent as he is. On a personal note, see if you can find out what kind of car he drives. Something understated but expensive would be my guess," Barry suggested. The car he had just described was the one he found parked at Amanda's the night Olivia sent him back.

"Not that I'm not appreciative, but why did Olivia call you?" Barry asked.

Brennon smiled. "Isn't it obvious? She cares about you. She also knows what it's like being attacked by those who are supposed to have your back. Maybe she has bigger plans for you."

Brennon saw the question on Barry's face. "She's

not confided in me, but I know she has an ever-growing business going on the side. She might need some help. I've been trying to steal her IT guy," Brennon confessed. "But there's that family connection. I also wouldn't be opposed to discussing some opportunities with you myself. I could always use a cop's brain."

Barry dragged a hand over his face trying to come to grips with it all.

"It's a lot to think about, I know. Now, tell me, how is Livie? I was on the phone with her earlier, and she sounded tired or in pain or both."

"Silas took her to the doctor. She's upstairs resting."

Brennon looked alarmed. "Is everything alright?" The Olivia he knew only had one speed, and it didn't include napping in the middle of the day.

"She will be," Barry assured him. "She needs to slow down and take it easy."

Brennon looked relieved. He patted his pants pocket and came out with a ring of keys he tossed Barry's way. "You should have your place back by the end of the weekend."

Barry caught them not feeling the relief he thought he would at having them back. Somehow, they felt tainted. "About your fee." He had been hesitant to bring it up because of the number of zeros that might be involved.

Brennon waved him off, unconcerned. "I'm sure we can work something out. I saw your condo, remember? Do you know what a place like that would cost where I come from? San Antonio isn't such a bad place." The lawyer stood to go.

"Take the weekend to think about what I said. You

have an opportunity here, but it has a finite window of time."

Barry stood and offered his hand. "Thanks. I never saw this coming."

Brennon clapped him on the arm. "It's like death. Most people don't."

Chapter Twenty-Two

It was a perfect weekend. Olivia stayed grounded. Barry and Will had a beer. More time was spent with friends. Life seemed almost normal, except for the grown man living in their downstairs bedroom.

Sunday morning Olivia and Silas were out for a morning dog walk when Olivia stopped to search the pet posters looking for additions to her neighborhood predator theory.

"You think it's Smythe?" Silas asked.

"At first, but with all the dogs, I can't help but think of Rose."

"Maybe we should consider it could be both," Silas suggested.

Done with the pet memorial, Olivia resumed walking toward home. "Rose is gone."

"Do you know where?" Silas was curious.

"Back to the only place she has left."

Silas was interested to know more. "Where's that?" So far it wasn't back to the grandmother.

"My mother. She contacted Brennon about helping someone who could be in trouble. I'm guessing that person is Rose." Olivia realized Silas had stopped following. She turned to find him looking like he had something to say. "Brennon didn't take the case if you're wondering."

"I think this is the part where I tell you I'm going

to look for Rose. I'm also planning on meeting your mother if she agrees," Silas said letting go of the secret he had carried for days.

Olivia went so still he couldn't read her. "Anything you want me to tell her?" Silas asked, breaking the heavy silence between them.

A collision of thoughts swirled inside her head. Olivia grabbed the one that kept rising to the top. "I bet she's sorry she left me behind. I'm not interested in a reunion. You and our daughters are off limits."

"Would you trust her?" Silas asked.

Olivia pondered his question but only for a moment. "I don't know her well enough to trust her. What I do know about her, I don't like."

"What's that?" Silas asked, wondering which Sarah Larsin topic she would pick.

"Samael Knight."

The choice surprised him, but it shouldn't have. It was the least personal. "What do you know?" They hadn't discussed the mysterious Mr. Knight since he got Jamie Smythe to slip a business card through their mail slot.

"Your little brother, Kevin. He is quite the cyber detective. He doesn't believe Samael Knight is his real name."

Silas hadn't told her, but Interpol thought the same thing. They were looking at identity theft but kept coming up empty.

"What about Deveroux? Is he going?" Olivia didn't like the thought of Silas being on his own, not in a place her mother called home.

"He left already. I had no idea, but Deveroux lives in Vegas. According to Patrick, he relocated there sometime during his career break," Silas said using the same euphonism the Bureau did for the time Deveroux spent in rehab.

"Barry and I both expected a visit from him but got nothing. Did he tell you what he wanted?" Silas had been conspicuously quiet about his dealings with the rogue agent.

Silas finally got Deveroux alone Friday afternoon after he dropped Livie off. It had been ugly, one reason he had avoided discussing it. Otherwise, he would have no choice but to act on his suspicions. If he went down that road, there would be no turning back. The Bureau was one big happy family until they weren't.

"I think Deveroux's compromised. The things he claimed Amanda told him about the barn didn't come from Barry. The only other person with access to that kind of information was Rose Corey. Tell me, why would Dr. Greene be involved with a patient?"

"I'm sure Rose promised something Amanda wanted," Olivia said simply.

"What could Rose possibly give her?"

"Access to Barry. A love spell. Who knows?"

Her response caught him off guard. "But those aren't real." As soon as the words left his mouth, Silas realized they were a mistake.

Olivia stayed silent, watching the tide of emotions roll across his face.

"Are they?" Silas asked, finally piercing the air between them.

"My great-grandmother's mother, Agatha, was a potion maker." Agatha was probably the reason Abitha became an Apothecary. "She was known for her love spells."

After Lily caught her up on the last two generations, Olivia took the books back and started her own reading. That's how she spent her time when she was supposed to be taking an afternoon nap. She was giving herself a crash course in family lore because she was going to need it.

"It's part of the persona of witches isn't it? Depending on which myth you want to believe. The one of the plump grandmotherly-type who can help you ensnare your beloved and reap riches beyond your wildest imagination. Or the picture that was painted at the sheriff's house? Only a witch powerful enough to summon a demon can do that."

The description stuck like a barb. No matter how long they had known each other, there were still parts of her Silas didn't know. He wondered if he ever would.

"Did Bartholomew tell you Deveroux thinks you're a witch?" Silas couldn't make himself ask until now.

"He didn't have to. It screams inside of him." And inside of her. Reading her family history books confirmed what she had always known.

Silas had to take a step back and change the subject. Wading into Olivia's world, he was losing his footing. "SAPD finally found Tennent's missing cruiser. It was abandoned three blocks from Deveroux's hotel. Too close for comfort for me," Silas admitted.

"You believe Deveroux could be involved with Rose?" Olivia wanted to make sure she heard him correctly. Her husband had few gut feelings, but when he did, they were dead on.

"I hate to say it, but I do," Silas conceded.

Her husband was also very loyal to the Bureau. "It

makes sense," Olivia conceded. "If Rose is involved with my mother, then Rose has to have more gifts than raising the dead."

"Patrick mentioned that in addition to alcohol indulgence there was suspicion Deveroux was also involved with prostitutes."

"Submerging yourself in a world full of sex has to be a slippery slope when you're a weak man like Deveroux. He would be an easy target," Olivia agreed.

"So, how involved in all of this is your mother?" Silas wanted to know.

"Since Roche and Ana were recruiting girls for her, I'm sure she provided Rose safe harbor when it was all over. Have you considered she might be the one who sent Rose to find out what the sheriff was going to say to the FBI?"

He had, but that wasn't what bothered Silas at the moment. "What you call recruitment, Deveroux calls trafficking." The words were worlds apart, and Silas was on Devereux's side with this one.

"I have no illusions about my mother, or if she was involved with those girls. But even the FBI hasn't been able to prove trafficking. The girls she is looking for are gifted in their own way. It is their nature, Silas, and they require guidance. I hope that is what she is giving them. As someone who is gifted, I can't disparage them. You have no idea how grateful I would have been for someone to show me the way. The gifts we have are our nature. The best we can do is learn to accept and adapt."

"Is that what you did?" Silas already knew the answer, but he wanted to hear her explanation.

"I'm lucky, I found a way to blend. I was able to

channel my gifts into a successful career. Still, it hasn't been easy. You witnessed that firsthand. Father Dominic and the Archbishop have often reminded me that if I had been born at any other time, I would not be so fortunate. It appears as if my mother was lucky as well. She runs a legitimate business." Olivia could tell the conversation was making Silas uncomfortable. "As distasteful as it might be," she added, hoping to soften the blow, but she was tired of doing that as well.

"If we really are the witches Deveroux believes us to be, don't you think we would have learned from history?" Olivia pushed him. "If Salem taught us anything, it's to hide. The best place is in plain sight. Like Rose did with taking the sheriff's old cruiser. It was a smart move. Refurbished or not, it still looks like a cop car, which made her invisible to the people looking for her."

Silas couldn't tell if Olivia was impressed or concerned.

"Rose is wise beyond her years. It's a problem." All this talk made Olivia realize the mess Rose was making. For everyone.

Sensing Olivia may have realized what he already knew, Silas told her the rest.

"Deveroux has a head full of ideas. He talks of secret societies. He thinks the FBI is using you to expose them. They want you as an ally and a teacher." It was the best summation Silas could come up with.

"All I've done is remind them of history. The Church has long preached there are demons. I just brought them into the light."

Or they followed you.

"It's an arrangement of necessity," Olivia

concluded, a bemused look on her face. "Thus, the increase in my fee. The Bureau will pay because they have no one else.

"Deveroux says the FBI is aware you are not the only gifted one. He talked about growing up in New Orleans and hearing stories about things like what happened at the sheriff's house."

It was something Olivia suspected, thanks to Pittman. Prisoners were in abundant supply. They were easy, available research subjects. The government certainly wasn't above it. "The only reason behind cooperation is enlightenment."

Her train of thought continued to unsettle him. "How did they gain enlightenment?" Silas asked, not sure if he wanted to know the answer.

"They assessed the threat potential. Thus, the bargaining."

Silas couldn't help but be chilled by the prospect.

"Don't tell me that sounds crazy after all the unexplainable things we've seen?" Olivia prompted, realizing she had lost him. "Deveroux made it very clear at the sheriff's house and at the briefing what he was talking about. The definition of paranormal is an occurrence, event or perception that has no scientific explanation. The same could have been said of genetics less than a century ago. Only in the last few decades have intuitive abilities been acknowledged, but that doesn't mean they haven't always existed. Sometimes it takes society time to catch up. Given other government entities have admitted to investigating them I'd say the FBI is last to the party."

Silas couldn't argue with her even though he wished he could. After experimentation usually came exploitation. This wasn't some theory they were discussing, but his family.

Silas wanted to make it all go away. "Maybe Deveroux's just crazy."

"No," Olivia snapped. "He's convenient. He spreads the word but no matter how strange, no one takes him seriously because he's damaged. I'm not the only one Silas. There are others out there."

Rose Corey and Larry Wayne Pittman sprang to mind. "Of course not." His words were hollow because Silas knew someone like Rose could ruin it for everyone.

"Kim met one. I'm going to track him down. I hope I can learn from him."

"Is that wise? Is it safe?" Silas protested.

Olivia laid her hand on his arm in an attempt to soothe him. "He's a nurse. Kim works with him. Your brother vetted him. I'll even take Barry with me." She didn't dare tell him Barry was as skeptical as he was now. "I can't go it alone. Not anymore. Our daughters need to know their world."

"What about our world?" Silas asked. An us versus them scenario was quickly constructing itself inside his head.

"They need to understand the past in order to find their place in the present." Olivia could tell their conversation was troubling him. They were reaching an impasse, but she had made up her mind. "I will not yield to the FBI."

"You just said it was a necessary arrangement," Silas protested. He didn't like where this conversation was going.

"Let me clarify," Olivia said. "The arrangement is

a necessity for the FBI. Not me. There are more of us then there are of them, and I'm done playing by anyone else's rules but my own."

It sounded like the speech she gave the day she quit the FBI. At the time, Silas knew she was angry. He thought they were just words. Today she was something else. Determined. Defiant. That's when it all came crashing down. Silas saw his wife through new eyes. To survive the monsters, she was forced to embrace the gifts she had once shunned. Olivia was evolving. Only now did Silas know why the FBI tried to suppress her. It wasn't because they doubted her skills. They feared them. If they could see her right now, they would know they weren't wrong.

Olivia shattered his thoughts by slipping her arm through his and steering him toward home. "Lily wants to dress up for Halloween and sit outside and hand out candy. It sounds like fun. Our daughters will be here soon. You and I don't have a lot of us time left."

"I leave tomorrow," Silas said, a solemn reminder of how this conversation originally started.

"You have to go? Now? Really?"

Silas nodded. "I think it's important we put this case to bed." Because he knew it wasn't just about this case. It was about something more.

Olivia slipped her arm out of his. The defiance was gone, replaced by sadness. "If you go, I fear you'll miss the delivery of the only children you will ever have."

****

Herschel Gaines was waiting for them in the lobby. Brennon wanted a third-party present in case he needed to file a complaint with SAPD. Brennon doubted it was necessary, but he was taking no chances with what they may find waiting for them. Forensics wasn't known for cleaning up after themselves. Brennon played hardball with the boys downtown and made no apologies about it. From the compensation package he carried in his briefcase, it appeared they got the message loud and clear. Kurt Preston also got what he wanted, Bartholomew off the force. He didn't care how much it cost.

The crime scene tape was off the door. Brennon took it as a good sign. Inside, the place was spotless. After a brief walk-through, Brennon waited on the balcony leaving the Texas Ranger alone with Barry.

Ranger Gaines bypassed the view in the living room to linger in the bedroom office. "It's a bad deal what happened to you," Gaines said when Barry came to join him.

Barry could only nod, still feeling stunned at being back in a place that a week ago felt like home. Now it felt alien. Barry wasn't even sure he wanted to be here.

"You know, it's none of my business, but I've seen a lot of politics in my thirty years. When the threat comes from the outside it's manageable. When it's an inside job, those never go well. I don't usually like lawyers but calling that one was a smart move. I wouldn't want to tangle with him. That's my two cents worth anyway," Gaines said.

Gaines stepped closer to the board, perusing the headlines, tapping his finger against the clippings. "As a free agent you're not restricted by jurisdiction. Looks like you've got yourself an interesting case right here. How did you catch it?"

"Following up for those who can't." Mark Austin would never finish the case that killed his brother. As for Olivia, Barry wondered what losing Jason really did to her. Barry would never tell Silas what he knew. Combing Jason's old laptop, Barry stumbled upon email exchanges between Jason and Olivia giving him intimate knowledge of the evolution of their relationship.

With Olivia living in Richmond and Jason outside of DC, it was their preferred method of correspondence given where they were in life. Olivia was working the night shift and writing her dissertation during the day while Jason was proving himself an up-and-coming journalist. Their relationship blossomed through words. Given Silas' proclivity for snooping Barry had since password-protected the exchanges. Silas didn't need to read them. Sometimes Barry wished he could forget them. Except they were what kept him focused on finding out the truth behind Jason's death. He didn't deserve to die, and Olivia didn't deserve to lose him.

"We all have a few of those," Gaines sympathized. "I've been thinking about one I caught early in my career. He was a regular, hard-working guy. Kept his head down, paid his bills, took care of his family. One day his wife hears him and the neighbor outside. She can't make out the words, only the raised voices. Next thing she knows her husband comes inside and grabs something out of the closet. He goes back outside without saying a word and blows the guy away. He calmly walks back in, sets the gun on the table and tells her he killed the neighbor. She said he told her to call the police. She didn't even know they owned a gun."

"What's his story?" Barry couldn't resist asking.

"He said his neighbor wasn't who he said he was. That there was something bad inside of him. The only way to make it to go away was to kill him."

"So, who was crazy? Your guy or the neighbor?"

Gaines shrugged. "My guy was convicted, but what I keep coming back to is in the interview room he confessed to killing others. People he didn't even know. All unsolved, random murders. Different methods. Looked like spur of the moment kind of thing. Kind of like with the neighbor. He could have read about them in the paper for all I knew. The first one dated back more than a decade."

"That would have made him an avid reader," Barry commented. "Dr. Osborne says the best way to get away with murder is not to kill people you know." It was what she said about Smythe. If he had kept killing the way he did with his first two victims, they would still be finding dead girls in parks. Instead, Smythe got tangled up with a demon. He went off script and got himself caught.

"Dr. Osborne is a smart lady." Gaines looked over at Barry. "She got you the attorney, didn't she? You would have never called the likes of him. Is she going to be okay?"

Barry nodded. "It won't be long now."

"Doesn't look like it. She's bigger by the minute." The ranger smiled.

"So, what happened with your guy?"

"There was never any evidence to link him to the other murders, so he only did time for the one. I was young. I hadn't seen a lot. I caught the bad guy. That's all I cared about. But there was this old cop, staring down retirement. He started looking into some of the unsolved ones. His explanation was it could have as easily been our guy as anyone else. He concluded from looking at the victims that whoever did the killings did society a favor. As for the one that happened on my watch, it came out later, when DNA became a thing, that the dead neighbor was also the neighborhood rapist. He ruined a lot of lives before he got himself shot. Maybe my guy knew what he was talking about. He just never said."

"So, the guy who killed his neighbor was some kind of vigilante?"

Gaines shrugged again. "You could call him that. I contacted the old cop who investigated the cases. The ones he looked into had shady pasts, just like the dead neighbor. My guy was jumping the gun, acting as judge, jury, and executioner. It made me think of the case Dr. Osborne and Agent Branch worked last summer, the one with the dead girls in Florida. The ones who murdered their friends." The case had been all over the news.

"I remember the cousin, the one that killed them said, 'they needed kill'n'. That stuck with me. Those psychic abilities Dr. Osborne has, how do we know there aren't more out there like her?"

A switch inside Barry flipped. Instinctively he knew it was part of being her fabled watcher. His job was to protect her. "What do you mean more?"

"People who see things we can't. Know things we don't. Maybe there are people who can see evil. Isn't that what the doc does? The older I get, the more possibilities I see. Some things can't be explained any other way."

Barry walked Gaines to the door. "How did your guy do after his release? Did he go back to killing?"

"Good question. He never got arrested again if he

did. He moved around a lot, though. Last I heard he ended up here in a nursing home across town. Over at Oak Hollow."

"Frank Pope," Barry said the name before he could stop himself.

The ranger gave him a crooked grin. "He's got to be well into his eighties by now. Don't tell me he made a liar out of me."

Chapter Twenty-Three

Barry's trek to his favorite balcony was slow. Brennon was leaning on the railing, his gaze fixed on the traffic down 281. It's exactly what Barry would have done in another lifetime.

"I found that in the kitchen," Brennon said, nodding toward the gift basket on the high-top table in the corner.

Barry peaked inside and saw a variety of whiskey flavors. The handwriting on the card he would never read looked like Katie's. He felt sure Frank was in on it, too. His bed was made, and it smelled like fresh laundry. He didn't call the cleaning lady, and Barry was pretty sure he left the bed unmade the last morning he was here. Looking back, it was a good thing for him he left when he did. All things considered; Barry was lucky. Maybe it was time he started looking at it that way.

"I received an offer from the city today." Brennon headed back inside for his briefcase, but Barry stopped him.

"I don't need to see it. Not right now. Just tell me, is it fair?"

"It's fair. But I never take the first offer."

Barry avoided going to the railing. Knowing Amanda had climbed over it, to meet whatever she was looking for, ruined it for him.

"Did you find out what kind of car Preston drives? Was it one of those new electric ones?"

Brennon smiled. "As a matter of fact, it was. How did you know?"

"A vehicle matching that description was parked outside Amanda's house the night of her party. After all the guests had gone. I think he was separated from his wife at the time."

"They're back together now and expecting a baby," Brennon informed him.

"Then at least we know he's fertile. Go back and tell them I know whose baby Amanda was carrying. Then ask for more. Preston will think Amanda told me."

"Did she?"

"No. She wanted it to be mine. I think that's why she didn't tell her family. She wanted to put it all back together."

"But you didn't."

"I never wanted it in the first place. I was trying to get over someone else."

"How did that work out for you?" Brennon asked.

"It's better. It's different."

"I'll approach them tomorrow," Brennon said. "I want them to think it's over." He patted Barry on the shoulder. "Take whatever time you need. I'll meet you downstairs."

"Are you really interested in the condo?"

"It would be a great investment opportunity."

Barry had done the math. The unit upstairs was listed for over two and a half million. His condo was smaller, but the location was the same, and he owned this place free and clear. It was a gift from his dad. It was the only thing the man had ever given him except a hard time. With the sale of the condo and his retirement, he would never have to work again. And he wasn't even fifty. Things could be worse.

Barry waited until he heard the door click shut behind Brennon before approaching the railing. He forced himself to look down and wondered what Amanda thought about in the end. As for him, he was thinking some things couldn't be put back together.

His perch over the city had been his sanctuary. Now that it had been breached, there was no going back.

****

Barry returned to find Olivia doing what she was when he left—staring at a computer screen—except the location had changed. She had moved to the dining table, and this wasn't her computer. It was Jason's that Barry mistakenly left out. He should have put it away. He had locked it, but that didn't do any good. Olivia knew the passcode. It was her birthday. Like the alarm code to her house was Jason's.

Realizing his error, Barry immediately felt guilty. "I should have put that away."

Olivia shook her head and avoided his eyes. Hers were red.

At a loss for what to do, Barry placated her with food. First, with the chocolate-covered almonds he dug out of his gift basket, followed by a steaming cup of pumpkin spice tea he brought with him as he joined her outside in the back. Barry felt like he was treading in Silas' territory, but since the incident with the flowers, they avoided the front porch.

Barry passed her the cup of tea and fired up the

grill.

"You're cooking again?"

"Are you saying you don't like my cooking?" he asked.

Olivia smirked at his uncharacteristic attempt at humor. "Absolutely not. It was delicious, but you don't have to cook."

"I want to. We have to eat, and I thought a change of scenery might be in order," Barry suggested.

Olivia took a long sip from the cup enjoying the easy ebb and flow between them. He was giving her an out on talking about Jason.

When she didn't take the bait, Barry moved on with something they had put off too long. "I saw Herschel Gaines today. He told me about Frank Pope. He said Pope reminded him of your guy down in Florida."

Larry Wayne Pittman. Confessed murderer. He might be dead, but after her talk with Silas about the FBI and theories of more like Pittman, Olivia decided to review some of her early cases. Maybe she missed more gifted—just as she did with Pittman the first time. If she found something that piqued her interest it could be another project for Kevin Branch. It was what she was doing before she took a trip down memory lane with Jason.

"Gaines made a good point. If you can sense evil, then it shouldn't be too much of a stretch to think other people can too. The natural reaction would be to kill it." Barry let the statement hang there signaling there would be no out this time. He watched and waited for her reaction.

Daisy was stretched out next to Olivia's chair.

Alvin was at Barry's feet. The outside lights flickered on as the sun dipped toward the horizon. He had just asked her to shatter this world as the two of them discussed things no one believed existed.

"Do you trust me?" Olivia began.

"With my life," Barry told her, his words gentle, but uncompromising. "You've been holding back on me."

"I thought you didn't like my information because it came from a killer," Olivia reminded him.

"I'm not ashamed to admit I was wrong." Barry reached over and gave her hand a squeeze. "I stand with you. We're in this together."

Olivia squeezed back in hopes of drowning out the words of a demon swimming inside her head.

"He promised he would always be there for you. It looks like he meant it," Alleracsap whispered inside her thoughts.

She didn't see the demon or even feel him, but he had been making the garden his own more often than she liked. His hovering began at the same time as her pregnancy. His proximity was too close and made her uncomfortable.

Olivia cradled her babies. She had to step into the unknown for them. They were part of two worlds, and it was up to her to teach them coexistence. Since her discussion with Silas, she felt more protective than ever. But she couldn't take on that role solo. The burden was too great. "I'll tell you what I know."

"Gaines' prisoner does sound like Pittman," Olivia confirmed. Barry didn't have to tell her what Gaines said, she had read Kevin Branch's assessment. "I believed everything Pittman told me. He killed those girls because he saw what was inside them. He called himself a cleaner—someone who does exactly what you said. He saw evil and he killed it. It was that simple."

The Archbishop had confirmed the story, but Barry wanted to hear her version. "What did Pittman say that made you a believer?"

"He spoke words my gran used and some I had never heard. Collector, watcher, alpha, hunter, seer, and teller."

"But you're none of those. You're something more," Barry emphasized.

"Pittman knew me as a reader. Just like Gran said." Olivia explained. "It meant I could read the energy left behind by the living."

Ana Lutz and Roche said the same thing, but they believed there was more to her. So did Barry. "I'm no expert, but you do more than read it. I saw what you did in the barn. I sensed the energy. It felt like a lightning storm. You used it. It's what shattered the lights and started the fire." And brought the thing that hovered in the corner.

"I was angry. I lashed out," Olivia confessed. Disposing of Andre Roche was exactly what she intended. The only difference was she planned to use a snake, not a demon. Roche should have been more careful about what he wished for.

"You were pushed. Ana wanted a demonstration," Barry said.

"You mean my mother wanted one," Olivia corrected him. She took a deep breath, caging the anger she felt for the woman who gave birth to her instead of unleashing it on Barry. She may have been too harsh with Silas the other day. He had been uncharacteristically distant since their discussion. The absence of him left her wounded; she didn't want to inflict another one.

"According to Pittman these abilities are genetic. People like him, like me, are all part of some ancient collective. It starts at birth."

"Not for everyone," Barry confessed quietly. "What does watcher mean to you?"

"Protector. Defender." For Olivia, the term was synonymous with sentry. Ironic, because that was the role Barry adopted from the beginning.

"As watcher, I'm in this because of our connection. I need you to know that when I said we're in this together, I meant it. Those aren't just words or empty promises." It was because of the guidance from Father Dominic and the Archbishop that Barry could express what he felt for her in such generic terms. "I know what they mean."

"It seems you've been holding out on me," Olivia repeated the response he gave her earlier. She didn't trust herself to say anything else. He had opened a well of emotion inside her.

"I've been spending time at the Archdiocese, but you already knew that." Barry paused, wondering if she would pick up the thread he was dangling, but she didn't. Part of him was relieved. Barry wasn't sure he was prepared for that conversation.

"After what happened in the barn I had to turn somewhere, to someone for my own sanity. Given what happened, the Church seemed like the most obvious choice," Barry explained. "A watcher can live their life never knowing what they can become. The gene is dormant until they cross paths with someone like you. There's a bonding of sorts that occurs. It's more than an obligation or a duty. It's servitude. That sounds like a collective," Barry said, surprising himself by using Pittman's words. "According to Church lore, there are many who are sensitive to the other side in one form or another."

Olivia had heard similar words from Father Dominic. "And how does the Church feel about those with sensitivities?" Olivia wanted to know. Dominic had always been vague. She doubted the Archbishop followed the same rule.

"The dark path is much easier to follow than the one full of light. The Church believes the ramifications of such…" Barry paused, unsure of what word to use.

"Gifts," Olivia said it for him. Her choice had been made. She refused to believe they were anything else.

"That they come with a price," Barry warned.

"…for someone like me," Olivia said it for him. "The one who lives in twilight and can touch both sides."

"The other side is as sensitive to you as you are to it. You hunt it as much as it hunts you," Barry said.

Hunt was one word for it. So was follow. Olivia kept the comparison to herself. "That worries the Church, doesn't it?"

To his credit, Barry didn't hesitate. "Someone with your skills could be very powerful if seduced by the dark side. As watcher, I'm here to make sure that doesn't happen."

He said the words without judgment or fear. Instead, they were gentle and full of understanding. Olivia took a deep breath, letting go of the pent-up anxiety she had been holding. He had given her exactly what she needed. Barry saw her for what she was, not what he wanted her to be.

For just a moment Olivia looked uncharacteristically fragile, but it faded with her heavy sigh. Barry was relieved he didn't confront her about Jason earlier. "What else did you learn from Pittman? The girls he murdered were the real killers, weren't they? Knowing that was his gift."

Olivia confirmed with a shake of her head. Media coverage was intentionally vague about the reasons behind any of the killings. It was for the best. The truth was ugly. In the public's eyes, Pittman was a confessed killer who died in prison. Only those close to the case knew the truth.

"The body of the missing girl we found, and the visions associated with it were enough to convince me," Olivia explained. The FBI might need forensics, but she didn't and neither did Pittman. "The other two missing girls are probably at the bottom of an empty crocodile pond. The girls Pittman shot killed their friends, which is why Pittman killed them."

"They weren't Pittman's first, were they?"

"No, but they were the only ones he confessed to. He said he could tell when something wasn't right with a person. He described a peeping tom, a thief and someone who sounded like a predator. The DOJ gave me his juvenile records. Kevin Branch did some digging. He can link Pittman to those and so many more."

"When I mentioned to Gaines I knew who Frank Pope was, his first question was if he was at it again," Barry said.

"I asked Kevin to look into him as well. Before and after his conviction. I believe he learned how not to get caught," Olivia explained, even though the thoughts didn't connect with the man she saw in the common room. Maybe due to his age and living arrangement, Pope assumed a new quest. Could a cleaner become a hunter? Or did a hunter need an apprentice? The thought teased her. She filed it away in the browser that was always open. The one that belonged to Rogan Poe.

"Gaines said when Pope killed his neighbor, his wife didn't even know he owned a gun."

"When a person is forced to hide, they become very good secret keepers. If not, they cease to exist," Olivia explained.

****

After dinner, Barry and Olivia moved back outside. It was a clear night, and the stars were in full bloom. "I'd forgotten how much I've missed doing this. Grilling and sitting outside. Having a yard," Barry mused.

"I thought one of the things you liked about your condo is there was no yard," Olivia reminded him.

"Yeah, well, that's when I was keeping cop hours," Barry explained.

"Sounds like you might have something else in mind," she pondered.

"I know of somewhere. I helped pick it out. Built the deck. Bought the grill. It's still available. The owners have been unwilling to sell. But I think I can change their minds."

Olivia took a long sip of her tea, waiting for him to say more, but he didn't have to. She could guess he was talking about Mark's parents, Alan and Belinda Austin.

They had been unable to part with Mark's house despite the burden of managing renters. It was the last piece they had of their son, and they weren't ready to let go.

Mark bought the house thinking he had a whole life ahead of him. It was heartbreaking that life ended way too soon. With both sons dead and their daughter in and out of mental health facilities, the Austin family was in ruins. Barry would never tell her, but Olivia knew through Jessica that he had been looking in on Alan and Belinda, stepping up as a son and maybe healing his own lack of family. At least that's what Olivia hoped. Barry deserved happiness.

"Are all the cases you found with Pittman and Pope still open? Unsolved?" Barry asked.

Olivia shook her head in agreement. "Gone completely cold."

"Are you compiling a database?"

"Working on it, but it will take more than me and Kevin Branch. I may have been able to verify Pittman's claims, but I still don't know enough." It was an unspoken plug for her request to join her to meet a so-called hunter. Barry might not be happy about it, but Olivia knew he would come around. If nothing else, because he would never let her go alone. "Looks like you're already doing some research. There's always more," Oliva coaxed.

She suddenly put down her cup and reached for her belly. Olivia motioned for him to come closer. Fearing something was wrong Barry moved without explanation.

With no reservations, Olivia reached for his hands and pressed them to either side of her abdomen. "Feel that?" She smiled. "They're both moving, at the same time. One of them is just waking up, the other one settling in for the night."

A smile parted Barry's lips as his hands rested on either side of her. "That's incredible."

"Did the bishop say if watcher duty includes them as well?" Olivia asked.

"I might need to check on that. Since this is genetic, what will they become?" Barry asked, settling back into his own chair. "Do you know?"

Olivia stroked the right side of her belly and then the left. "Genevieve and Gwendolyn. They each have their own gifts. I don't know who has what yet, but one is a seer, and the other a teller. Seers see the future. Tellers tell the past. They are the reason I've been having visions of both. I would assume it's because we share the same body. At least I hope so. I look forward to all this sharing going away once I deliver." Olivia flashed him a pained smile and continued to cradle her offspring.

Silas was right when he made the ultimate request to Barry. *You love her. I know you do. It has to be you.* Olivia had seen a future where Silas didn't exist.

Since they were talking about the future, Barry thought he should ask. "How accurate are these visions?"

"Two for three so far. One was a past event that happened to the agent I worked with on the Pittman case. The other was of Silas. I saw his death. He had complications after his knee surgery which could have killed him. According to Pittman his Nan was a Seer. She taught him time is fluid and that the future isn't set. It's only real at the time of the vision."

That's why Olivia believed Silas' time had passed.

At least that was what she told herself.

"And the third vision?"

"That one is still a mystery. It was of Mark, a woman, and a child. A boy, I think. Since that was not what happened, I thought of it as some altered version of what his life could have been." Just like what could have happened to Silas had she not been there.

The night had been full of revelations. Barry had one more. "I would say you're three for three," he said solemnly. "Maybe it was a version of what could have been, but Mark was a father even though he never knew. The boy's name is Aiden. Katie Morgan, the forensic tech, is his mother. They were together the night before Mark died."

****

While Olivia went inside to soak in the tub before going to bed, Barry retreated to the porch. He sipped his drink, surveyed the neighborhood, and waited for Lily. It was her last day of a four-day stint. Olivia said she was proud of him for embracing change. His response was he might as well rip the band-aid off.

Barry greeted Lily in her driveway. He liked the way her eyes lit up at seeing him. He pressed against her, enjoying the feel of her.

"Suddenly I'm not nearly as exhausted as I thought I was," Lily whispered.

"A wise woman once told me it's okay to take it slow; if it's important," Barry told her.

Lily stopped, but he didn't let go. Her cheeks blazed red. "I'm sorry, I'm being presumptuous." Lily bit her lip.

"No, you're not," Barry consoled her. "I'm just saying I want it to be for the right reasons. What's happening here is important."

Lily smiled. "Not because I've only been with one man in the last thirty years?"

Barry tried not to laugh as he pressed his lips back to hers. "I wanted you to know, with Silas gone, I have other obligations. But I wish I could be here with you."

Lily stole a glance next door. "You're right. Tonight, your place is with her. I'm not going anywhere."

Chapter Twenty-Four

Deveroux didn't answer his phone all day. Considering Silas was in the guy's town, he'd hoped for more consistency. Still, he had planned ahead and rented a car with the idea of pursuing his own scenic route. Silas had never been a Vegas-type guy. He showed up when expected for the obligatory meetings, bachelor parties, and destination weddings, but to him, the place felt dirty. It was too loud and too tacky for his taste. He wasn't a strip club kind of a guy, either. Silas might have enjoyed an overactive single life, but he did have a type. He liked a challenge and good conversation. Silas enjoyed hearing how people who didn't hunt monsters lived. Not that he shared anything of himself, but he was a good listener. He ultimately realized it was the ability to share that was a key component of being with Olivia. Maybe that was why he had been so unsettled by their conversation on their Sunday morning walk. They were nowhere near being on the same page for what was staring them in the face, and he got the distinct feeling Livie was holding back on him.

His drive-by of Sarah Larsin's businesses was pure research. He and Deveroux would get the run down tomorrow, but Silas wanted to see for himself. In a world full of too-bright lights, Sarah Larsin's establishments stood apart. As a strip club, *Red*

Sparrow was the only one that looked as expected, but the billboard was classier than its flashing neon neighbors. *Zoar* was branded as a Gentlemen's Club and looked like a five-star restaurant where reservations were required. Her flagship business *Delilah's Den* was located an hour outside of town. *The Den* was one of only twenty or so legal brothels in Nevada. It looked like a resort. No prices were listed on the website. Silas could only assume the old adage "if you have to ask" applied. Those looking to make a reservation were encouraged to book early. As of today, the earliest available overnight stay was more than four months away. If what he heard was true, and Sarah Larsin cultivated specific types of girls, Silas envisioned a platinum card membership with a mysterious set of oligarch clients to go with them. No such perk was mentioned on the website.

The different locations meant overlapping law-enforcement jurisdictions. Silas wondered if that was deliberate to keep them from talking, or purely for marketing purposes. If Sarah was anything like her daughter, there were multiple levels to any decision.

As a result, Silas made several unscheduled stops visiting each jurisdiction. A flash of his FBI credentials earned him a high-level overview of what local law enforcement thought of Ms. Larsin and her business practices. The locals were cooperative, if not overly complimentary.

There were no reports of trouble from any of her establishments. More than one joked that a call-out would be the only way they could get a peek inside. Too pricey for their paychecks. She didn't even have a record for code violations. She also reportedly went above and beyond, setting new industry standards. She was known to be a fair employer who was generous during the holidays. She gave back to the community, especially to homeless teens. The cynic in Silas wondered if the visits weren't some recruiting strategy. Surely, he would get a different story when he met with the local FBI boys.

By the end of the day, Silas still hadn't heard from Deveroux. He left another message feigning comradery, attempting to elicit a dinner invitation. Olivia was right about Deveroux being an easy target. It was troubling that a man with Deveroux's proclivities would settle in Las Vegas. To Silas, it didn't seem like an attempt to run from his demons but to get closer to them. Deveroux's excuse had been that his work brought him here more than anywhere else. Deveroux's marriage ended sometime after the move to DC and before the rehab stint. With no kids, Deveroux was adrift.

Silas made it easy on himself and decided to have dinner at his hotel. That way, if he wanted more than one bourbon, it wouldn't matter. Before committing to Livie, Silas would have been perfectly content with a night like tonight, full of possibility if he so desired. Instead, he felt lost and adrift in his own way but didn't seek the same refuge as Deveroux. There were plenty of women looking for company. He saw more than one female look his way while he enjoyed his meal.

When his plate was gone, and he and Livie had said their goodnights, Silas focused his attention on the Monday night football game on the big screen. He was looking for an escape, not yet ready to return to his room, where he would only miss the life waiting for him back in San Antonio. He was halfway through his first bourbon and debating another when the blonde approached. Physically she was just his type. Small and petite like Livie, enough breast to garner attention, a toss-up on whether she was a professional conversationalist. She snagged his attention but his lack of interest shut her down.

He was toying with his glass when the waiter appeared with another, along with a carafe of blood-red wine. "I didn't order this," Silas told him.

A woman slid into the booth across from him. "I did," she said with a ready smile.

Silas stared across the table to find himself looking into a slightly older version of his wife. All except for the eyes. The ones staring back at him were blue, not fiery green, but they were just as hypnotic.

Sarah Larsin slid a tip large enough to cover his meal and then some toward the waiter, who promptly scurried away like he had prior instructions.

Sarah Larsin trained her eyes on him, expecting something. Silas got the message and filled her glass which she tipped toward his fresh bourbon. "Cheers, Agent Branch. Or may I call you Silas?"

The familiarity was unnerving. So was the way she looked at him. She was in full appraisal mode, almost like a predator assessing a target. If he was anyone but her son-in-law, he would be a plaything. Silas steeled himself and stared back until she finally retreated.

"You do seem immune. I thought it was just the girl and that I was mistaken."

He should have known. "You sent her?"

"Of course, I did. It's what I do. I wanted to see what kind of man you are."

"The married kind."

Sarah laughed. "Marriage is a legal contract. Commitment is something else entirely. It does seem your wife has you under her spell." Sarah took a sip of her drink, and the smile disappeared. "Rumor has it she is more like her father. Glad to see there's something of me in her."

"About her father." Silas took a shot in the dark, knowing it was a non-topic for Livie, but he had to try. He was looking at his only source of information.

"Couldn't pronounce his name. Never saw him again. End of story."

Silas noted Sarah gripped the wine glass a little harder, and the practiced smile was nowhere to be found. He had tried too hard, too soon. He decided to pull back.

"I called your offices. I planned on coming to you," Silas told her.

"You have FBI written all over you. Not that it's a bad look; you carry it well, but it's bad for business. I can't have you show up at my place during working hours. Discretion is of utmost importance as you can imagine."

As reported, Sarah Larsin was a woman accustomed to being in charge.

"And yes, I do like to be the one in control. I'm sure my daughter is like that as well. Or you wouldn't be so tame."

This woman was playing with his head. Maybe because she looked so much like Livie. Sarah Larsin had been young when she gave birth, but the two could pass for sisters. Sarah's version was different though, reminding him of Livie when a storm was brewing inside her.

"Don't worry, I can't read minds, not like her. I can occasionally catch glimpses, but really, I just read people. Mine is an acquired skill, important in my business. Like yours. My daughter's skills were gifted. There's a big difference." Sarah drained her glass, and Silas reached over to pour her another. "Ask me whatever you came here to ask me. The night is just beginning, and it is time for me to go to work."

"Why did you call Brennon Kaine? And who did you call him about?" Without Deveroux to interfere, Silas was asking what he wanted to know.

"I called him because I knew you would come running. It was as much an invitation as a warning."

"About?"

"Rose."

Use of the first name only told Silas Sarah Larsin did know her.

"She's a problem. A loose cannon actually," Sarah told him.

"Did she kill the sheriff?" Checking Ms. Larsin's familiarity, Silas avoided calling Jim Tennent by name.

"I think you know the answer to that question. Before you ask, I had nothing to do with it." Sarah held her hand up like a pledge, her red, gleaming nails looking like daggers. "I merely suggested she speak with him. The rest, Rose took into her own hands, and apparently it ended rather messily. She has certain inclinations that are not encouraged." Sarah shook her head, lost in her own thoughts.

"Like raising the dead?"

"Did she, now?" Sarah raised a brow, genuinely curious.

"Looks that way. At least that's what your daughter

believes."

"I'm sure she's correct."

Sarah tapped a lacquered nail against the table, signaling to Silas her obvious displeasure at the news.

"The agent I'm working with is curious about the girls you procure. The ones you had Ana and Roche looking for," Silas ventured. This was a first blush for his mother-in-law, and Silas was aware he was probably on a very short clock.

"Andre Roche was never part of the deal. Ana, like Rose, couldn't follow instructions."

"So, you're innocent in all of this. Just a business woman?" Silas was the one pissed now.

"There are girls out there, like me, who need my help. They need guidance because no one understands them or what they are. Some find their way on their own, some don't, that's what Ana was for. Then there are others, not just girls, who never find their way anywhere except into trouble. The likes of Larry Wayne Pittman come to mind."

She sounded too much like Livie. Silas switched gears and took another shot in the dark. "Does the same apply to Jamie Smythe?"

"You don't know? Jamie is one of those people you signed up to catch before you got involved with my daughter—a psychopath."

"I know that," Silas told her, sounding annoyed.

Sarah looked at him curiously. "My daughter must have failed to inform you. I know she's figured it out by now. She has her own personal demon with *It*s own agenda."

Silas swallowed hard. Of course, he knew about the demon, but it was one thing for Livie to talk about it in the dark. To hear it from a woman so far removed from their lives filled him with unease. It was another reminder he was surrounded by a whole new world. The walls were closing in, and he needed to catch up or get left behind.

"The way I understand it, Jamie Smythe caught the attention of some low-level demon. Then another caught wind of it and saw an opportunity to right a wrong."

Sarah sensed his dread. "It's best you leave the nefarious dealing of demons to my daughter. I hear she's a natural." Sarah reached out to pat Silas' hand but drew back at the last minute. "Let me help you where I can. Believe it or not, I provide a valuable service."

Silas' features were still clouded, but he stayed on track. "This goes way beyond me," he warned. While Silas felt Livie wasn't being totally open with him, he didn't want to tell her that the conspiracy theories he attributed to Deveroux were true. Silas confirmed them with Patrick. There were shadowy subagents ready to draw lines in the sand with antics such as Rose's killing of the sheriff. Those same agents were ready for an "us versus them" scenario, and they sounded as dogmatic about their agenda as Livie.

"Mason Deveroux?"

Sarah flashed another smile, one Silas hadn't seen, a cross between pitiful and sinister. He couldn't determine which.

"He's compromised. Surely you know that. More ways than you can possibly imagine."

Silas was more than happy to keep all about Deveroux quiet. Just as he had done with Livie.

"Compromised, how?"

"I'm afraid he found Rose a little too enticing. Playing with the dead isn't her only gift. Surely my daughter knows that as well."

"Kind of like the sheriff?" Silas asked.

"Let's hope your agent doesn't end up like him," Sarah said with an arched brow. She drained her glass and prepared to leave.

"I have follow-up questions," Silas warned her.

"Of course, you do." She smiled. "You're just like the government agency you represent. Always wanting more. Call my office. I'm sure we can arrange another meeting." Sarah slid to the edge of the booth but stopped herself. "Did my daughter have anything to say to me?"

She sounded curious, not regretful. Then again, Silas was sure she was a woman good at hiding her intentions. Still, he took it as a rare slip of emotion on her part.

Silas saw no reason not to tell her. Maybe she would show him something else. He wanted to know more about Livie as a child, whether she did or not. It could be important. "She said she was sure you were sorry you left her behind."

Sarah tried a smile again but couldn't pull it off. Her eyes drifted somewhere else, beyond this place to another life perhaps.

"Of all the things I've done, there are two transgressions that forever changed the course of my life. One was staying the night in a hotel room with a man who wasn't a man at all. The other was leaving my daughter behind. I admit it. She scared me. If it's any consolation, by the time I figured out what she was, my mother had already taken her from me. The legal system wasn't so forgiving back then, not to mothers like me. In my defense, I was young and foolish—both times. As for Olivia, you should be grateful my mother raised her. Otherwise, you might have found yourself hunting her instead of bedding her. Nevertheless, everything works out in the end. Those who taught me about her assured me she would find her way back. Looks like she's on her way."

Silas knew he would be unable to unhear those words.

"I'm eager to see what kind of mother she becomes. You should. too. There will come a day when your daughters scare you, too. Now, take care of yourself. My granddaughters need a strong father figure, and even though we just met, I far prefer you to the alternative. Unfortunately for you, their meeting is inevitable. You should settle your business here and hurry home."

Not until after she left did Silas realize it wasn't Barry she was warning him about.

Chapter Twenty-Five

A dark-haired girl weaved past them on the narrow walkway, a bounce in her step. Olivia noted Barry's lengthy backward glance and felt especially pregnant as she climbed the stairs. Pheromones from the girl led them to their intended destination. A banquet of smells seeped beneath the door, prickling Olivia's senses. She let Barry do the knocking, but she stepped forward, forcing him to yield the point position to her.

They heard footsteps on the other side. No "*who is it?*" just the turn of the knob. A tall man, wearing nothing but distressed jeans, opened the door. The pants hung on the hips of his well-sculpted body, the top of them still undone.

A new aura rippled across Olivia. The essence reminded her of Silas, but it was fleeting as something more powerful crashed over her, sweeping it away. This new wave was wild and totally untamed.

"May I help you?"

The words sounded far away. Slamming the door to the primal sensations, Olivia found her focus. The dark eyes staring back at her narrowed as a bemused smile sliced his lips.

"Dr. Osborne, I presume." He watched Olivia's eyes taking him all in, traveling to his bare feet all the way back to his bed-tasseled ebony locks. "I could say it's a surprise, but then we both know that would be a

lie. I wouldn't want us to start out on the wrong foot."
He reached for the T-shirt that was flung over his
shoulder and took his time slipping it on. He was
surprised at the fumble of his own fingers as he secured
his jeans.

Barry didn't like the prickling sensation inching up
his neck. "Mr. Poe?"

"At your service, lieutenant," the man in the
doorway replied, his eyes never leaving Olivia.

Barry sensed he was interrupting some kind of
moment. "Mind if we have a word?" He wedged
himself in between them severing whatever was going
on.

"Did you want an invitation?" Poe asked.

Olivia saddled up next to Barry. "That would be
the polite thing to do." The smile she flashed was more
sinister than sincere.

Poe's eyes finally landed on her abdomen. "I guess
it would." He stepped aside, giving Barry a brief once-
over as they entered. "Your timing is impeccable."

"I took the liberty of checking your work schedule
to make sure you were off," Olivia snipped.

"Not what I meant," Poe said, closing the door
behind them. This close to her, Poe could feel her
heightened senses and raised his. "Welcome to my
humble abode."

Olivia surveyed her surroundings. The living room
was tidy. Minimalistic, even with the obligatory couch
and chair, each accompanied by a table. The pieces
looked like they came with the apartment. The space
was silent. Even the flashy big-screen TV was dormant.
Other than it, the walls were bare. The only other piece
of furniture was a bookcase tucked away in the corner.

There were no personal items on display, but the shelves were laden with books, some leather-bound. They were the only things in the room that belonged to the mysterious Mr. Poe. Olivia resisted the urge to wander over and run her fingers along the spines, seeking the words hidden inside. She had no doubt some would reveal themselves to her with a touch.

To her left was a kitchen. There was a four-seater dinette with one chair pulled out, an open laptop in front of it, and a steaming cup of coffee nearby. On the right was an open door leading to a bedroom. Olivia could see the edge of an unmade bed. The smell of the girl was tangled in the sheets.

Told you your timing was impeccable.

Olivia turned at the voice inside her head.

"Since you reminded me of my manners, would you like something to drink?" Poe asked, using his words this time.

Olivia shook her head.

"Let me guess, too early for you?" Poe asked, eyeing Barry.

Barry bit back an equally sarcastic remark. His dislike for this guy was rising by the minute. He was relieved Olivia invited him along. "We're just here for a little chat."

Poe pointed Olivia to the recliner, clearly his choice of seat. "I recommend that one. Better for your back," Poe said as he strode into the kitchen to snag his coffee. He returned to casually plop himself on the couch. He focused his attention on Olivia while keeping Barry in his periphery.

Barry parked himself across the room against the mantle so he could watch both. They looked like two boxers sizing each other up.

Poe took the first swing. "So, what took you so long? And why did it take a priest to get your attention? I'm surprised you even associate with them, you know, considering," Poe asked as he sipped his coffee.

Olivia slowed her breathing, keeping herself on track. This was her show, not Rogan Poe's. "Enlighten me."

Barry felt the tension rise in the room along with the tone of her voice. She wasn't caving to Poe's dominance. He wondered if this was what she was like across the table from a suspect. To the point and unwavering.

"I want to know why your patients keep dying. And not just here. It seems you have quite the history," Olivia continued.

Poe seemed pleased at the revelation. "You checked me out, I'm flattered," he said with a tantalizing smile. "I am hurt, however, that you don't remember."

The room went still as his words pulled her into a memory.

Olivia wanted to flee, but the recliner swaddled her in comfort as the familiar scents of cinnamon and lilac beckoned her. Wispy grey shadows flooded her periphery, masking a sun-streaked room. The sensation reminded her of the visions she experienced early in pregnancy, only this one was different. She wasn't looking in. She was immersed.

The recliner was gone. So was the comfort she felt. This new place offered nothing but emptiness. As her eyes adjusted to the dark, Olivia heard strained breaths coming so far apart any one of them could be the last. It wouldn't be long now.

"Livie."

Olivia heard the whisper, even though she knew Gran could no longer speak.

Olivia threaded her hand through the bedrail between them. Gran's hand escaped the blanket. Ice-cold fingers gripped Olivia's with a strength they shouldn't have.

"Please, Livie."

Olivia's heart skipped a beat. They were Gran's words, but they were in her head. It hadn't been that way in a long time, not after Gran taught her how to shut them out. "Please, Livie—help me fly. Set me free."

Olivia's breaths came in short bursts, unlike the long paces of Gran's. She forced herself not to listen. With every raspy sound, she feared it would be Gran's last. The connection was weak and fading like the sun surrendering to twilight.

"I see the light, but the dark is coming. It's almost here."

Olivia could end her suffering. The key was in the pain pump. Gran had made her promise she would, but it was a vow made in vain.

Rogan Poe's defenses crumbled, as he lapped at the flow of her power.

"Exi. Capits mei," Olivia hissed.

Barry cocked his head her way, unsure what he had heard.

Poe struggled to shake himself free.

Olivia watched Poe waiting for him to return to the present. The change in demeanor was disarming. He used it as a weapon, but not this time, not with her. The scales between them had shifted. He would never be able to invade her again without her consent.

Poe's eyes slid toward the lieutenant, looking for an easier target. "You put your hands on your hips to remind yourself of the badge and the gun you wore for so long, but they're not there anymore. You're not here as a policeman. Please tell me you know what you are."

"I know I'm the one asking the questions," Olivia snapped, claiming the control that should have been hers all along.

Poe's attention returned to her.

Under Poe's scrutiny, Olivia's insides stilled. Her babies weren't squirming. *Were they listening? Did they feel him, too?*

"Are you here to accuse me of something?" Poe feigned surprise when it was clear she was waiting on him.

"Nurses make the best serial killers. Opportunity. Means. Skill set," Olivia broke it down for him.

Earlier, she had rejected the idea of Poe as a killer. She was merely using Oak Hollow as an excuse to get him talking. From where Barry was standing, it didn't look like she needed one. Poe was enjoying her company, seduced by her attention.

"Preach, sister," Poe told her.

"I'm not your sister."

Her voice sounded as menacing as the smile she flashed earlier. Barry hadn't seen her like this since the barn.

Poe yielded with a nod of his chin. "You're right— you're something else entirely."

"Why don't you tell me what you are if not a killer?" Olivia challenged him.

"I think you know. That's why you're here. You talked to good old Larry, before he died or maybe since, who knows?"

Olivia ignored him. She wasn't ready to discuss Larry Wayne Pittman, or how Poe knew about that. Not yet, because that would involve Samael Knight. For whatever reason, Olivia preferred to avoid him. The fact Poe knew she could commune with the dead didn't faze her. She could only look in so many dark corners at a time. Accepting herself and her gifts wasn't one of them. Not anymore. She had chased them into the light.

"You seem interested in indulging me. Why not give it a try?" The smile she flashed Poe wasn't the sinister one.

Poe shifted in his seat with her newfound attention while Barry felt a clutch in his stomach as he watched them. Two alphas looking for control.

Poe put down his coffee and cleared his throat. "I am a means to an end. Death comes for us all. Sometimes the ones in my care ask for it. When they still can. Don't tell me you don't know. The key I left in the pain pump wasn't an accident."

Olivia stared him down but made no move to answer.

Poe shook his head. "Fine. You want to see mine first? I'm not shy." He had regained his footing. His smile was more seductive than sinister.

"Is this the part you tell us you're an Angel of Mercy?" Barry spoke just to shut him up.

"Don't confuse me with the winged ones," Poe snapped but quickly reigned in his emotions. "I'm not that vengeful." The smile faded.

"A hunter then?" Olivia prompted.

Barry swallowed against the bile rising in his throat. What they talked about in private was no longer private. Part of him hoped Poe wasn't what she thought he was, and that he would laugh them out the door. Otherwise, Barry feared they would never be free of him.

"That's a word given by others. I prefer the word *gardener*. I pluck the weeds when they pop up. Hunter implies I kill things. You know there's only one thing that can do that. If you haven't met one of them yet, I'm sure you will. Maybe Gabriel because he does like to send his messages. Or if things get really bad, maybe it will be Michael the defender."

Olivia dismissed his narrative. She wasn't ready to hear it. "So, you're not a cleaner?"

Poe made a face, part pity, part annoyance. "No. Poor bastards. They know just enough to get themselves in trouble. Theirs is a rudimentary skill. An evolutionary downgrade I call it."

"Is that what Mr. Pope is?" Olivia asked. If there had been homicides at Oak Hollow, he was responsible, not Poe.

"Was. He's the Angel of Mercy now. He can see where the dark ones are gathering. When he can, he eliminates the host before they can take hold. We both know what that looks like. It's not pretty."

"Poe's not your real name, is it?" Barry asked. More to remind them he was still there. It looked like they had a lot to talk about, but Barry couldn't leave her alone. Not with this man.

"Have you seen my real name? Poujet?"

"I can see why you changed it," Barry conceded.

"Pope is very similar. Are the two of you related?"

It was a random question really, but Olivia was learning to feel her way in the dark with Poe, like absorbing a new language. Once, she heard only in whispers. Now truths came in loud and clear.

"Great uncle. He's the brother to my mémé."

"Mémé," Olivia repeated the name, the vowels short. It was a term of endearment. The tenderness in his voice was unmistakable.

"It's French for grandmother. I'm here to see Frank to the other side."

"Like you did for my Gran?" Olivia asked. Barry had mentioned Poe worked in San Antonio once before. The key to the pain pump was an offering.

"It's safer that way. For those of us who know what lurks in the shadows. And you couldn't do it," Poe said tenderly. His reminder was a condolence. Doing what she couldn't was a burden he was willing to carry for her.

Barry felt a definite shift in mood. A sudden thaw seeped between them, changing them from advisories to comrades. Barry sensed what was to come. Silas was going to like this guy even less than he did.

"So, you're not behind the deaths?" Olivia asked.

"Only when I'm needed. Protection is the preferred choice along with banishment."

"That's why you put the salt on the window sills?"

"I chose the ways of the old."

"That's your mémé talking, isn't it? That's why you added the cumin? Something spicy."

Poe liked her use of the word, and the way it sounded on her tongue. "*Ma Cherie*."

Her sun baby did a somersault at the sultry sound of his voice.

"The winged ones are the only ones who can truly kill with those flaming swords of theirs. But they don't. They won't. They leave it to us to keep the peace. The ones trapped in the middle."

Poe's gaze finally moved back to Barry. "You know what he is, don't you?"

"Watcher." Barry said it before she could.

Poe clapped his big hands together. "Thank God. I didn't want to be the one to tell you. I hear it's a tortuous, confusing job. It also means you're not the father. But you should do your job now and look after her. The color is starting to rise in your cheeks, Olivia. Go home and take care of your daughters. They are our future."

Chapter Twenty-Six

"How full of shit is he?" Barry asked as they drove from Poe's apartment. Barry had hoped Olivia would be the one to start, but she had been eerily quiet. Barry looked over at her hoping for a reaction. Instead, he found her cheeks were still red, and her hand was pressed to her side. "Are you okay?"

"I'm tired that's all," she said, her tone was dismissive. Olivia fixed her gaze out the window, away from him. "Rogan Poe is only full of himself, as far as I can tell." Her hands moved from her side to massage either side of her temples. "I told you we needed to see him. He didn't disappoint."

Maybe that's what Barry didn't like. He believed Poe as much as she did. He had his own sixth sense on this one. The problem was Rogan Poe was like Silas Branch on steroids. "What did he say to you?" Barry asked.

Olivia shook her head. "You were there."

"I know I was, but there was a long silence. I thought I heard you say something to him."

Barry watched her take a deep breath. She was preparing a response, meaning she knew exactly what he was talking about.

"I told him to get out of my head," Olivia confessed.

"Did you say that in English?" Barry wanted to

know.

"Not sure. If you didn't understand it probably came out as Latin," she explained.

Her response told Barry he didn't want to continue that line of questioning. He moved on to something equally troubling. "He was coming on to you."

Olivia finally turned to look at him. "Really?"

Barry wasn't sure if she was kidding or trying to deflect the truth. "That's what it felt like."

"Poe was trying to rattle me, that's all. His type is obviously the sexy, exotic creature we passed on our way inside." Olivia wasn't sure the woman didn't have her own kind of gift, something her mother would be interested in. Once in Poe's apartment, Olivia could differentiate between the sultry scents. It made sense. Poe was someone who would stick to his own kind.

Their kind.

The thought was lodged inside Olivia's head, a permanent fixture. Expanding her world opened her mind to phrases like us and them. "Maybe because death surrounds him, Poe is attracted to life."

It sounded like psychobabble. Barry didn't believe it and wondered if she did. "So, there was nothing going on between the two of you?" Barry decided he wouldn't stop until she gave him something.

"I felt an energy flow," Olivia admitted softly. "It was oozing out of him."

There was feeling behind her words, Barry just wasn't sure what kind. He found himself holding his breath, thinking she was going to tell him, and then she shut herself down, erasing any preconceptions he might have had.

"I used it—like I used the energy in the barn."

"This wasn't like the barn." Barry preferred anger over the dance he had just witnessed.

"This was familiarity, not anger," Olivia said, choosing her words carefully. "It got him talking, didn't it?"

Barry resisted telling her Rogan Poe would have talked even without her help. He was as eager for the meeting as she was. The comment about the priest told Barry that Poe had been expecting it. Maybe he needed to revisit Poe's history.

"I've never met anyone like him. I've never met anyone like me," Olivia said.

She sounded wistful. "What was Pittman or even Kim?" Barry asked, desperate to dissolve Poe from her memory.

"You heard what Poe said about Pittman, about cleaners," Olivia reminded.

"I heard something that sounded like a class designation within this collective," Barry rephrased, his words sharper than hers.

"It's a skill set," Olivia corrected him. "As for Kim, she has her own set of gifts, but they are nowhere near the level of Poe's. It's like meeting a long-lost relative who shares the same beliefs, sees the world the same way. We operate on the same frequency. It's a step beyond speaking the same language. Truthfully, it's comforting to know I'm not alone anymore."

Now that he got her to talk, Barry almost wished he could tell her to stop. "How are you going to explain this to Silas?"

"Silas will come around like he did with you. The exchange between us will slow after a few visits. Poe will learn how to control it."

Olivia definitely had more faith in Poe than he did. Barry was also trying not to be disturbed by her likening Poe to him.

"So will I. It's like learning how to shudder someone's thoughts. Silas will understand," Olivia assured him. She and Silas were bonded by something more than love. Silas was also invested. This wasn't just about her.

Barry still looked unsure.

"You have to trust me on this one," Olivia said, finally giving him her full attention.

That sounded like they were going to see more of Rogan Poe. A lot more. "It doesn't make me like him," Barry admitted.

"You don't have to like him. You just have to trust him. If there are as many gifted out there as Pittman said, we have to. It can't be just you and me anymore." Olivia's hand went back to her abdomen as she said it.

Strangely, Barry did trust Poe, no matter how he felt. He also knew she was right. They had to stick together. This was bigger than both of them. It's what she'd been trying to tell him about Silas.

"There's someone out there who can raise the dead. I hope there's not more like her," Olivia mused.

"As disturbing as that is, I think you're at the top of the food chain." From the look on her face, Barry wasn't sure if she was happy about the designation. Maybe she was still trying to decide.

"Let's stop and get something to eat. My head hurts," she said instead.

****

Deveroux was a no-show for the briefing at the local field office. The only consolation was the text waiting for Silas when he woke up. Deveroux was chasing down a lead and would circle back. The message didn't stop Silas from calling him. He wasn't surprised when he was shuffled straight to voicemail. He didn't bother to leave a message. Whatever he said wouldn't make a difference.

Silas showed up for the meeting with his local counterparts as scheduled, hoping they had information for him.

"Deveroux's not with you?" Agent Dennis asked.

Patrick had briefed Silas earlier, telling him the assistant agent in charge, Leo Dennis, was a good guy. A solid agent who didn't need much to get up to speed.

"Afraid he couldn't make it," Silas said, hoping his inner turmoil didn't show. "You know Deveroux?"

"We met when he first came to town a few years ago looking into the same thing you are. He called the other day with the information on your person of interest. I heard he had a rough go of it. Just wondering how he was doing."

Silas wondered the same thing. "Anything on the girl, Rose Corey?"

"Not a thing, pretty much like your main inquiry. Ms. Larsin is interesting. She's been around a long time. A steady climber, which says a lot given the tricks of the trade, no pun intended. It's a rough business. Transient employees, unpredictable clientele, and muscle from the outside."

Considering Dennis' use of the word muscle, Silas thought of the mob. "Is she connected?" Girls, sex, and drugs were a reliable business. One is always in demand no matter what the economy.

"Not locally. Maybe not at all."

"So, she's a lone wolf?"

"She's certainly not a sheep," Dennis grinned at his own pun. "Her connections are in the old country, just not the Italian kind."

"Where?" Silas was genuinely curious. Deveroux claimed there was an international connection.

"Persia."

"Why?"

"I'm pretty sure it has to do with her largest stockholder, Samael Knight."

Silas did his best to look passive, hoping the agent could give him more information than he already had, which wasn't much. "What do you know about Mr. Knight?"

"Just like the other players in this game, not a lot, except he bankrolled Ms. Larsin in the beginning. How that connection happened, no one knows. She came here with little to no money and certainly no connections. How she landed a big financial fish like Knight is a mystery. What she accumulated before that was on her back. She's got the rap sheet to prove it. A decade later, she owns her own strip club and several other very successful establishments. These are only photos we have of the guy." Dennis passed him the same photos of Knight that Silas had already seen. He'd thought they were grainy because they were digital, but these were the same.

"We can't even get clear facial recognition on this guy. The overall physical description fits someone of Iranian descent. Darker skin. Eyes as black as night is a common description. I hear he gives people the heebie-jeebies, if you believe in that sort of thing. Having worked for the BAU I'm sure you know what I'm talking about."

Silas nodded. He did. "Some things can't be explained." He felt the heebie-jeebies a few times himself. The first time came when sitting across the interview table from a twelve-year-old boy Livie was interrogating. Another was the night he entered the house he now called home and shot Jamie Smythe. The most recent was his trip to the sheriff's house.

"For someone so successful, I'd say Ms. Larsin is mundane. She remains compliant. She has loyal employees and very loyal customers, which says a lot in her business. She has a specific type of clientele, rich and looking for complete satisfaction. Her girls are top notch. She has had her share of complaints over the years."

Silas perked up. This was something he hadn't heard. "What did her clients say?"

"This is where it gets interesting," Dennis told him. "No clients. Just wives and family members, complaining about the amount of money their loved ones spent in her establishments."

"Extortion?" Silas asked even though the suggestion didn't feel right.

Dennis shook his head. "No. More like addiction. There have been numerous claims drugs are used to entice the clientele and enhance the experience."

"Any findings?" Silas knew cocaine and methamphetamine could be absorbed through the skin.

"Ms. Larsin submitted her girls to testing. No dice, so to speak. No drugs, just glitter and a few interesting trace herbs. Rumor has it she must have some fancy chemist working for her. Nothing tested is considered an aphrodisiac." Dennis smiled.

Silas knew Sarah Larsin didn't have to employ anyone except the right kind of girl. There were no drugs, just natural pheromones. He knew because he was an addict, too.

"Most she's had are a few heart attacks out at the Den. That's why she employees a full-time nurse onsite. I hear there's also one at the gentleman's club on the strip," Dennis reported.

"Is she offering anything special or kinky?"

"Apparently, she doesn't have to. The rumor is these girls get inside your head and make it a full-body experience, no whips or chains required. So far, it seems to be true, but however they do it, it's drug free. Maybe these girls do have some special allure. Who knows? She's broken no laws, as much as some wish she would."

"Any employee complaints?"

"None," Agent Dennis assured him.

That seemed strange as well. "Are they afraid?" Adult entertainment was often an abuse-ridden vocation.

"I don't think so. It's more like some kind of a bond. Like a sisterhood," Dennis said.

"So, is Mason Deveroux wrong?"

"I get that he's concerned about trafficking and all. The Middle East connection is interesting, but that's all it is. An interesting urban legend. These girls might all be similar in their talents, but there are no signs of trafficking. They get to Ms. Larsin on their own."

"Do you believe it?" Silas asked. He needed another perspective, one that wasn't tainted like Deveroux's or his.

"Does it matter?"

"To Deveroux it does," Silas told him.

Agent Dennis' eyes cut to the corner, away from Silas while he considered the question and the reasons behind it. They were both watching Mason Deveroux implode. No one wanted to see that in a fellow agent. "Whatever Sarah Larsin has got going on is so deep, she'll never get caught. I hate to see Deveroux wreck his career over it."

With a confession out of the way, Silas pressed the question Agent Dennis hadn't answered. "What do you think is going on?"

Dennis hesitated. "I don't know. It's different. Hard to describe. Kind of like a haunted house. Is it real or is it imagined?"

Silas thought it was an interesting analogy.

"All I know for sure is Sarah Larsin is smart and she's crafty. While that bothers some people, it's not against the law. She treats her employees well, pays her taxes, and gives back to the community. What more could you want?"

Silas left the meeting feeling that he was at an impasse. He called Patrick to give him a rundown. Nothing on Sarah Larsin and nothing on Rose Corey. And Deveroux was MIA. Silas was getting ready to pack it up and return home tomorrow. Livie would enjoy the surprise.

"Is Sarah Larsin on some keep-away status I don't know about?" Silas decided to take a shot in the dark.

Deveroux had said more than once he had been told to stand down. At the time, Silas had chalked it up to obsessiveness on Deveroux's part. When Patrick confirmed Deveroux's rants about secret societies, it confirmed Livie's belief that Deveroux was damaged goods. Despite the truth he was spouting, the FBI would let Deveroux twist in the wind and watch the self-infliction from afar. Knowing that, Silas couldn't help but wonder what the FBI was still keeping from him. It sure sounded like Sarah Larsin was untouchable. Or was it what Livie had warned him about? Lessons of the past. Hiding in plain sight. Is that what Sarah Larsin was doing?

"I wouldn't know. I got cut out of the loop when you transferred to San Antonio," Patrick admitted.

The answer took Silas a minute to process. He had been in San Antonio for more than a year. Government bureaucracy was slow and cumbersome. That meant somewhere in some dark crevices of the FBI this topic had been discussed long before Agent Mason Deveroux arrived. If Patrick was out of the loop, how or why was he so forthcoming? Silas recalled Patrick's warning about moving to San Antonio. "*It could have unforeseen effects on your career.*" At the time, Silas thought it was about him moving away from the BAU. Looking back, maybe it was about him moving to be with Olivia.

"I guess maybe now is the time to tell you Jon Sharpe requested a transfer out of San Antonio. Things are too spooky for him—his words," Patrick said.

Silas remained silent.

"Word is, the powers that be, are fast tracking Will Ibarra to be your sidekick. Based on his recent assessment, he doesn't scare easily and is open to alternative explanations."

"None of this is protocol," Silas was saying it as a friend and not one of Patrick's former agents.

"Look, I don't have to be in the loop to know that

whatever freak show happened down in Texas has gotten a lot of people who like to stay in the shadows wondering if they should step out into the sun and make their intentions known. Paring Will Ibarra with you is a pretty good indication of where things are headed."

"Do I get any say in this?" Silas asked.

"It's the Bureau, what do you think? If you don't want it to get that way, then you should find Ms. Corey before she decides to conjure more walking dead people."

The statement told Silas everything he needed to know. More changes ahead.

****

Eating helped her headache. Still, Olivia asked Lily to come over and take her blood pressure. At least it wasn't as high as the last check at her doctor's visit, but it was up more than it should be. Olivia's solution was a nap. Barry wondered if Rogan Poe had felt it, and that's why he sent her away.

Barry called Lily back for a recheck as soon as Olivia was awake.

"How is she now?" They were outside on the front porch, out of earshot.

"Better than earlier. She has to take it easy. If it keeps going like this, one day it won't come back down."

"What happens then?"

"The babies come out."

Barry was clueless about pregnant women, but even he didn't see Olivia lasting until January.

"Just so you know, I won't be around to check on her tomorrow," Lily said, rescuing him from the rabbit hole he had just fallen down. "I have another meeting with my attorney and then probably a realtor, followed by an afternoon in-service at the hospital. Olivia said she knew someone else who could take her blood pressure. She didn't mean you, did she?"

"No."

"Well, make sure she gets it checked. Take her to the doctor if you have to," Lily insisted.

"Did you bring that up with Olivia?" Like with Silas and the house rules, Barry needed a game plan.

"Her pressures are borderline, not quite at the tipping point yet, but she's probably not sharing all her symptoms. I know what she's doing. She's buying time. She knows as well as I do, if her pressure readings keep going up, her doctor won't hesitate to deliver the babies. They're viable, but still small. She wants to keep them inside of her as long as she can."

"At her own risk?"

Lily gave him an awkward shrug. "Hypertension is a leading cause of maternal mortality. You really don't want to hear this," she told him. His face told her she was right. "We need to take this one day at a time. The best thing you can do is take care of her tomorrow. Who's helping you with that?"

"She met a nurse today," Barry said.

Lily smiled. "Well, that's good."

"Not really."

Lily gave him a quizzical look.

"Long story," Barry said.

The look on his face told Lily that was all he would say. "When is Silas coming home?" she asked instead.

"Not sure."

"Well, maybe you should find out," Lily suggested. "Tomorrow is Halloween."

Chapter Twenty-Seven

"A demon was here," Rogan Poe said upon entering.

His eyes strayed to the mark on the floor as the flashback played for him. The smell of sulfur engulfed him while he watched the light show inside her house play out the night Jamie Smythe came for her. The priest stopped *It* by plunging his silver cross into Jamie's foot, giving them enough time to escape into the bathroom. Since demons were once angels, they were immortal. The best Olivia could do was drive out the demon. It's why she took out the host with a bullet.

"That was his greeting," Olivia said, shaking herself free. She had relived the experience as it played out for Poe.

"I can see that," Poe answered, his eyes moving around the room, landing back on her. "*It* visits frequently. Probably more so now," Poe said eyeing the baby bump. "*It's* watchful, to the point of hovering. Am I correct?"

"Yes."

She seemed hesitant, but at least she wasn't keeping it from him. They were off to a good start. "*It's* not here for your offspring. *It* would take them if you offered. But *It* can't, not without your consent. A demon on the property is a deterrent against our own kind. Unfortunately, you have more to fear from them in your condition."

"They would be unwise to come for my children," Olivia snapped back.

The tone in her voice sent a chill down Poe's back.

Olivia saw the look on his face no matter how quickly he tried to hide it. "I'm not sure where that came from," she admitted.

Poe reached out to touch her but stopped himself. "It's an awakening. Motherhood does that." He tried to smile but knew he wasn't doing a good job reassuring her.

"But that's not what you're here for," Olivia said. "My children are not what you seek."

"No," Poe replied softly, clearing his throat and the air between them.

Poe passed on her offer of something to drink, leading her over to the couch instead to get her off her feet. "Let me do this first, and then I'll get us something. I know my way around a kitchen."

Olivia imagined he knew his way around a lot of things.

"Your watcher's not here. I'm surprised." Poe said. He saw the blood pressure cuff, but he brought his own.

"I didn't tell him when you were coming," Olivia said.

Poe smirked at the comment but quickly slipped into nurse mode. "How are you feeling?" Poe asked over the ripping sound of the cuff.

Olivia eyed him carefully as he appraised her. "You tell me," she countered.

"From the history you gave me, this thing says you're borderline. But it's still early. I mean it. How do you feel? Headache, spots before your eyes, epigastric pain?"

Before she could answer, Poe reached over without warning and flipped up the light blanket covering the lower half of her body. With the folds of fabric, Poe could forget she was pregnant. Beneath the fuzzy pink blanket, her feet were bare. The yoga pants exposed her toned calves. His hand encircled her ankle as he scanned for hints of swelling, "Only a trace amount of edema. That's good."

"Better than yesterday. My toes looked like little smokies," Olivia said, shaking her foot free and flicking the blanket back in place. She looked into his face and couldn't help but stare. "What happened to your eyes? They were dark yesterday." The eyes staring back at her were crystal blue. She reached for his chin to bring him closer, and he reacted with a quick jerk beyond her grasp, but he didn't break eye contact.

"These are my eyes. I'm sure you've been told yours glow when you are angry or excited." Poe leaned back and watched hers dim. "They are subliminal signals we send each other. Pheromones are the trigger. It doesn't happen to all of us. Certain teas can help."

"Help with what?" Olivia wanted specifics.

"The flow of energy. Suppression from outside influences."

Olivia wondered if that was why she didn't feel him so much this morning. She told Barry it would improve with time, but until the demon triggered him, all she felt was a void. She had known Poe would find a way to control it. Olivia never imagined it would be like this. "The tea is what my Gran would call kitchen magic."

Poe gave her a lazy smile, and she felt a

reactionary spark. "For the not so gifted, yes. Most witches do their work in the garden or the kitchen. Others," he said, gazing at her, "are free to roam."

"What kind?"

"Of witch?" Poe wasn't sure she was ready for that discussion. He knew he wasn't.

"Tea," Olivia clarified.

"Hyssop. I had a cup this morning." He would definitely need another when he left. Good thing he stocked up after her visit yesterday.

"Hyssop is used for purification. Hyssop branches were dipped in lamb's blood to paint the doorposts of the Israelites so as not to incur God's wrath during the first Passover," Olivia repeated the story Gran told her.

"You know more than you claim. It also removes hexes or stops them from taking hold." He hoped.

"I mean you no harm." They were more words that came without warning.

Again, Poe resisted the urge to touch her. "Not intentionally. But in case you didn't notice, our energies were," he hesitated at what word to use. "Tangled, yesterday. I need that to stop. We can't work together if we're caught in some kind of tug of war. I'm sure it will be better once you're not in your condition." At least he hoped so.

Poe watched her slide her arm protectively over where her daughters nestled inside of her. "Dealing with three of you all at once is a little much. Even for me."

"So, they are gifted?" Olivia inquired.

"You know that already. They're strong, like their mother," Poe said with a glint in his eyes. "You will require help with them," he cautioned.

Olivia watched as he packed away the blood pressure cuff and stethoscope.

"Barry thought what was happening yesterday was something else." Olivia waited for Poe to explain.

"Let me guess, attraction? Desire?" Poe finished for her. The look in his eyes told her Barry wasn't wrong. Neither was she.

Olivia noticed the darkening of his eyes. "I have a husband," she told him. "Please tell me what this is." It sounded like a plea.

"Oh, I'm very aware of your husband." The bravado was gone, replaced only by repentance. "I can smell him all over this house. He's an alpha, probably more." Poe's eyes strayed to her midsection again. "Historically, gifted women like you being blonde, pale, and small in stature were preyed upon by predators, human and otherwise. They survived and ensured the bloodline was continued by using their charms to bond with an alpha male. An alpha-alpha is the best choice, but not as common. With those matches, a chemical connection is formed."

"Typically, those exposed to predators develop instincts that include a heightened sense of awareness," Olivia explained. "Could that explain the ability to sense evil?" she suggested. Poe seemed to ponder the question. Olivia wasn't sure if he was thinking or evading.

"Those experiences also induce intense feelings of fear and panic," Poe countered.

"Are you discounting my theory?" Olivia questioned him.

"I'm simply testing your hypothesis. Do you experience feelings of fear or panic?"

She considered not answering truthfully and wondered if he would know. "Not typically," Olivia admitted, watching Poe carefully for a reaction. Her answer seemed to confirm something he already knew. "But at the heart of it, aren't we all just animals?"

"Until we become something else. You're an evolution. A combination of many things." His eyes grew dark as he said it. She knew hers flashed in return. As much as he didn't like Barry, Poe almost wished the Watcher had stayed so he could, watch. Her and him.

"An evolution of what? What am I?" Olivia asked, rousing him from wherever he had gone.

Poe smiled, slow and measured, not mischievous like before. "Not now. We have to leave something to talk about another time."

"Tomorrow is never promised," Olivia said. Again, the words came out of nowhere. Maybe this was another side effect of being around Poe, but if he wasn't ready to talk about it, she wouldn't press him. He had his reasons. She sought him for guidance. She had to start letting him lead. Besides, there were other things she needed to know.

"So, when one of my kind crosses paths with another alpha male, like you." Olivia didn't finish her sentence, waiting for Poe to do it for her.

No doubt it made for bloody times. Poe decided to side-step the history lesson and focus on the positive. "I harbor no malcontent, but your energy is powerful, and seductive. Still, your husband, the infamous Agent Branch, has nothing to fear from whatever stirs between us. Your bond to your husband is strong. I can feel that, too. The only way to break it would be an unbinding ceremony or death. For me, drinking the tea will help.

Eventually it will even out."

What Poe didn't tell her was, she could break through his defenses even with the tea. They were meager in comparison to hers.

"How do you know all of this?" Olivia asked, feeling melancholy, missing something she never had. "Did your mémé teach you?"

Poe smiled at thoughts of his grandmother. "She did. I had to call her last night. Between her illegible handwriting and the fact it was written in French, I was having a hard time translating her recipe for the hyssop tea."

Olivia wished for one more conversation with Gran. She would tell her of Silas and her babies. "I think I'd like to meet her."

Mémé had never been more than fifty miles from her beloved Bayou. "She made the same request."

Olivia's face was a mix of confusion and delight. "She did?"

"You are a legend," Poe told her, but it was another story for another time. "Now, let me get you something to drink and you can show me those crime scene photos you promised. I brought you some chamomile tea, Mémé's recipe, if you allow it." Poe offered her his hand.

Olivia slipped her hand into his. "Of course."

Poe was surprised at her grip. She was small but powerful. She would be menacing with babies to protect.

"I trust you," she whispered.

His eyes went dark. "Your trust is not misplaced." Poe hoped it was a promise he could keep.

****

Barry and Brennon met with the city attorney, and Barry signed his career away. His retirement was secure along with a hefty sum to be paid in additional installments. Barry wasn't worried about his financial future. The way he lived, his retirement would have been enough. At the same time, a realtor was at his condo doing a video walkthrough for Isaac Kaine. After the signing, Barry took a detour with Brennon in tow. The attorney insisted on coming.

Amanda's service was held the afternoon before. Brennon had strictly forbidden him to attend. Her family needed their time to grieve. Ultimately, time was the only thing that could help find a resolution. Brennon cautioned him there might never be one. Amanda didn't leave a note, but the family had decided Barry was the reason. Learning she was pregnant only made things worse. There was nothing Barry could do. Not now, maybe not ever. Still, he had his own good-bye to say.

Barry brought with him a dozen orange tulips. They were Amanda's favorite. He thought they were pretty, but they never lasted long. Maybe that meant something. A symbol of some kind. Amanda never found what she was looking for, including life. It brought tears to his eyes at the waste. Barry bent down to lay them with the other flowers when he noticed another dozen identical to his. The tulips weren't something her family would have given. Like his, they arrived after the ceremony. Barry could tell by their freshness.

Brennon noticed them as well. "I did what you told me to do," Brennon said. "I told Preston you knew who the father was. It was after that they came back with the other offer." It didn't stop Brennon from suggesting they hold out for more, but Barry was done. The DA's swift response was the validation Barry needed. It was never about money.

Barry drove Brennon back to the condo where their morning began. Barry met him there after he picked up some more things, including the suit he was wearing. He had gotten it for his last court appearance. This was only his second time wearing it. Now, he didn't know when he would ever need it again.

Brennon suggested a celebratory lunch, but Barry passed. He wanted to get back to Olivia. Brennon shook his hand and rode the elevator up to the condo. The realtor was waiting.

****

The vehicle in front of the house caught his eye. It looked like a tank with four doors and big tires. Barry was debating on a closer look when he heard the front door open.

"The extra room makes moving easier. Pretty much everything I own fits in the back," a familiar voice said from the porch.

Barry steeled himself for the confrontation and redirected his path toward the house. Poe's jeans were nicer today. The t-shirt was gone, replaced by a sweater fitting for the cooler weather, but lightweight enough to show the rippling muscles beneath. When Poe wasn't taking care of people at the Alzheimer's Unit, he obviously spent time in the gym. He carried a little black pouch with him.

"What are you doing here?" Barry asked.

"Making a house call." Poe smiled. "Her pressures are borderline. I managed to keep her off her feet. If you can do the same, she might have a good day."

He sounded like Lily with the one-day-at-a-time plan. Poe made a move for the steps, but Barry took his position at the bottom, blocking his path. He didn't care if Poe was bigger and younger.

Poe caved first. "She called. I came. She's right about having a necromancer on her hands. Nasty business. I've never seen one outside the bayou. This one's just getting started, but she's only going to get better. If she's smart, she'll go to ground and hone her skills before making another appearance."

"We are talking about Rose Corey?" Barry confirmed. Olivia said she wanted to discuss Sheriff Tennent's case with Poe, but he had assumed they would do it together. He didn't like the way it made him feel knowing she met with Poe alone.

"Yes. I hope she's the only one."

"Is she still around?" Barry asked, thinking about the porch light incident.

"Depends on how many loose ends she needs to tie."

"And who is she loyal to now that Andre Roche is dead?" Barry pressed.

"I know Ms. Corey was found with Roche, but I told Olivia I think she may have mistaken who was the apprentice and who was the teacher."

Barry was lost. "How do you figure that?" Supposedly the Roches were into voodoo magic.

"I heard the theory on Roche's mother, but Corey is an interesting name, with roots in Salem. Giles Corey, a farmer, was accused of witchcraft. They tortured him by placing weighted rocks on his chest while they questioned him. Corey was the only man in America to die from 'pressing'. It took him three days, but he never entered a plea of any kind. If he had, his sons would not have inherited his lands. His apparition still walks the streets, just another type of walking dead. My guess is Rose came by her skills through the family tree. In my estimation, she has gone rogue."

Barry studied Poe. He believed him, but he wasn't going to say as much. After a few beers, Will Ibarra had told him about the scene at Tennent's place. Barry had seen photos for himself, but what got him was how Ibarra said the place made him feel. Barry had the same feelings for a place he had never been and a person he had never met. Poe's history lesson explained all those things. Rose was a threat. Not only to them but to the natural order of things.

"Something else you want to ask me?" Poe asked, snapping Barry out of his wanderings.

"So, this is how it's going to be? You're part of the gang, now?" Barry asked.

"I've always known she was here," Poe admitted.

"You've been here for two years. And you're just now coming around."

"That somehow makes me suspicious?" Poe's tone had an edge to it.

"It makes me curious. Why not stay the first time, when her gran died? Why come back?" Barry demanded.

"You think I'd tell you something I haven't told her?"

Maybe that was what Barry didn't like. Poe and Olivia were having conversations without him, about things he and Olivia had just discovered. Maybe he didn't want to share her with Poe.

"There was curiosity about what she would do not

working for the FBI. Then there was Jamie Smythe and then the barn. It was the incident that sealed the deal."

One night, one event changed all their lives.

"Is Sarah Larsin someone who's interested in Olivia?" Ana Lutz had said as much. Now Barry said it.

"She's one. Samael Knight is the other. Sarah answers to him. She might have left her little girl behind, but she'll never be free of the daughter she helped create. She is responsible for letting her go."

"And you. What do you get out of all of this? A fancy place for your grandmother to live? That fancy ride over there? How much did that set you back or is Sarah Larsin paying for that too? Or Samael Knight?" Both were shots in the dark, but Barry hoped to bait him. He had reread Poe's history the night before. He knew there was something bothering him. Regardless of what Olivia said about how lucrative travel nursing was, Poe seemed to have more outgo than income.

Poe's eyes darkened. "I'm a simple man. I travel light, no wife, no kids, no attachments. My ride, as you call it is a practicality in my situation and my one indulgence."

"What was the girl we saw leaving your apartment the other day?"

"A consenting adult. We're way more alike than you would like to admit," Poe challenged him.

Barry stiffened at the suggestion. The accusation hit too close to home.

"As for Samael Knight, I don't make deals with the likes of him. He's only a few steps away from Lucifer himself. And Sarah, there's no working with her without that abomination. As for my grandmother, she doesn't need to be living all alone in the swamp."

If not Sarah Larsin, then who enticed Poe back to San Antonio? "Where does your loyalty lie?" Barry asked.

"To the woman inside. I just had to meet her first. She had to accept me."

Barry advanced, climbing the steps to join Poe on the porch, not liking his words. Barry was about to say something about them when something else caught his attention.

"It's the eyes," Poe confessed. The lieutenant had noticed the darkness was gone, just like Olivia. "Don't tell me you haven't noticed how hers change with her moods?" Barry's stare never wavered. No doubt measuring his truthfulness. "I'm handling it." Poe reached into his pocket and dug out a small burlap sachet. He tossed it to Barry. "I even brought one for you."

Barry caught it and held it up to the light.

"Don't worry. It's just witch hazel bark. Keep it in your pocket. It eases grief over a lost love and reduces that passionate burn that keeps you up at night."

Barry noticed Poe pushing another one down inside his own pocket.

"I told you it was confusing…being a watcher," Poe told him.

"You don't know anything about me," Barry said, feeling angry all over again.

"I know you're one tough son-of-a-bitch to deal with her without some kind of magic."

"Then tell me, if she has a watcher, what does she need you for?"

"You should hope you never find out."

Chapter Twenty-Eight

His trip to Vegas was starting to feel like a waste of time. Silas never heard anything more from Deveroux after his morning text. Following his meeting with Agent Dennis, Silas received a phone call from Marco, Sarah Larsin's personal assistant, inviting him to meet with some of Rose's former coworkers at the strip club *Zoar* before opening.

Silas didn't see his mother-in-law. Instead, he spent his visit flanked by several scantily clad women who all were more than willing to talk about Rose Corey. They referred to her as a hostess and not a dancer. They also educated Silas on how the business worked. Technically, none of the girls were employed by Ms. Larsin. They were known as independent contractors, which left Ms. Larsin free from having to keep detailed employee records, an ideal situation for someone who wanted to fly under the radar.

Basically, the only thing Sarah Larsin was responsible for was not hiring girls who were under eighteen. Silas recalled from his briefing with SAPD that Rose's age was in question. Silas wondered if the girls had been coached to refer to Rose as a hostess. Sarah Larsin was a rule follower when it came to operating her business. The hostess job description was vague at best, other than escorting patrons to their tables. Given their jobs, Silas knew working on the side was a definite possibility. However, without having to ask, the girls were quick to say Ms. Larsin forbade them from seeing patrons outside the confines of the establishment. If the girls wanted to move up to something more than dancing, and they were over twenty-one *Delilah's Den* was always open.

As reported by both the FBI and local law enforcement, Silas got a firsthand show of how appreciative these employees were of their employer. Silas thought he knew why. Unlike most sex-driven businesses in Vegas, neither these girls nor the girls at *Delila's Den* were controlled by outside pimps. Independent contractor was a misnomer. Most owners partnered with pimps to monitor the merchandise, but not Sarah Larsin. The girls working for her had no pimps, which meant more freedom for them. Silas was smart enough to know that removing the pimp role left a vacancy that he didn't believe went unfulfilled. Silas guessed someone with close ties to Ms. Larsin filled it, probably Samael Knight. Not surprisingly, the girls were reluctant to talk about him, and Silas didn't press. Knight wasn't who he was looking for. At least not now.

No matter what was really going on, according to the girls, being with Ms. Larsin was far better than being anywhere they had been before. Their stories were eerily similar to Livie's. Growing up, these girls realized they were different. They never fit in until finding Sarah Larsin. Like Livie, they were looking for structure and understanding. Livie found hers hunting monsters. These girls entertained them or, in some cases, they were them.

The whole arrangement gave Silas a mob-type feel

or in more archaic terms indentured servant. Maybe that's what stroked Deveroux's radar. Silas could feel himself slipping down that shadowy rabbit hole if he spent too much time thinking about it. Whatever it was, according to these girls, they had it good.

As for Rose, she had come and gone over the last eighteen months, not an uncommon practice. Ms. Larsin's door was always open, especially to those she had worked with before. Apparently, Sarah had her own set of loyalties. Piecing together a timeline, Rose's first contact with Sarah Larsin would have occurred after the incident in Atascosa County, making Ana Lutz the likely connection.

None of the girls claimed to be close to Rose. She was too freaky even for them. One of their former workmates rented a room to her until she found Rose chanting over her dead cat. Rose admitted to killing it so she could bring it back to life. Silas asked about speaking with the roommate, but she'd split two months earlier, after the incident with Rose. That was also the last time any of them saw Rose.

The timeline confirmed what Silas already knew. Rose's grandmother was telling the truth when she said she had no idea of her granddaughter's whereabouts. The only missing piece was where Rose may have spent the last couple of months. Given her history, it could have been anywhere. Her mode of transportation between Nevada and Texas was also in question. The girls assured him any one of them could obtain altered identification given the type of clientele they came in contact with daily. Ms. Larsin would have frowned on that as well.

The uptake in activity and the dimming of the

lights told Silas he had spent more time there than he realized. Happy hour was approaching. "One last question," he said, as the girls stirred with the change in atmosphere. "What happened to the cat?"

The girl who introduced herself as Lolly Pop was the only one who stayed to answer. "It came back of course. Roni found it sitting at the end of her bed in the middle of the night. She said its eyes were red. She threw it out the window."

Escaping the dimly lit background and returning back into the desert sunlight, Silas felt immense relief the interview was over. The tickle of pheromones piqued his senses upon arrival, and while the girls paled in comparison to the wave surrounding his mother-in-law, Silas wondered if they were what wore him down. There was definitely some underlying force at work, natural or otherwise. Maybe that's why there were four of them. There was strength in numbers. As for Silas, at any other time in his life, he would have enjoyed himself immensely, but he believed being with Livie provided him some kind of armor. Her own mother had said he was under Olivia's spell. Maybe it wasn't merely a figure of speech. Or perhaps Sarah Larsin had wanted to test its strength.

Silas hit up the first convenience store he could find and indulged in an energy drink. Back in the car, with a clear head, he reached out to Will Ibarra on the status of the sheriff's case. There was little progress, other than Jim Tennet's body remained at the morgue with Meeks while the family bickered over who would claim it.

As far as Rose Corey was concerned, Will did have other information. Prints in the sheriff's truck as well as his abandoned car matched the unknown prints at his house. Comparing those to Rose's employment records at Barry's condo sealed the deal and solved a mystery of more unknown prints found at Dr. Amanda Greene's place. Some of Dr. Greene's neighbors reported sightings of a young girl matching Rose's description the week before Amanda's death. Amanda's family denied knowing anything about the girl. At the same time, they admitted they rarely spent time at Amanda's new home. In the weeks leading up to her untimely demise, they saw little of her. Amanda's excuse was she was working hard at her new job. Not only had her family been unaware of her pregnancy, but they also didn't know the real reason behind her departure from the lucrative practice where she had worked following the death of her husband, former Dallas police detective, Eric Greene.

During their conversation, Silas hoped Will would mention his supposed fast-track to the San Antonio field office, but he didn't. Silas knew Will was reluctant to relocate but had resigned himself to the inevitable. Personally, Silas would be happy if Will stayed in San Antonio...as would Livie. She hoped Will would eventually pop the question so he and Jessica could start making their own family. Family and friend building had become his wife's new passion.

On his way back to the hotel, Silas drove by Deveroux's condo after obtaining the address from Patrick. Deveroux's parking space was empty for the second time that day. Silas wondered what else the agent could be working on. He left a voicemail update for Patrick and ended his day with dinner alone in his hotel room where there would be no interruptions. Silas sent his thanks to Sarah Larsin and her staff, via a phone call back to Marco, but also heard nothing in return. Just like the silent Deveroux.

Silas woke up early, already feeling restless. Other than meeting his mother-in-law, the trip to Vegas had been a waste of time. He should be home.

Silas decided to surprise Livie and return early but was disappointed to learn the only available flights were later in the day. He might not make it home for trick-or-treating, but at least he would be there before Halloween was over.

Booking a flight home didn't satisfy Silas' restlessness. There were still too many empty hours ahead, and there was still something wrong in Vegas. Silas could feel it.

On his way to breakfast, Silas drove by Deveroux's place again. The gate was closed and with no one to tailgate inside, Silas was forced to pull forward and speak to the guard on duty. According to him, Deveroux moved out a month ago. For security reasons, he couldn't give out the new address, even if he had it. A flash of FBI credentials didn't change his mind.

Despite Deveroux's lack of a return call, Silas left a message with Patrick, requesting an updated location on Deveroux. Too anxious for breakfast, Silas opted for more coffee instead. While in line at the overcrowded coffee bar, Silas missed Marco's call. Ms. Larsin's assistant left a message with an invitation for a mid-afternoon meal with Ms. Larsin at *Delilah's Den*. Silas was weighing the benefits of saying goodbye to his mother-in-law, when Patrick called back.

"Okay, you've made enough noise that someone's listening. I relayed what you said about Deveroux's domicile, only to learn, he bought a house about a month ago in some new housing development outside of the city. Deveroux dubbed it his death house as he prepares for retirement. He filed the official paperwork about the same time. Anyway, Deveroux's team started calling and got his voice mail just like you. Now there's no answer and no phone signal. The cell phone has either been turned off, disabled, or is out of range. Either way, it doesn't bode well for the agent in question. This is what got him sent to rehab last time. He went on a bender and went radio silent. We're waiting to hear back on the phone's last known location."

The whole scenario heightened Silas' feeling of angst. "How long is that going to take?"

"Unsure. This is where I remind you to be careful of what you wish for. In the meantime, since you are the closest, we thought you might do a drive-by and welfare check. I'm sending you the address now. I'm warning you. Last time they found him passed out in his own piss and vomit. He had to go to the hospital for medical detox before rehab would take him."

"I thought you were blowing me off last night when you didn't call back," Silas said, hearing the ping on his phone signaling the arrival of the coordinates Patrick promised.

"Family obligations. My oldest, Allie had a basketball tournament. Given your genes I'm sure at least one of your girls will be an athlete. You'll learn how to triage. How is Olivia, by the way?"

"She told me the other day the babies are coming this year and not next."

"Two added tax deductions," Patrick tried to make

light of the news, still trying to adjust to the new family-oriented Silas Branch. "I'm surprised you made this trip at all."

Silas regretted he left Livie upset about the trip. He would make it up to her. "I couldn't resist the possibility of meeting my mother-in-law. It was important. Family. Future."

"Did you?"

"I did. It was brief, but enlightening."

Patrick was eager to hear, but Silas wasn't in a sharing mood. "Go find Deveroux and get yourself back home where you belong. Let me know what you find," Patrick told him instead.

****

The drive to Deveroux's chosen retirement home was a familiar one. Silas made it not two days ago when he checked out *Delilah's Den*. The close proximity was a coincidence not lost on Silas. He decided to call Marco back and tell him he accepted Sarah's lunch invitation. He might as well, seeing he was going to be in the area.

Deveroux's neighborhood was still in the development stage with lots of construction and several houses in varying degrees of assembly. Silas followed the GPS commands and stopped at the entrance. With only a handful of streets, he had no trouble finding Deveroux's address. Deveroux's mailbox was up and marked. In the driveway sat the standard Bureau sedan Silas had been tracking for days.

Silas turned in the cul-de-sac at the end of the block and pulled alongside the curb to the closest completed but empty house. He watched Deveroux's place before proceeding. The house to the immediate left was still under construction but looked near completion. There were various vans in front that looked like flooring and cabinet makers. The house on the other side of Deveroux's place looked occupied. Two houses down, a white non-descript van that looked like it could double for surveillance or home improvement piqued Silas' interest. He let it go. For all, he knew it could belong to the Bureau looking for their rogue agent.

Silas pulled out his phone and made one last attempt at telephone contact. Nothing. He pocketed the phone, checked his gun, and headed up the driveway. The dust on the car told him it hadn't moved in at least a day, but it was hard to tell in a desert. The car was in the farthest spot from the front door, making Silas wonder if there wasn't another vehicle parked inside. The garage door was solid, without windows, so he couldn't get a visual. There was one large window in the front of the house, with the inside shutters closed tight. No one answered the door.

A privacy fence was up, and the gate was closed but not locked. Silas tried not to disturb the freshly sodded backyard. The back windows were shuttered like the ones in the front. Silas headed for the covered patio with a sliding glass door. The blinds on it weren't closed all the way. The disarray he saw inside had nothing to do with a recent move-in and everything to do with why he was here. Just like the gate, the door wasn't locked.

The smell hit him, making his eyes water as he surveyed the carnage. The scene reminded Silas of the sheriff's house. The room was full of bloody footprints that shouldn't be there. With the nose of his gun leading the way, Silas was just beginning to process what he was seeing when he smelt something else. Instinct took over and he fled to the door, the roar behind him filling his ears as a blast of heat stung his neck.

As the darkness reached out to grab him, Livie was all he saw. Silas knew their first night together on his couch would be a memory he would carry for the rest of his life.

The stark crimson lace against her pale skin. Her rapid breaths. The rise and fall of her breasts as she leaned in closer. Silas had never seen anything he wanted more.

The glow of her green eyes as she bent down to kiss him was the last thing Silas saw before his world faded to black.

Chapter Twenty-Nine

Olivia woke from her nap with her heart pounding. She slid her hand to the tightening in her side. She lay there, waiting for the contraction to pass. When she could breathe easily again, she sat up, trying to make sense of the jumbled images in her head. She reached for her phone and called Silas.

While Olivia was doing that Barry caught sight of movement outside the house. Twice in ten days, law enforcement had shown up unannounced. The sight of Jon Sharpe heading up the walk gave Barry an immediate sense of dread. He opened the door before the agent could knock.

Olivia didn't get off the couch, but Barry heard her plant her feet on the floor. She had been restless since she woke. Sensing her mood, Barry ditched his plan to discuss Rogan Poe. Something was wrong, but he didn't have the chance to get it out of her before the FBI arrived.

"Why didn't Patrick call me?" Olivia asked after Agent Sharpe's greeting.

"He knows Silas is out of town. The Director thought a check-in wouldn't be a bad thing. Professional courtesy and all." Sharpe attempted a smile but couldn't finish it.

"I don't believe you. Patrick and I used to work together. He knows he can call me."

"He didn't want to alarm you." The agent linked his hands in front of him.

Olivia assumed it was because he didn't know what else to do with them. "What do you think showing up here is doing? Why are you here?" Olivia asked again.

"When was the last time you talked to Silas?" Sharpe replied with his own question.

Olivia's eyes narrowed, trying to glean what she could out of him without invading his thoughts. "Who wants to know? Patrick or the Bureau?"

Sharpe's eyes shifted away from her and to the right. It meant he was accessing his imagination and not his memory. Was he trying to decide what answer she wanted? If he had to choose, she already knew the answer, so she saved him the trouble.

"I have no doubt Patrick is the one who asked you to come here, so you're not lying. If it was just Patrick asking, however, he could have done that himself," Olivia explained.

The agent sighed. He knew leading with anything other than the truth wouldn't work. All he could do was deflect. "The Director wants to know how long it's been since you last talked to Silas," Sharpe rephrased.

The mention of a timeline confirmed something was wrong. Olivia's hand went back to her side, feeling her muscles tighten again. "I haven't spoken to Silas since last night." She purposefully kept out the part about only getting his voicemail every other time she called. "Just tell me what's going on. I know how this works."

Barry noted the change in her voice. She was also pressing her side. She had been doing it since the agent arrived, maybe before.

Sharpe's unease returned.

"Don't make me ask you again," Olivia cautioned.

Her words sounded like the hiss Barry heard in Poe's apartment. At least she was speaking English this time.

Sharpe cracked. "Silas has been trying to track down Mason Deveroux since he got to Vegas. The address he had for Deveroux was wrong. Director Monahan gave Silas the new one. It's about an hour outside of the city. Silas hasn't checked in and he's not answering his cell. That was almost three hours ago."

Olivia felt short of breath as much from Sharpe's confession as the continuing pain in her side. She also felt the beginnings of a headache. Maybe it was the same one she had when she went to sleep. Barry must have noticed because she saw him making his way to her when Sharpe's pocket buzzed.

The agent saw a chance for escape and fled to the front porch.

Olivia intercepted Barry's advance with her phone. Dr. Tammy Murdoch's name was on the screen. "Call and tell them I'm having contractions. They're not stopping like last time. And I have a headache."

Barry hit the number and stepped aside to make the call.

Jon returned and surrendered his phone to Olivia.

"Livie. It's Patrick." He knew it was a gamble sending Sharpe over there, but he was buying time and looking for information. Learning Silas had booked a plane reservation home that morning gave him hope Livie could share some light on his whereabouts. But according to what Sharpe just told him, the trip home must have been a surprise.

"Sorry, if I worried you, but Deveroux is MIA. Silas went to check on him. I'm told the cell reception out there can be spotty."

"Get to the point, Patrick. I'm not in the mood." Her words were clipped as the tightness spread across her belly.

"Maybe I was premature in sending Agent Sharpe. I just got some good news. It looks like Silas is at Deveroux's house."

Olivia closed her eyes and concentrated on slow, even breaths. "Meaning you found his car. But not Silas." No return call from her husband told her that much.

Patrick should have known better than to think he could fool her. "Las Vegas agents are on their way to assist. Now, tell me what I can do for you."

"Find my husband and tell him I need him to come home."

"He has a flight scheduled later this evening." It was a false hope. Right now, it was the only kind Patrick had to offer.

Olivia didn't hear his answer. She was too busy watching the fluid pool on the floor at her feet. "Tell him to hurry."

****

Agent Dennis had to walk away to make the call. Otherwise, his caller wouldn't be able to hear anything he had to say.

"Tell me something," Patrick Monahan demanded.

"It's chaos." It was an understatement. The whole place looked like a warzone. Dennis knew what one looked like. He had been to one in another place full of sand. "The street is on lockdown while the local gas company makes sure the lines are shut down. We're waiting on them for the all-clear. My partner called for air support so we can get our own set of eyes. The lieutenant on sight did confirm, however, Deveroux's place is ground zero."

"Shit."

"Shit is right," Dennis agreed. "I don't know how long it will be before we can get in there."

"Any casualties, so far?" Patrick asked.

"A dog." Dennis heard some guys saying it looked like some kind of trauma to the throat but disregarded it as not pertinent to their situation. Their stakes were higher. "I know you are worried about your guy. I had lunch with him yesterday. I like him. From what I'm looking at, we better hope neither he nor Deveroux was inside that house."

****

Lily was waiting for them in Labor and Delivery. Her in-service session had just ended when Barry called. A nurse and a woman, Barry assumed was Dr. Murdoch, whisked Olivia into a room. Lily followed them while telling him to wait in the hall, explaining they would be doing some kind of an exam he didn't want to see.

Barry watched the parade of people in and out of Olivia's room until they all blurred together. Barry wasn't sure how long he waited, but whatever it was, was too long. He was about to say to "hell with it" and barge into Olivia's room when he heard a voice behind him demanding to see Dr. Osborne.

The Labor and Delivery department was a locked unit relying on an intercom system and a secured entry.

Kind of like a prison. The girl manning the door told the caller he would have to wait. Barry went over and told her to let him in, Dr. Osborne was expecting him. Barry didn't even care that he was here. He couldn't do this alone.

Rogan Poe rushed through the door, ignoring the girl who attempted to usher them around the corner out of the way. Poe's eyes were focused on the door behind Barry. A woman emerged with another one on her heels. The one in the front had to be the doctor. Rogan Poe sidestepped Barry and blocked her path.

The doctor surveyed the two men, not finding the one she wanted. "Where's Agent Branch?" Dr. Murdoch asked.

"Not here," Poe replied.

The doctor eyed his scrubs, looking for a name tag, but didn't find one. "Who are you?"

"Rogan Poe, friend of the family."

Dr. Murdoch looked at Barry. "Are you Lieutenant Bartholomew?"

Barry barely had a chance to nod before Poe interrupted.

"How is she?" Poe's tone was laced with concern disguised as demand.

"Hello, I'm Dr. Murdoch," she said, pausing a beat, letting Poe catch up to the fact she was the one in charge. "Olivia asked me to speak to both of you. We verified her water did break. She is in active labor and her blood pressure is severely elevated." Dr. Murdoch eyed the scrubs again. Barry had seen cops do the same, looking for common ground. "In an ideal situation, I would like to hold off on delivery for at least twenty-four hours."

"My patients are at the other end of the life spectrum," Poe explained. "I'm out of my depth here. What happens if you can't?"

"This isn't an ideal situation. If I can't bring down her pressures, soon, we'll have no choice but to deliver. Any idea when her husband is going to get here?"

The phone in Barry's pocket began to buzz. It was Olivia's. He saw Patrick Monahan's name on the screen. "Give me a minute."

Dr. Murdoch headed for the desk while Barry walked down the empty hall, leaving Lily and Poe in his wake. At least Poe stayed put.

"Livie, what's going on?" The voice sounded strained.

"This isn't Livie," Barry replied.

"Lieutenant Bartholomew? Agent Sharpe said you were with her. I sent him back to her house, but she's not there," Patrick Monahan explained.

"We're at the hospital. The babies are coming. Where is Silas?"

The pause on the other end was too long. "I'm sorry to hear that. I called to check on her because she didn't sound good."

Barry's gut clenched at the attempt to stall. "I'm sure she would feel better knowing where her husband is."

"About that. I'm actually glad you answered the phone."

****

Barry never thought he could feel such emotion for a man he had spent so much time despising. He took a moment to compose himself before he turned back around. There was just Poe.

"Your girlfriend went back in to be with Olivia. Where is Agent Branch? Why isn't he here already?" Poe managed to sound judgmental and demanding all at the same time.

Barry put his hand up as if that would somehow deter Rogan Poe. "He's been in Vegas the last few days."

"He's what?" Poe didn't even try to keep his voice down. "He left her? Now?"

"Look, I don't have time for you to have a meltdown or whatever this is. He's not here and that's the bottom line."

To his credit, Poe took it down a notch.

Barry watched him sort through his emotions and relax his shoulders. "When is he going to get here?" Poe's words were measured as if he had run them through some sort of filter before they left his mouth.

Barry hated the next part. It was just him and Poe and there was no way around it. It was like some sort of survival test. Barry took a breath of his own. They needed Olivia here as the intermediary. "There's been an accident. Silas was checking on a missing agent. By the time the other agents arrived, the place was on lockdown. There was some kind of explosion. They found Silas' rental car, but there's no sign of him."

Poe closed his eyes while he practiced more measured breathing. His face was unreadable. "Is Agent Branch dead and they just don't want to tell you?"

It wasn't something Barry had considered. He couldn't. Not now. "No one knows. They can't get inside." Out of the corner of his eye, Barry saw Dr. Murdoch approaching. He took the lead this time because Poe was still processing. And he needed this conversation to end.

"Agent Branch isn't going to make it back," Barry said before she could speak.

Dr. Murdoch looked alarmed. "What exactly does that mean?"

"He's missing," was all Barry could say.

"I don't care what kind of lies you have to tell, but no one tells her," she warned. "I've been watching the monitor. From the looks of her pressures, delivery isn't far away So, which one of you is going to take his place?" She asked looking at Poe.

He looked to Barry. "It has to be you."

The door swung open again. It was Lily. "Olivia wants her phone." Lily held her hand out to Barry while Dr. Murdoch slipped back inside.

Poe intercepted the handoff. "Someone needs to be with her for this," he said and followed the doctor.

Lily opened her mouth but closed it again when she saw the text alert on her own phone. "They're getting prepped for delivery," Lily told Barry, her mind already racing ahead to what she needed to do. "I told the NICU and Olivia that I would stay. They gave a lot of people the night off to be with their kids since it was Halloween. No one was prepared for a twin delivery tonight."

Lily reached for Barry, and he wrapped his arms around her. She gripped him tighter. "Who is that guy and where is Silas?"

"Rogan Poe, her nurse friend. And no one knows."

****

Poe watched Olivia as Dr. Murdoch laid out the plan. She didn't cry. She just accepted it. Once it was just the two of them, she asked for her phone. He asked her if she wanted to be alone to make the call. It was only then she started to cry.

Olivia struggled to keep her voice steady. "Silas Branch. If I have learned anything about faith, it's that there are no endings. Not real ones anyway. Just new beginnings. We can do this. Whatever is asked of us. Our daughters, our family, they are the most precious gifts anyone has ever given me, and you did that. You. I love you so much. Never forget. Ours is a merciful God."

It was the last coherent conversation Olivia had as Dr. Murdoch pushed meds and dulled her senses. Poe didn't leave her side. He stayed with her while Barry left to change into scrubs.

Will Ibarra was waiting at the nurses' station. He flashed his badge to gain entrance.

"I'm here for you, brother." Will pointed to the waiting room wanting Barry to know he wasn't alone. "I couldn't keep Kim away, and Jess is on her way."

Barry nodded.

"How are things?" It was a simple question, but Will knew sometimes, in these situations, those were the best.

Barry handed him his phone. "Do me a favor and call the Archbishop. I can't bring myself to do it."

Will passed Barry the phone as he came back by. "He's coming. We'll be waiting for him."

Barry couldn't speak. All he could do was nod.

He slipped back into Olivia's room to find Poe on his knees at her bedside, his head bowed to the hand he held. "*Mon allégeance est à vous et ceux que vous aimez. Une vie pour une vie. Une âme pour une âme.*" There were tears in his voice.

It sounded like French. Barry wanted to ask him what the words meant, but the room flooded with nurses.

They were out of time.

Chapter Thirty

Olivia was seizing by the time they got to the operating room.

Both Olivia and Silas missed the birth of their daughters, but the girls were not alone. Barry stood witness as Genevieve and Gwendolyn Branch came into the world just after midnight as All Hallows Eve surrendered to All Saints Day.

****

"You should never have left them," Poe said, his voice a sharp whisper. He had already gotten "the look" from the nurse across the hall. Poe knew what it meant. He had used the same cautionary glare more than a few times in his career. The nurse was considering how hard it would be to get him to leave.

"How am I supposed to know what a code pink means?" Barry snapped.

Poe stood up slowly, forcing Barry to look up at him, using his presence to intimidate, a useless tactic. Silas Branch had done the same thing.

"Keep your voice down. People are dying." Death was coming. Poe could feel it. He tried to shake it, but he couldn't push past it. He told himself it was his surroundings.

"Look, I know you don't like it, but one of us has to stay and one of us has to go." Poe's eyes traveled past the lieutenant to rest on the woman they were both trying to protect. She was too still and too pale despite the blood they were pumping into her veins. Due to multiple complications during her cesarean section, the doctor elected to keep her intubated. Barry was staring at her, willing her to wake up. She looked more dead than alive.

Poe reached down and grabbed Barry's wrist holding it up so he could see the wristbands the hospital gave him, one for each baby. "These are your free pass into the NICU," Poe reminded him.

Barry seemed to snap out of it. "It has to be me," Barry conceded.

Poe lowered himself back into the chair next to the bed, resigned to wait. Barry bet he was good at waiting. He was a good soldier.

Glad to leave Poe behind, Barry headed for the elevators with a nurse on his heels. She caught him at the double doors, outside Poe's view.

"You're leaving him here?" she asked, sounding desperate.

"I have to check on the babies," Barry insisted.

"Now?"

Barry heard the implication in her voice. He had just come from the NICU. He only left because they kicked him out. Barry neglected to tell Poe that part. "We heard the code pink. He's a nurse. He told me what it means," Barry explained. It wasn't just Poe. There was another meaning in the nurse's words, one Barry didn't want to think about. He couldn't go there, or he would never leave.

"The code pink alarm goes off for babies in Labor and Delivery and Post-Partum. There must be dozens of babies down there. It doesn't mean it came from the

NICU or was even your babies."

Barry didn't bother to correct her. He was there when they were born. Genevieve and Gwendolyn were the closest things he would ever have to children of his own. Already he felt the same protectiveness for them as he felt when he met Olivia. It felt like a transference. Especially now that Poe was here. He was the one looking out for Olivia now.

"Rogan Poe's name is not on the list," the nurse said, changing tactics.

Poe made the cut when they were in Labor and Delivery, but for whatever reason, he fell off the list when Olivia was transferred to the ICU following her emergency c-section. Maybe because Barry had been the one to accompany her. The hospital was big on protocol, which was a good thing, but not now.

"He's an old friend of the family." Barry could tell the nurse didn't believe him. "I vouch for him. Your patient would vouch for him if she could. Right now, you should throw the list out the window."

Lost in a sea of emotion, wanting to stay but needing to go, Barry went with the familiar. On reflex, his hands moved to his hips. It was his go-to move to get what he wanted, but the badge and gun were gone. Barry wondered how long it would take him to remember that.

"Someone has to go check on the babies and that's me." He held up the NICU entry bracelets as a show of good faith.

The nurse didn't waver. "We have an excellent NICU," she repeated. "Her babies couldn't be in better hands. There's nothing you can do for them. Let the staff do their job. She needs you more."

Since his tough guy stance wasn't working, Barry tried the truth. "That's why Rogan Poe stays. I don't want her to wake up alone."

If she wakes up... Barry saw the unspoken words in the nurse's eyes and turned his back on her, determined to walk away. He didn't get very far.

"The neurologist is on his way. He's going to want to talk to her husband." It was her final plea.

Barry stopped in his tracks, took a deep breath, and turned back around. "That's not me."

The nurse swallowed. "Where is he?"

Good question. "Not here," Barry said, using Poe's words.

****

Barry had to pass through two secure doors, to get where he was going. The first stop was through Labor and Delivery, the way he had come in hours ago. By now they knew who he was and waved him on. From the looks of things, there was a flurry of activity. He assumed it had to do with the code pink since the Neonatal Intensive Care Unit was just down the hall. Hospitals, like law enforcement, loved their acronyms. They knew him there too, but they kept him waiting in the ante-room. Barry grabbed a gown and put it on, feeling like he was entering a crime scene. He stopped at the sink and started the hand scrub they taught him hours before.

Lily appeared after the nurse who had let him in scurried out of sight. "What are you doing here?" Lily was whispering just like Poe. It must be a nurse thing.

The huddle where he left Genevieve and Gwendolyn caught his eye, and he ignored the question. "What's going on?"

"We have more deliveries pending. The full moon is bringing them in droves." Lily saw him tense despite the bulky paper gown.

"You didn't answer my question," Barry snapped, resisting every instinct he had to barge in and take control. The pained look on Lily's face snapped him back to this world, the one that wasn't his.

Lily laid her hand on his arm, ensuring he remained in place. "It's Genevieve."

She was the oldest, the one Olivia referred to as her sun baby. "What about her?"

"It's her eyes. They're freaking people out. They're violet and I swear to God they glow when she gets excited."

All Barry could think of was how Olivia's eyes changed. "What does that mean?" Whatever it was, it couldn't be normal.

"You want the scientific version or the paranormal one?" Lily let out a strained laugh.

"Scientifically what does violet mean?" Barry had a bad feeling already.

"Albinos have violet eyes, but that's not it. She has no other characteristics. It's why the neonatologist called in his partner for a second opinion."

"What's the paranormal one?" Barry asked.

Lily shifted from one foot to the other. "It's Halloween. People like to tell tales."

"Tell me those tales," Barry insisted no matter how uncomfortable she looked.

"Violet eyes are a sign of spirit people, or witches. There's also something called the Genesis myth. Those born with violet eyes are said to be mutants; full of vitality and abnormally long lifespans." Lily watched him looking for any reaction that told her he might know what she was talking about. She found none.

"Ross tried to tell me about Olivia. Like everything else he said, I thought they were lies. Until I found that black thing in my shower. I shot at it, but what did Olivia do? She called a priest. I've been reading her family history. Her past includes more than just an ancestor from Salem. Genevieve's eyes are the way they are because of Olivia." Lily told him.

"Her daughters are special, like she is," Barry confirmed. "Don't try to understand it. Not now."

"Is that why that man is here? Rogan Poe? What is he?" Lily asked.

"He has gifts, too. Not the same as Olivia, but he understands the dangers."

"Danger of what? Who's in danger? You don't mean?" Lily looked over her shoulder toward Olivia's daughters. The lights were dim behind her because the place never slept. "Who would they be in danger from?"

"Who or what," Barry said struggling with his own answer. "I'll explain everything later, I promise," he assured her. "Tell me about the code pink. Poe said it means an infant abduction." All along Barry hoped he was wrong, but he could tell by Lily's reaction he wasn't.

"It was just a drill," she said.

She sounded like a nurse. Barry had been here long enough to know that usually meant there was no good answer. "I don't believe you."

"We have them sometimes." Lily didn't look at him as she said it.

Barry had grown used to her looking at him. When

she didn't, he noticed. If she was going to play nurse, then he was going to play cop. "But probably not in the middle of the night," he suggested. "Something triggered that alarm." Like it or not, Rogan Poe was right to send him down here.

"Hear me out," Lily insisted seeing the look on his face. "Every baby gets an ankle monitor."

"That part I know," Barry told her. He vaguely recalled some nurses explaining the process in the delivery room. Each monitor had a built-in sensor that went off when the baby got too close to an exit, but there was too much going on for him to listen. He probably only remembered that much because it made him think of parolees.

"Each baby is assigned a number," Lily explained. "When the sensor is activated, it flashes across all the computer screens like the missing persons alerts you get on your phone."

"So, which baby sounded the alarm?" Barry asked again.

"It didn't have to be a real baby," Lily told him.

"Not a *real* baby?" Barry snapped before he could stop himself. He was too tired for this.

"You've heard of 'ghosts in the machine'? Sometimes we have a random, out of date number that pops up. It must have been one of those," Lily said with confidence. "That must be why they called administration." She squeezed his arm. She had been gripping it the whole time. "That's how I know it wasn't real," she whispered.

Lily was bobbing her head up and down like he was supposed to go along with her. She flashed the same smile she had used all week to seduce him. This time he was immune. She didn't know him well enough to know how his world worked. There were no coincidences. "Can anyone confirm anything you've just told me?" Barry asked.

"You're making this sound like a crime."

"It's the way I think." Lily was back to looking at him, but her eyes weren't as soft this time, and the smile had faded. Maybe he was scaring her. Barry couldn't worry about that right now. He fumbled under the gown to get to the phone on his hip.

"You're going to have to wash your hands again," Lily scolded him.

Barry ignored her while he fired off a text. When he was done, he looked up to see the doctors still huddled around the babies. "They're probably going to be here awhile, aren't they?"

Lily nodded. Her arms were crossed, closing herself off from him. He had scared her.

"Text me when they're done. I'll be back," Barry said, pulling at the yellow paper gown he had just put on.

Lily stood by, looking numb. "I told you it's probably nothing. Just a computer glitch."

"I can't take that chance," Barry said.

****

Barry knew he had made a lot of mistakes in his life, but selecting Will Ibarra to take Mark Austin's place wasn't one of them. Will was young, and he was tech savvy—all the things Barry wasn't. Will was still at the hospital, supporting him as any good partner did.

Barry found Will just where he said he would be—huddled in a corner of the almost deserted cafeteria. Kim was with him. Not far away was the Archbishop.

Barry felt minimally guilty getting the seventy-something year-old-man out of bed. Poe wasn't happy about it either, but their reasons were different. Barry needed the Archbishop here if things went bad. The Archbishop didn't look like a man who minded the late hour. He came dressed in a simple priest's frock and was at his own table listening to a hospital employee who looked like could use some guidance.

Barry slid into the empty seat across from Will and Kim where Will had a steaming cup of coffee waiting for him. "I stopped them before they could throw it out. It's old and has been cooking awhile, just the way you like it," Will said trying to break the solemness of the moment. Barry had already texted him about the possibility of a security threat.

Barry rehashed what he knew about the code pink. "Does this *ghost in the machine* theory sound plausible to you?"

Will shrugged. "Technology is great, until it isn't. That theory sounds like old-school problems to me. Not something you would find here in this hospital." Will had a lot of time on his hands. He had researched the hospital, realizing Olivia couldn't have found a better place to deliver. "They have a state-of-the-art NICU. Doesn't make sense they would be using some outdated system. It also begs the question, why would someone decide that tonight is a good time for a drill?" Will asked using air quotes on the word drill to make a point. "But, hey what do I know?"

"They wouldn't." It was Kim. She was so quiet Barry almost forgot she was there. "I just went through a mandatory safety in-service at my job. Alzheimer units have similar patient monitors because those patients like to wander. It's a common symptom. Every monitor has a number just like you said, but once it's on the patient, whoever put it on them is required to label it in the system with either the patient room number or name. Otherwise, when the alarm sounds and the monitors start flashing, how are you supposed to know which patient is in danger? I'm not a nurse yet, and even I know that. Whoever gave you that information doesn't know what they're talking about. If you don't believe me, ask Poe. He'll tell you." Kim stood up and stretched. "The grill is open. Anybody want anything?" she asked.

Barry and Will both shook their heads in silence.

"It's easy to forget she's a kid," Barry said once Kim was out of hearing distance.

"She has a point," Will said. "It sounds like something that should be looked into. What do you want me to do?"

"Find someone in security. Talk to them and see where it leads. Talk to someone in administration if you have to. Lean on them like the FBI agent you're meant to be," Barry said. "I want answers." Barry also knew he wouldn't be the only one. Rogan Poe wasn't going to like hearing any of this, and Barry didn't want Poe taking matters into his own hands. Despite what he felt hours ago, Barry couldn't afford to have Poe get kicked out of the hospital.

Will watched Barry withdraw into his shell, the one he used like armor. "Hey, I didn't tell you, but I got my assignment already. After my training at Quantico, I'll be coming back here."

Barry was glad to hear the news, but it also reminded him of something else. He had given Will

Olivia's phone. He didn't want to ask, but he wanted to know.

"No news," Will told before he had to ask. It was the elephant in the room.

Barry wasn't sure if the old adage, "no news is good news" applied. It was after midnight in Vegas as well. Who knew if they were still searching or waiting for the sun to come up. Barry pushed aside thoughts of Silas. He had to turn that part of this nightmare over to Patrick Monahan. The BAU director had informed him that he would be taking the red-eye from Washington to Vegas to oversee the recovery operation. The last time they spoke, Patrick promised he would come to San Antonio to deliver bad news to Olivia if it came to that. No matter Patrick's promise, Barry knew he would be the one left to pick up the pieces. He couldn't think about that, either.

Barry stared off, lost in other thoughts, but Will still needed answers.

"So, before I go lean on hospital security, do you want to tell me where you got your information? I think you should also ask yourself if the person who gave you faulty information did so because they didn't know or because they didn't want you to know."

Chapter Thirty-One

Agent Dennis met Patrick Monahan at the airport, using the drive time to update him on the recovery progress or the lack thereof.

"Still nothing?"

"They spent the night containing the fire. Deveroux's house is a total loss. There was damage to the adjacent dwellings as well," Agent Dennis explained.

"Casualties?"

"None that we know of, except someone's dog. Only one of Deveroux's neighbors was home. It blew out their windows and those of Agent Branch's rental car. The only reason it wasn't worse is most of the area is still under construction."

"Cut to the chase, when are we going to know?" Patrick asked what Agent Dennis was avoiding.

"No one's been inside yet, they're waiting for the heat to die down enough for a safety assessment. Deveroux's new home was ground zero. Hopefully, they can get in there today. So far all I have is there was a non-descript white van seen leaving the scene just after all hell broke loose. Maybe your agent hitched a ride somewhere."

Without contacting his pregnant wife? A text message from Lieutenant Bartholomew giving him an update on the happenings in San Antonio was the first thing to light up Patrick's screen as soon as he turned his phone back on after touch down. Silas Branch was now a father to tiny baby girls and his wife was in the ICU. The news only upped the ante. Patrick knew he should text back, but he couldn't. Not until he found Silas.

"We should start calling local hospitals," Patrick heard himself say.

****

Poe found Barry in the hospital chapel. "Did you come here because you wanted to be alone or because this is where you thought she would go?"

Barry stiffened at the intrusion. It was annoying how this guy got under his skin and inside his head.

Poe didn't wait for an answer. "Just so you know, she wouldn't come here."

Barry kept his focus ahead and not behind.

"You think because she follows the light, she worships at the altar?" Poe shook his head even though Barry wasn't looking. "She probably hasn't set foot in a church in years. She probably can't. Even if she wanted to. It's too uncomfortable; physically, I mean. All the emotions."

Barry let out a heavy sigh and turned around to find Poe with his arms spread, resting on the back of the pew. He had quite the wingspan. He also looked as haggard as Barry felt. At least Poe was human. "You're telling me Olivia is allergic to church?"

Poe didn't answer, just gave a little shrug.

The man had succeeded in disturbing his peace, yet now he was radio silent. "I came here because I figure if there are demons there must be angels," Barry confessed. He also came here to be alone before he had to deal with Poe again. Barry wasn't praying, although maybe he should be. He was just waiting for his thoughts to settle. A chapel seemed like the most peaceful place to do it. Barry couldn't remember the last time he prayed. Not even when Mark died. It was too late when he found him.

"They all started the same. I think people forget demons were once angels," Poe said. "If you really want to know, the angels are scarier than the demons in an unwavering zealot kind of way. They are single minded and without mercy." Poe wondered if it was because the angels had seen God's wrath.

"You sound like you like them even less than the demons," Barry commented.

Again, Poe shrugged. "At least you know where you stand with the angels. Demons are always willing to make a deal." They had received God's wrath, but they had survived. They knew deals were possible. Poe was feeling philosophical. Maybe it was the chapel.

In an uncharacteristic move, Poe reached out and touched Barry on the shoulder. "Be careful what you pray for," Poe warned him. He started to slide down the pew and slip away. Barry wondered where Poe was going. The Archbishop was at Olivia's bedside so she wasn't alone.

Barry paved the way for the Archbishop with a phone call to the ICU nurses' station. Apparently, it didn't matter that he wasn't on the list. Barry didn't know if it was because of who he was or because that meant the staff could rid themselves of Poe for a while. Barry hoped Poe wasn't on his way to kick him out.

"What's that supposed to mean?" Barry asked, delaying Poe's departure.

"They won't answer your prayers. The angels won't come for her." Poe was mater-of-fact.

"You have no faith?" Barry challenged him. "I heard you praying over her—something in French."

"It wasn't a prayer. It was a vow," Poe confessed. "My allegiance is to you and those you love. A life for a life. A soul for a soul. Those were the words I said to her. It's not about faith. It's about balance. It's why I said I had to meet her first."

Poe's eyes narrowed as he studied Barry. "After all this time, you still have no idea what she is, do you?" The men in robes had done her watcher no favors.

Father Dominic and the Archbishop had confirmed Pittman's story and taught Barry how he became a watcher, but they had not addressed Olivia's role or why or how she was the way she was. Barry assumed it was her ancestor in Salem, but looking into the bottomless pools of Poe's eyes, Barry realized the holy men had been holding out on him. And then he remembered something Lily had said. Before he could answer, Poe started talking.

"Her kind is rare." Unpredictable was the word Mémé used, but Poe wasn't inclined to share, not all at once. "She gets to walk on both sides of the lines, between this world and the other. Temptation is great. Why do you think she needs a watcher?"

Barry wasn't ready to hear what Poe had to say, at least not about himself. "What usually happens to her kind? Is she rare because there aren't many or because of something else?"

Poe shrugged indiscriminately. "Haven't you read history? And I don't mean what happened in Salem. That was a tea party compared to the real thing centuries before. Do you have any idea what happened to people with her abilities? Thumbscrews, quartering, hosting a funeral pyre, only it's lit while you're still alive. And that was only for the ones they caught. I have to believe the skillful ones, like her, were never found. As her watcher, you would have been subjected to the same fate. Be thankful for the passage of time. Olivia is fortunate she found a way to use her gifts. The FBI was perfect. She gets to be herself and hunt the monsters they can only dream about catching."

"Is it genetic? Is it divine intervention?" Barry asked before he could change his mind.

Poe flashed one of those lazy smiles he usually reserved for Olivia. "The story is as old as time. Genetic, yes. Divine, no." Barry looked like he wanted more, but Poe hesitated. Once he told the story there would be no taking it back. Barry would not be able to unhear the words.

"Save your prayers, watcher. The angels will wait, and they'll watch, like the cross-bearers upstairs," Poe told him. "She is a rarity. It wasn't supposed to happen anymore. It's why there was a great flood and a man named Noah built an ark. According to legend, there's only one way to become what she is. It's when a witch, the kind like her mother, sleeps with a man possessed. And lives." Poe stopped there giving Barry time to catch up.

"It is about more than just an ancestor from Salem." Barry repeated words he had already heard that night.

Poe's eyes narrowed at the statement. How did this man know only parts of the story? What kind of game was the old one playing? Poe should have known better than to trust him. As a rule, he didn't trust easily, Barry Bartholomew was different. Poe did not know this man, not really, not yet, but ultimately they were both bound together on the same quest. One by fate. One by promise. Barry deserved more than half-truths.

"Let me just say this. If Olivia needs saving, it will be the demons who do it. They're the ones interested in genetics. They see her as one of their own."

****

Will staked out the Labor and Delivery waiting room and followed the security guard down the stairwell. The guard was talkative after Will flashed him a badge and mentioned the FBI. They parted ways with the guard's promise of getting him in contact with someone in administration. Will elected not to tell Barry what he had learned. Not until he had something concrete. He also needed some sleep before he had either of those conversations. He should get Kim home where she could get some sleep so she would be there to relieve Jessica when Adelyn woke up.

It was about that time Olivia's phone went off in his pocket. Will pulled it out hoping it was Silas. Instead, it was someone named Kevin.

—Sorry for the early morning text, but I have some information on that nurse you asked me to look into. Call me as soon as you get this.—

At that point, Will decided he should just give the car keys to Kim and tell her to go on home. He wasn't leaving anytime soon.

****

The sun was just starting to pierce the sky. It shouldn't be long before he could get out and stretch his legs. Patrick was sitting in Agent Dennis' car thumbing through emails on his phone waiting for the all-clear to walk the grounds surrounding Agent Deveroux's house.

There was a sharp rap on the car window, causing Patrick to jump, a reminder of all the caffeine he had consumed in the last however many hours. Patrick started fumbling for the button to lower the car window when he saw what Agent Dennis was holding in his gloved hand.

"Found this in the backyard of Deveroux's place. It belongs to Agent Branch," Dennis told him.

The window wouldn't budge. In frustration Patrick exited the car altogether, joining Dennis in the street. "You're sure about that?" Patrick asked his eyes never leaving the shiny black phone.

Dennis pulled out his own phone and hit the button that would connect him with the last number called. The phone in Dennis' gloved hand came alive. At the top of a screen full of missed calls was the number for Leo Dennis. "I figured it was the fastest way to find out."

The background of the home screen was a picture of a beautiful blonde woman.

"I'm guessing, is that Dr. Osborne?" Dennis asked as the screen faded back to black.

Patrick nodded as he watched Dennis drop the phone in an evidence bag.

"It's interesting we didn't find anything else. Not his keys, his wallet, no change, nothing but this. Interesting, don't you think?" Dennis probed. "Looks professional."

Patrick was stoic as Dennis handed him the bag.

Especially if you own a white van and don't want anyone to track your location.

Agent Dennis walked away, and Patrick got back in the car. He had no idea who to call first.

****

The feeling inside of his head felt more like a blow to the head than drugs. At least the ringing in his ears was subsiding. Now it felt like they were full of cotton. Not that he could hear anything around him. It was as silent as a tomb. He couldn't see anything, but he wasn't blind. It was just dark. He could make out shapes, outlines of what he thought were windows that were shuttered or draped—maybe both.

The last thing Silas remembered seeing was Livie's eyes. He thought he was dying. He tried to move and that's when the pain in his leg reminded him he was very much alive. That's also when the face appeared out of nowhere.

"Special Agent Branch, so good of you to join us. Remember me?"

Epilogue

Alone at last, Rogan watched the sunrise, basking in its light. He found himself wanting a cigarette. Smoking was a brief habit he toyed with in his youth. He gave it up when he decided he didn't want to be dependent on anything.

Once the sun cleared the horizon, he made the call, relaying the night's events.

Mémé was silent for a long time. "You needn't worry. The words were as much for himself as her." Rogan assured her. "They won't let her die. My guess is her mother didn't sleep with just any demon."

"Her survival is what I worry about," she finally said. "How strong is her watcher?"

"He's in love with her."

"Problematic, but not uncommon. He's not why you needed the hyssop tea, though, is it?"

Rogan's lack of response was her answer. He could never lie to her.

She began to murmur.

"Remember your English, Mémé. She doesn't know French, and I don't have time to teach her."

"You would be a poor teacher," she scolded him.

"She needs you. I need you," Rogan said with earnest.

"You, more than you realize," she said, her English perfect.

Rogan didn't expect an answer to his next call. It was too long after dawn, but the message needed to be delivered. It was short and to the point.

"If you had anything to do with what happened outside Vegas today, you'll have me to answer to."

The reply came in the form of a text.

—*Maybe you should reconsider your position. Wouldn't your life be better if he was dead?*

****

"Where am I?" Olivia asked.

"Do not look so frightened," Alleracsap reassured her. *"Seeing me does not mean you are dead."*

"What does it mean?"

"You are taking a rest, courtesy of the medicine men caring for you. It has left your mind open, even more so than in sleep," Alleracsap explained.

"What about my daughters?"

"Very well—better than you, actually. They are strong like their mother. The second one is especially feisty. The drive to action is a trait from her father. I am speaking merely in biological terms. Your first one is contemplative. That one you, will need to watch carefully. Anyway, Others are watching over them."

Olivia felt a lurch in her empty womb. Not only were her babies physically gone, but she could no longer blanket their thoughts. *"Others?"*

"You doubt me?" Something akin to a low, rumbling growl emanated from his chest. Alleracsap felt pleasure at her lack of reaction. Grown men, adorned with robes, didn't fare so well when hearing it. Olivia was comfortable with him.

He could shed all the disguises and be himself. *"Have I ever lied to you? Did I not tell you how sorry I was about Jason? I also recall telling you how much your Watcher loves you. He will not leave you no matter how many times you reject him."*

It was all true. Alleracsap had never lied to her. But that's not all he said either. *"I only rejected him once,"* Olivia pointed out.

"We shall see," Alleracsap told her. *"As for the Others, you remember from the lessons Ginny taught you. My name is Legion, for we are many—you know the verses. Your little progenies are much too valuable, like you, for any harm to come to them."*

"Why am I here?" Olivia demanded.

"You have a Seer and a Teller, but you already knew that. The Teller came first; let her tell you a lullaby. They are not just sweet songs sung to the young. They are things of lore. That is why you are here. To see your past and remember what it was like."

"Remember what was like?"

"The magic inside of you. It can help you find the answers to some of your questions." Alleracsap's tone was full of promise.

"Like what?"

"What's the first thing that comes to mind when you realized you were not like the other little girls?"

Olivia looked up and saw the sticks of floating colors. If she spun them fast enough, they changed. Blue and yellow made green. *"What color are my father's eyes?"* It was the first question—the only question that came to mind.

"You are on the right path." The voice didn't sound like Alleracsap. *"It is time to resurrect all that you have buried, my child."*

A word about the author...

I've been a registered nurse for more than thirty years, but my first passion has always been writing.

Growing up the youngest child of older parents I spent a lot of time entertaining myself. I discovered my love of writing through reading and when I ran out of books, I wrote my own. I have lived in San Antonio, Texas for almost twenty years and have adopted it as my own. I love the diversity of this city and its endless supply of ghosts which make it the perfect setting for the Olivia Osborne series. When I'm not writing I can be found with my family and any number of cats.

LisaComptonbooks.com

Thank you for purchasing
this publication of The Wild Rose Press, Inc.

For questions or more information
contact us at
info@thewildrosepress.com.

The Wild Rose Press, Inc.
www.thewildrosepress.com